THE SWEETEST GIFT

Seraphina smiled up at him and he felt the breath knocked out of his very experienced, entirely masculine body. He was dizzied at the effect Seraphina had, given the fact that he was himself no greenhorn among the fairer sex. She was more beautiful than anyone he had ever encountered, but the attraction was more substantial than that. She understood his music and therefore his soul stripped bare. He understood her wiles and her mischief—had he not those selfsame impulses deep within himself?

The stars twinkled in the deep, dark sea of sky. Their lustre was reflected in Seraphina's eyes as she looked at him, missing a step as she did so. He helped her correct her balance, pulling closed the coat that had opened during the stumble. He trembled a little at the sight that greeted him. Pure white on delicate cream, her pearls shimmering and dancing like a veritable constellation of heavenly stars.

"Angel, my angel," he breathed. . . .

MADRIGALS
AND
MISTLETOE

HAYLEY ANN SOLOMON

Zebra Books
Kensington Publishing Corp.
http://www.zebrabooks.com

ONE

Miss Seraphina Camfrey yelped as two stray pins wedged their way into her person. She knew it was useless to complain. Cordelia could be *so* unfeeling when she had her mind fixed on a task.

"Stand still!"

Seraphina squirmed and did her best to oblige. The cream satin felt delectably soft, but she was mindful of the sharp points that held her in their thrall.

"I can't see why we can't simply send for Miss Davenport!"

Her sister looked scornful. "And pay an excessive amount for something I can throw together in an afternoon? If you ceased fidgeting, we would have this done in no time."

Miss Camfrey sighed and allowed her thoughts to wonder to the pleasures of her first truly grown-up soiree. She wondered if it would be any more entertaining than her court presentation had been. Deadly dull, she had thought it, despite having been in a *passion* of anticipation for months.

"Do you think the Prince of Wales will attend?"

Cordelia, her mouth full of pins, shook her head and reached for some of the pastel riband she'd procured from a delightful little shop just south of Conduit Street.

"I think not." She jabbed the pins into their cushion and looked up for the first time. "He is taking the waters in Bath, though what good *that* can do the man I am sure I am at a loss to fathom!"

Seraphina giggled. "I hear it is really terribly nasty."

"Oh, excessively! One gulp has me choking."

"I am glad we are safely in London then!"

"So am I. You may step out now. I think I have the measurements."

With relief Seraphina exchanged the satin for her morning dress of pale muslin. She waved away her maid, who was hovering in the background, and wrestled with the ties herself. When she'd done, she turned inquiring eyes on her sister.

"Who *will* attend this evening?"

Cordelia, abstracted and a little teasing, fluttered her hands vaguely.

"Miss Caroline Daventry, Miss Jane Sneddon, Lady Charlotte Sinclair . . ."

Seraphina threw the button box at her sister. "Don't be so provoking! You know what I mean!"

Cordelia's mouth curved. She thought she did. "With the war at an end there will be any number of beaux to take your fancy! Lord Rochester, Captain Cardross—"

The younger Miss Camfrey did not wait for her sister to continue. "They say the Duke of Doncaster has returned."

Cordelia's brows shot up. "Roving Rhaz? I should think you are setting your sights too high."

Seraphina shrugged her shoulders dismissively. "I do not seek to *marry* the man, only to meet him! Lady Gussington says—"

"Far too much!" The words were prim, but Cordelia's shoulders shook in silent amusement. How her sister, just out of the schoolroom, came by her snippets of gossip she never could tell.

"Did you call him Roving Rhaz?"

Cordelia's fine grey eyes lit with ready laughter. "Awake to every suit, are you not? Yes, I did and I take leave to tell you it was quite shocking of me!"

Seraphina waved this aside airily. "I hope you do not intend to turn missish, Delia dear! Roving Rhaz sounds so delectably—"

"Wicked?"

"Yes . . ." Seraphina was not sure. She imagined someone tall with compelling eyes and a magnetic charm. Not wicked perhaps, but sinfully attractive nonetheless. She shivered in anticipation, her eyes glazing over in a pleasant daydream.

"Seraphina!" Cordelia's eyes were laughing as she scolded her errant sister. "Have done with mooning, I beg you! You would do well to practice on your harpsichord if you have so little else to employ your time."

Seraphina made a terrible face and grimaced quite comically. "I'd rather be dragged backward across St. James's Square! You *know* the cacophony I can make!"

"If you practiced, it would not be a cacophony! Besides, *all* young ladies need to play. This very evening is a case in point. Think what the soiree would be like without entertainments from the guests. Hideous, I assure you."

"Yes, well, thank heavens I am not being called upon to play! If ever I am, I shall simply claim a genteel headache and make good my escape."

"Hmm?" Cordelia deftly turned the hem and affixed a pearl rosette to the border. Truth to tell, her own thoughts were wandering, though not in as errant a direction as those of the irrepressible Seraphina. It was Lord Winthrop with his bluff country air that occupied most of her thoughts.

Whilst she wished that his bushy red whiskers were not quite so thick, it mattered not a whit to her that his tailor was not quite of the first elegance. Henry Winthrop did not need close fitting greatcoats of the first stare, for he spent more time in the stables than he did in the drawing rooms. This, Cordelia conceded, was just as well, for the gentleman had neither the wit nor the address to prosper among the bon ton. Still, he was good-hearted and had the noted distinction of offering for her hand. Since she was one and twenty, this was no small consideration. Cordelia fingered the ring that encircled her finger and sighed.

The time for romantic nonsense was over and done with. She must have done with her foolishness and marry the good Lord Henry. He might take an unflattering interest in her horses and her housekeeping, but he would undoubtedly be kind. Besides, it had been arranged for an age. Henry must not have been out of leading strings when her mama and his planned the match. It would be churlish to cry off now when she had the advantage of three seasons behind her. Unaccountable, then, that a little voice at the back of her head protested.

Cordelia pricked her finger and winced. Better she concentrate on the job at hand. She held her handiwork up to the sunny window and nodded. If Seraphina did not turn heads, she would eat a mongoose. The cream satin was just perfect. Demure enough for a debutante, but also an engaging foil to her rich auburn hair.

"Cordelia!"

She was startled to find her mama had entered the room.

"I wish you would not waste time cobbling gowns together! Miss Davenport should be sent for. I am sure she could do with the work."

Cordelia nodded, but continued her stitching nonetheless. No point bothering Lady Ancilla with financial concerns. She'd simply shrug her fine-boned shoulders and disdainfully recommend the bills to be consigned to some bureau drawer or other. Though marvellous in her own way, Ancilla had no *notion* at times. Cordelia fleetingly wondered how her poor father had coped. No doubt he'd simply indulged Ancilla shamefully, meekly making good the outrageous debts as they were incurred. This satisfactory state of affairs might well have continued had his life not been cut short by a hunting accident. Since the land and title had been entailed to the next heir, the Camfreys had been obliged to take up the dower house and curtail much of their expenditure.

It had been this consideration, of course, that had led Cordelia to accept Lord Winthrop's most obliging offer. As Lady Winthrop, she would be able to sponsor Seraphina into society and maintain her mother's own standard of living. If she sighed for something more, she was simply succumbing to an unusual fit of the dismals.

"I hope you are wearing something utterly divine tonight, my darling!" Ancilla smiled fondly. "You should be the belle of the ball with your high cheekbones and natural ringlets. If I were not so positively in my dotage I would envy you, Cordelia, my love, for no one could have a trimmer figure or neater pair of ankles than you."

Miss Camfrey flashed her mother a brilliant smile. "Don't say that or *Seraphina* might take a pet! Besides, *you*, my dear mama, are hardly in your dotage."

Whilst Ancilla was evidently pleased, she was not to be turned from her subject. "What *are* you wearing, Cordelia?"

"I thought the pink crepe. I could sprig it with lemon—"

Mrs. Camfrey threw up her elegantly gloved hands in horror. "*Not* the spencer again! I told you to get rid of it!"

"So you did, Mama, but I thought, with a little refurbishing—"

"No!" Ancilla's tone brooked no argument. "You will come with me, if you please! If you are absolutely hell bent on refurbishing—and I see you are—I daresay I have any *number* of gowns I'd be glad to see the back of."

"Yes, Delia! *Do* say you will!" Seraphina, naturally good-natured, allied herself to her mother's cause. Faced with such pressing encouragement, the elder Miss Camfrey had little alternative but to submit gracefully. Truth to tell, the thought of draping herself in a shimmering satin with an overlay of dove grey lace did much for the restoration of her humour. By the time Lord Winthrop's ponderous barouche was announced, she found herself to be in perfectly good spirits, her strange fit of the dismals all but gone.

The elder and younger Miss Camfrey did not have long to wait before being announced and making their curtsies. Lord Winthrop, with obvious relief, scratched his name on both their dance cards, performed his obligation manfully and disappeared into the card room for the remainder of the evening. Ancilla, seeing that her chicks were in high fettle and excellent looks, adjured them to have a merry time and dismissed them summarily, the role of chaperone wearisome to one who still felt young and deliciously carefree herself.

That being so, it was up to Cordelia to ensure Seraphina was well seated in the anteroom, where the entertainment was to begin. This she did, whispering brightly under her fan to nod to Lady Bricknell, acknowledge Lord Eddington and outstare, if she could, the odious Countess of Glaston. This Seraphina applied herself to with much relish, for there was nothing she liked better than a good spat. Forced to be sorry she had spoken, Cordelia nudged Seraphina to behave.

Downcast but not entirely subdued, the irrepressible Miss Camfrey turned her attention to some of the soiree's notable oddities, commenting with ceaseless appreciation on the fall of Sir Charlton's cravat, the luminescence of the candles, the remarkable resonance of the room, the ice carvings laid out at table, the elegant footwear of the Marchioness of Slade and the intriguing features of Lord Byron, who seemed to possess a brooding presence that was entirely at one with his strikingly handsome features.

She caught his eye once, and he slightly inclined his head, causing a shiver of delighted anticipation to course through her veins. Cordelia smiled indulgently at her sister, loath to dampen the high spirits. She remembered *exactly* how she'd felt three years ago at her first social gathering. There was a hush as their hostess, Lady Dearforth, clapped her hands and called the gathering to attention.

Out of the corner of her eye, Seraphina caught sight of Miss Lila Mersham and visibly recoiled. Lila had been a venerable bully at Miss Caxton's Seminary for Young Ladies. She wondered fleetingly if age had improved her and thought not. She was gowned in an unflattering shade of violet, and her scowl seemed quite prodigious. Seraphina inclined her head regally and turned her eyes to the hostess. She was aching to laugh, for Lila looked most put out by her presence, especially since the Camfreys took precedence in the seating arrangements. Lord Winthrop, it appeared, was not *entirely* without uses!

Lady Dearforth outlined the programme in a ringing voice and politely called upon Lord Stanley's distinguished tenor to edify the audience with a rendition from Purcell's secular motets. This he did, much to the company's polite enjoyment. Lord Byron was next, reading an extract from *Childe Harold* with such potent vigour that both Miss Camfreys were moved to tears.

It was fortunate that the Misses Wexford were up next, for their technically perfect rendition of Bach's *Toccato* and *Fugue in F Major* proved most satisfactory in calming—not to say boring—the younger Miss Camfrey in particular.

Perhaps it was the heat of the room or the lateness of the hour, but whatever the reason, it seemed to Seraphina that the organ was a singularly pompous instrument. As her eyes drooped, even the lilting tones of the harp and spinet, coupled with the exacting melodies of the harpsichord, seemed dull to her untried ears. All around, she was aware of a ceaseless, excited hum, but she was struggling too hard not to yawn to pay much attention.

Cordelia looked anxious. Lord Winthrop had disappeared into the bowels of the card room. If she knew him, he'd not give either of them a passing thought for several hours or more. This in itself did not bother her, but the sight of Seraphina, slightly swaying, did little to alleviate her concerns. Just as she was casting her eyes about for a footman, she felt the most unnerving sensation shoot through her being and rock her to the very core.

In the centre of the room, looking for all the world as though he owned it, stood quite the most magnificent man Cordelia had ever had the felicity of noticing. His stark black evening coat yielded faint glimmers of light where a thread of silver laced its way through superfine fabric. His knee breeches—a skintight confection of doe's leather—were almost indecent. Cordelia tried not to notice how every muscle of his impeccable body was outlined for those interested enough to look. It appeared that most were, for every eye in the room seemed to fall upon his person.

For an instant, their eyes locked—silver grey on deep, dark black. She felt a strange light-headedness creep through her being and wondered, for an instant, if the heady sensation was shared. She thought it was, for the man raised his gloved fingers to his lips and saluted her silently. She blushed furiously and chided herself for being such a shatter-brained widgeon. Still, when the programme recommenced, her back felt warm as if by a glance he could strip her naked. She was perfectly certain he *was* entertaining himself with the sight of her derriere, for the burning sensation remained with her throughout Lady Kemble's recital and the Air on G that followed.

Three seasons—*three seasons*—and she had never met this paragon—or was he a rogue? She was indignantly inclined to think the latter, but then, thinking was rather difficult as she was currently circumstanced. She mentally crossed off all the possibilities. *Not* Captain Peters or the Earl of Pemberton, not Lord Fallow—he was away with the prince regent. Sir Epsom Curruthers was said to be rotund; the Barnaby twins were far too young. He could be a captain of the dragoons or an envoy of some sort—he had that air of authority.

Her thoughts teased at her, not the least because next to this absolute nonpareil, poor Lord Henry Winthrop came up far the worse for scrutiny. Still, she fingered her ring. Artifice, charm and unholy good looks did not always make for exemplary husbands. Her lips twitched ironically. On the contrary . . .

Several simple madrigals followed, sung unaccompanied by a series of select young ladies both solo and in unison. At last, the end of the programme was reached. Both sisters clapped automatically as Lady Dearforth thanked the last formal participant, Lady Amelia Trent. Her singing had been passable, but what her voice lacked was made up for abundantly in her skill at accompaniment. Her fingers had flown across the keyboard, her eyes oblivious to the pages of music obligingly being turned by Lord Kilpatrick. As the audience applauded, she gathered up her score in a flutter of self-consciousness and made to resume her seat.

Cordelia turned to Seraphina, anxious to get her moving before she was caught in the crush.

"Wait!" The loud, familiar and unmelodious voice of Lila Mersham rang out through the throng. Lady Dearforth, understanding that she was being addressed, indicated to her guests to resume their seats.

"Miss Mersham?"

The eyes of the crowd were upon her. Not even her mother, the Countess of Glaston, could bid her be silent. Lila's eyes sparkled with the sudden attention. She curtsied and adopted an admirably coy expression that both Camfrey sisters found quite sickening.

"Beg pardon, ma'am! I thought I might introduce to your attention our newest debutante, Miss Seraphina Camfrey!" Lila's eyes narrowed slyly, but she maintained her simpering stance. She smiled effusively across the room, her eyes meeting those of her victim with a strange, menacing gleam. "Seraphina was wont to sing to us at Miss Caxton's Seminary for Young Ladies. Perhaps she might favour us with a madrigal? Byrd or Gibbons was ever a favourite!"

Miss Seraphina sat stock-still, her fan quivering appallingly in her hand. It seemed hours before she stirred, or Cordelia made faint protesting noises, but of course, it could have been no more than a matter of seconds. By that time, every jewelled head in the audience was unremittingly turned in her direction. There could be no crying headache—it would be churlish when her hostess was smiling at her with such gracious encouragement and half the room were clapping politely, murmuring, "Hear, Hear," in spirited tones.

Cordelia thought she ought to take out the smelling salts, for Seraphina looked deathly pale and unusually anguished given her devil-may-care nature. As she was opening her reticule, Seraphina stood up and made an acknowledging curtsy. She was nothing, if not brave, the youngest Miss Camfrey! Cordelia bit her lip and prayed for the best. Not Byrd! Seraphina only ever practiced Handel, for she adored his counterpoint and had a strange aptitude for that which she admired.

In the event, it turned out to be a Purcell that was suggested to her. "Lost Is My Quiet Forever" was forwarded as a suggestion from Captain Sanderson, who also offered to play the opening bars. As Seraphina made her way to the front, Cordelia felt her fan snap between her fingers. Whilst she could still overwhelmingly feel the scorching scrutiny of the gentleman behind her, she no longer cared. All her thoughts were concentrated on her sibling. Cordelia prayed that the younger Miss Camfrey's first season was not to be her last, for an outright humiliation would be something she would surely not bear. She prayed, too, that against all odds Seraphina could live up to her name and sing like an angel.

TWO

Seraphina thanked Lady Dearforth and took the score from her hands. It was a complicated piece, hand inscribed, but she was, at least, familiar with the rudiments. She glanced at it frantically again, trying to recall the words, key and register. All eyes were upon her and it made not a whit of difference that, apart from Cordelia, she could easily be regarded as the most becoming young woman in the room. It was probably this very fact that had set off Lila's malicious lark, so even if she *had* been aware of her appearance, it would have been cold comfort.

She was surprised how steady her hands were in the circumstances. She would dearly like to have caught Cordelia's eye, but Captain Sanderson had taken up his position and was waiting for her nod. Her heart thumped quite dreadfully and she hoped that the lump in her throat would make little difference to her performance. She looked at the notes again and they seemed to be swimming in front of her. She tried to remember the advice of her string of singing masters, but could recall none, save that she should keep her hands at her side and take a deep breath before she began. Impossible! She could take the breath, but she needed her hands to read the score. Time seemed to be racing by and the whole chamber had become significantly silent.

Feeling as if she was rushing headlong over a precipice, she turned to the elegant Captain Sanderson and inclined her head.

The music began, and suddenly shaking from head to foot, the younger Miss Camfrey opened her mouth to sing. Too late she realised how unsuitable the melancholy piece was for her own, untried soprano. It required suspensions between melody and bass that even the most gifted singer would have found challenging. After striking the wrong key, far too high for the accompaniment, she faltered, of a mind to begin again. Her face was whiter than the cream satin she'd chosen to effect and several of her auburn tendrils had worked their way loose from her pearl pinned topknot. Only her eyes were defiant as she trembled on the low notes and sang, "Forever," hopelessly flat.

Cordelia ached for her sister and turned, hoping to make her way quietly to the front. When the performance was over, she would take Seraphina briskly in hand and urge Lord Winthrop to have the carriage sent round. Her eyes flickered upward to meet the unwavering ones of the nonpareil she'd encountered earlier. She caught a hint of amused sympathy in his expression, before he quietly gestured her to resume her seat. Cordelia never did know why she obeyed, but unhesitatingly she did.

With a few short strides, the stranger somehow forced his way through the riveted throng. A startled Seraphina found her hand gently clasped in a grip of comforting strength. Then, before she had a moment to take a single disastrous note more, the gentleman smiled eloquently and set the key, his tenor a fine mask to the lady's halting attempts. The duet prospered, Seraphina taking enormous comfort from the dark stranger at her side. When she missed a bar or could not catch the text fast enough, he covered for her with smooth, unfaltering aplomb.

Finally—it seemed forever—the ordeal was at an end. Miss Camfrey held her head high and bit her lip, for she was in full expectation of being society's little joke for the rest of the season. In this, she was mistaken, for the burst of applause that met her ears seemed quite unaccountable. Cordelia was by her side in an instant, bewildered and unutterably grateful for the gentleman's intervention.

He would brook no thanks, however, claiming it as his privilege to have served such a beautiful maiden. At this, Seraphina positively preened, but Cordelia looked at the gentleman suspiciously, the hint of a blush on her personable cheeks. The gentleman's eyes had never left her own and she had the giddying sensation that *she* was the maiden of whom he spoke. She shook herself sternly, for there was no good to be gained by such speculation.

"I must add my gratitude to my sister's, sir!"

"Must you?" His eyes looked whimsical and intensely black. Cordelia felt he must see her heart hammering through the dove grey satin and intricate lace overdress. He didn't, for he was concentrating on the pink flesh that spilled becomingly out of the gown rather than on the fabric itself.

He drew her slightly aside and lowered his voice. "I trust you intend leaving?"

Cordelia nodded.

"May I ask that you stay, rather?" He drew her aside confidentially and Cordelia felt the warmth of his hand through his fine leather gloves. When he released her, the warmth remained, a burning patch on her satin clad arm.

"After this debacle I feel we should leave. Perhaps it

is a matter of the least said, the sooner mended. If we stay, we are bound to invite malicious gabble mongering." Cordelia could not for the life of her discover why she was making these confidences to a stranger. Perhaps it was his warm regard or the quiet, authoritative confidence he exuded.

She was surprised to see the gentleman smile a little wryly. "At the risk of sounding *odiously* puffed up in my own consequence, I am prepared to wager a sennight's wage that your sister's musical debut will be considered a vast success."

"Surely that is doing it a bit brown, sir? Why, you heard—"

"Sometimes what one hears and what one sees are two entirely different things." Cordelia looked mystified at this cryptic remark, but the gentleman did not see fit to enlighten her. Instead, he suggested again that the sisters stay to brave out the evening, for that was surely the best strategy to quell catty tongues.

"So you noticed, sir?"

"Lila Mersham? She has nothing but my contempt. A spiteful, ill-bred lass, but a troublemaker unless I miss my mark. Stay and the dust will settle."

The gentleman refrained to say that his *own* hand would probably raise more dust than Lila's ever had. He sighed. No doubt the ladies would discover that of their own accord. He only hoped he had not done anything precipate enough to raise expectations. On this thought, he politely returned Cordelia to her sister and made a charming bow. Bidding them both a fair evening, he vanished into the throngs, leaving the more sober Miss Camfrey to face her bright-eyed sister and dampen some of her overhigh spirits.

Seraphina, it seemed, was an instant success. She was being hailed far and wide as society's newest diamond. The fact that she could not sing did not seem to weigh too high with the gentlemen, each of whom assured her fulsomely that either her voice was heavenly—a tarradiddle even Seraphina could not, with equanimity, accept—or that entertainments at soirees were deadly dull and not, on any account, to be taken seriously.

Cordelia could accept this, for there was no doubt her scamp of a sister was in excellent looks. What she was more puzzled about, however, was the interest of the various high sticklers, who made a point of introducing themselves and issuing select invitations. Lady Jersey *herself* did them the honour of a conversation, admonishing them to present themselves to Almack's the following session. It did not signify, for the ladies had already come by vouchers through Ancilla's friendship with Lady Cowper, but nevertheless Cordelia was fully sensible to the honour done them.

The evening flew by without further incident. Lord Winthrop handsomely offered another dance to his betrothed, who had not the heart to refuse. As Cordelia tucked her graceful hand in his, she was overcome by a slight depression. She should not be making comparisons—they were unkind—but next to that of the enigmatic dark gentleman, Lord Henry's padded frame seemed rather square. He still affected a wig and powder, choosing to adorn his frogged coat with all manner of seals and furbelows that, rather than increasing his consequence, diminished it. Cordelia could not help but feel that the austere simplicity of her captain—for she thought of him as that—spoke volumes for his taste. As she executed an exceedingly pretty entrechat, she could not help wishing things were different.

Vivaldi's poignant notes hung in the air as the dance finished and Lord Henry drew her from the circle. For the first time, he seemed to notice her shimmering gown with its low-cut front and high waistband, drawn together skilfully by a ribbon of dove grey satin sprigged with silver.

"You look ravishing tonight, Cordelia!" Miss Camfrey smiled and murmured thanks. Lord Henry appeared to be regarding her as though seeing her for the first time. "Shall we take a stroll in the gardens?"

Cordelia glanced outside. The night was starry and refreshingly cool. The offer was tempting but slightly improper, given the fact that Ancilla was nowhere at hand. Still, Lord Henry was her betrothed, and if she could possibly stir up a spark in him, she would be glad.

"Seraphina . . ."

"Oh, leave her!" Lord Winthrop sounded rather abrupt.

Cordelia raised her eyebrows somewhat at this incivility. Seeing this, Lord Henry emitted a short laugh and apologised, explaining that he was a deuced new hand at doing the pretty and should not *Mrs.* Camfrey be minding her youngest?

It was useless to explain that she should, but was hardly likely to. Cordelia had *long* since assumed the mantle of responsibility for her family, finding Ancilla in just as much need of a watchful eye as her sister. Ancilla at forty had just as much vitality as she had at seventeen. High spirits, bounteous good looks and a comfortably good nature made her sought after wherever she went. She was proud of her two magnificent daughters, but just a little puzzled that they should be so grown-up or that she, Ancilla, should have charge of them. Whenever she furrowed her brow and contemplated the matter, it always came down to a laughing shrug of the shoulders and a concentrated attempt to dismiss the matter from her mind entirely.

Cordelia was loath to share this state of affairs with this stranger who was to be her husband. Instead, she replied amiably that Seraphina would probably be anxious for company, this being her first come-out soiree.

At this, Lord Henry chortled rather rudely but with a good deal of amusement. Taken aback, Cordelia could only ask him what the jest was, for certainly she could see nothing in her words to have elicited such a response. She noted that Lord Henry looked a good deal pleasanter when his eyes smiled and was glad.

"That demmed sister of yours has no need of company, Cordelia! I may be rather behind hand with society, but I do have eyes and ears you know!"

"How so?" The older Miss Camfrey was still puzzled. She smiled politely and moved aside as a couple made their way back indoors.

"She is *feted* with admirers! Greville Winters positively scowled at me when he thought I was engaged for the waltz! I told him I'd already *done* my duty by her and I have, what is more."

Cordelia ignored the smug tones of one who has sanctimoniously performed a distasteful task. She was used to Lord Henry, by now. If he had been talking of a horse, no doubt his eyes would have shone with ardour. Too much to expect him to muster up enthusiasm for a mere female. Still, his words were curiously interesting.

"I have not seen her this age, being caught up in first the quadrille, then the Scottish reel and . . . oh! any number of dances! She has admirers, you say?"

"Being treated like a demmed diamond of the first water! No accounting for tastes if I may make so bold."

Cordelia bit off a sharp reply. No sense in coming to odds with her beau or expecting him to have the gloss of social finesse high society usually demanded. Lord Winthrop had clearly not *meant* to insult her sister. It was just his offhand manner of expression that offended her sensibilities. She determined not to refine too much on what was, after all, a small matter.

"I am glad to hear it, though I am at a loss—"

Lord Winthrop snorted. "Talk of the card room, it is! I may be a little green about the gills but I am not a clodpole entirely!"

Cordelia politely inclined her head and assured him the thought had not entered her head. He looked at her sharply, but seeing no hint of irony in her wide grey eyes, he nodded in satisfaction.

"Seems that Doncaster fellow has taken a fancy to the chit. Of course, that is enough to set the whole ton on their heels! The man is such an arbiter of fashion that every dandy must needs follow his lead!" Lord Winthrop shook his head at the unfathomable nature of society.

Light—a tiny, dim lantern glow of light dawned in Cordelia's brain. "Are you saying that her popularity is due, not to her own vastly entertaining nature but that of . . . Doncaster, you say?"

Her companion tapped his foot impatiently. "Exactly so! You have the right of it, my love."

Cordelia could not quite like the term of endearment. Still, as his betrothed, she must needs grow accustomed. His lordship, fond of the sound of his own voice, grew expansive. He helped her through the narrow, gilded door and followed her into the shadowy night. Clouds were cloaking the stars, so it was darker than Cordelia had expected. She shivered a little, but Lord Winthrop failed to notice. He was warming to his theme.

"Doncaster seems to have the most extraordinary effect on all he encounters! He has not been back from Paris above two months and the whole demmed world is falling about trying to tie their neckerchiefs in the Doncaster Dash! I have no time for it, I say, not but that

he *does* have the most promising stables! Bought Red-
mond's greys for an unholy sum but he had the right
of it. An excellent matched pair if ever I saw one. Hasn't
stinted on the bloodstock either. Took over the entire
Charleston stable saving a few feeble beasts that found
their way in there God knows how. I saw him at New-
market and again at Tattersall's. Cool as a cucumber he
was, as if he were not bidding for six matched stallions,
jet black and high steppers if ever I saw them!"

His tone took on an excited pitch of indignation. Cordelia, whilst not sharing his preoccupation, nevertheless
found herself listening avidly to every word that fell
from Lord Winthrop's lips. This was a novel experience,
for she had not, up till now, found much to arrest her
interest in his conversation. She stifled the lowering suspicion that her polite attention stemmed not from
maidenly interest in her betrothed but from a most un-
maidenly interest in the man of whom he spoke.

Lord Winthrop continued. "Mind you, I don't approve of the Four Horse Club and that I tell you
straight! They turned down my membership, which
only proves to you what a feckless, nohow sort of a
bunch they are. Notable horsemen indeed! If they can't
recognise a bruising rider when they see one, they are
not worthy of their standing. I shall talk to Doncaster
about it directly."

Cordelia, with admirable restraint, refrained from the
rather obvious retort that hung from her lips. She
smiled and touched Lord Henry's arm placatingly.

He looked down in surprise, far too caught up in his
indignation at the infamous Four Horse Club to recall
the reason he had brought her out here in the first
place. The sight of her creamy flesh reminded him
anew. Cordelia noticed the direction of her glance and
smiled. Like all young women—even those past their
last prayers at the grand old age of one and twenty—she

was not averse to appreciation in a gentleman's eye. Lord Winthrop raised his quizzing glass to her, then commented she was like to catch her death of cold in that "newfangled fribble."

His words were like a dash of cold water to the older Miss Camfrey, who could not help replying that whilst the gown was in the latest mode, it was by no means newfangled, her mother having worn it to Lady Dennington's masquerade an age ago at least. Lord Henry snorted and considered the point won. "If Ancilla has had a hand in the gown I daresay it is *dashed* too fast!"

Cordelia felt her cheeks stain red. Her delicious bosom rose and fell as she attempted to answer mildly. Whilst she had much to say to her mama in private, she would *not* have her gossiped about, even if the man doing the talking was her intended.

"Recall to mind, your lordship, that it is my *mother* of whom we speak!" The severe tones were lost on Henry, who was looking past her towards the footmen setting up impromptu trellises outside.

"Dashed if I don't have a mind to one of those ices!"

Cordelia gave up in disgust. When Lord Henry, quite forgetting her presence, ambled off to secure his place in the long line of waiting guests, she shook her head and made her way inside.

"I see you took my advice!" The voice nearly overset Cordelia, for it so neatly matched the one in her head. She whirled around to find Doncaster negligently propped against a wide, alabaster pillar. If possible, he was more handsome than she remembered him, though his nose was straighter and his mouth slightly wider than she had first supposed.

"Indeed, sir! Though I now find I have more to thank you for than I had immediately imagined!"

He looked amused. "There is no accounting for tastes, is there?"

"Possibly not, though I suspect that in this case society is more discerning than it *usually* proves to be."

His eyes softened. "May I take that as a compliment? It is refreshing for I am so used, you see, to being served Spanish coin."

"A sore trial, I am sure! Yes, I did mean it as a compliment though I am sure I may have overstepped the bounds somewhere!"

"You mean beautiful young women do not *usually* commend admiring gentlemen?" His tone was suddenly flirtatious and Cordelia looked up, colouring.

"Don't talk flummery to me if you please!"

"Is it flummery to say I admire you? I *could* have said your eyes shimmer like candlelight and the curves of your mouth are infinitely"—there was a hushed pause before his dark eyes burned into hers, and, in a low, breathtakingly intimate tone, he whispered—"kissable."

Cordelia felt as though she was stunned. All her three seasons had not prepared her for such brazen, *flagrantly* romantic and *quite* unsuitable conversation.

She decided to ignore the wild fluttering of her heart and the intimate smile that lurked in the depths of bold, black eyes. "Now *that* would be flummery, sir!"

A decided twinkle entered my Lord Doncaster's eyes. "A sense of humour, too," he murmured, *quite* unrepentant and in just as familiar a tone.

"Do stop it, sir!"

The twinkle turned into a gleam. "I do believe, Miss . . . ?"

"Good heavens! We are not yet introduced!" Cordelia's hands flew to her mouth. "Miss Camfrey, sir!"

"Excellent! I do believe, Miss Camfrey, that you must be the first among your sex to depress my pretensions!"

"You must lead a charmed life, then, Sir . . . ?"

"Lord, actually!"

"Yes, I had suspected as much. At first I thought you must be in the military—your authoritative air, you know—"

His lordship cocked his head to one side and folded his arms, a distinct light of enjoyment flitting across his near perfect features. "And now?"

"Oh, now I am certain you are a lord, for all the world is kowtowing to you! Besides, I have it on the best authority you are a member of the Four Horse Club."

"True, though it is extraordinary how fast word travels."

"Yes, well, that is so, of course! Society is bound to gossip—so very diverting."

"I am glad to hear I am a source of amusement, ma'am!"

"No, that is not what I meant—"

"I am teasing!"

Miss Camfrey dimpled and she peeked outrageously at the impeccably clad gentleman. "I suspected as much. It is tremendously refreshing to have someone understand my irony."

"Tremendously refreshing to *hear* it, Miss Camfrey! The world takes itself too seriously!"

"I think so, too. But come, sir! I have very prettily exchanged names with you, but you have not, I believe, returned the favour!"

"Only because it would be improper to be so forward!"

Cordelia wrinkled her nose. "Shall I fetch my mama to introduce us? I hope you don't intend being so absurd, my lord!"

"I revel in absurdities, Miss Camfrey!" She rewarded him with a smile that shook him to the core. Their elegant repartee was going farther than he had first intended, but he wondered, rather ruefully, whether that mattered. "Well then, since you insist—and I defy you to suddenly kowtow to me—I am Rhaz, Lord Doncaster.

Cordelia's head felt as though it was spinning. She did not know why she should feel so faint with surprise, for it was no secret that the duke was back. He was looking at her rather wistfully, so she recovered her poise in an instant and allowed the laughter to shine through her speaking, misty grey eyes.

"Ought I to curtsy, your grace?"

"Quite probably. It seems to be what every young lady *does* when she sees me. Quite unaccountable, really, when I stand six foot two in my stockinged feet. You'd think they would try to *stretch,* rather than sink!"

"Perhaps I should stretch then!"

His ready laughter was tinged with a hint of devilry as he murmured subtly and with a wealth of unspoken innuendo, "How eminently suitable, for then our lips will be practically touching!"

As Cordelia registered his meaning, the words hung like dew between them. A heartbeat of wild yearning, then the light went out of Cordelia's eyes. The duke saw it and raised quizzical brows.

"I was funning, Miss Camfrey!"

Cordelia waited until her heart was beating at a more manageable pace.

"Your grace, I think I should tell you I am betrothed." She was in an agony that he should think her forward for making too much out of his flirtatious gallantry. He seemed to understand something of her feelings, for he took her hands lightly and maintained the same rallying tone.

"I should think so! The men of England would not be such slow tops to let a diamond like you pass through their fingers!"

Cordelia smiled, relieving that she had set the tone for their dalliance, if such this could be called. More

like the unbridled enjoyment of one mind's wit meeting
with an answering comprehension.

"I must go."

The duke nodded, though for once he was silent.

Cordelia hesitated, then addressed him with sad fi-
nality. "Good-bye then."

Once again, his grace nodded. As Cordelia made a
small, self-conscious curtsy, she heard a faint, self-mocking murmur. She could *swear* he had reverted to French,
erasing her firm farewell with a warmer, more promising, "Au revoir."

THREE

"I suppose your grace will think it *entirely* the thing to jaunter around the country with no more—no more I say!—than two portmanteaus and a little slip of a halfling for a tiger!"

His grace the Duke of Doncaster did not seem at all perturbed by this monologue, but bent his mind, instead, to the intricate task of fastening his shirtsleeves and pulling on a skintight coat made exactly to order. His valet, catching sight of the excellent fit, allowed himself a small sigh of vicarious pleasure before continuing on his tirade.

"Mark my words, your grace! Your Hessians will disgrace me."

"Ah, there is the crux of it, Jennings! Your overweening pride among the upper servants! You harangue me day after day simply because I refuse to increase your consequence by filling two of my carriages with . . . with . . . what exactly *do* you wish me to convey?"

"Only what is proper, my lord! Your hunting dress, your evening garb, your greatcoats, a mere dozen starched cravats—"

"Only a dozen? For shame, Jennings!" The humour in his grace's mellifluous voice was unmistakable.

Jennings scowled and ostentatiously handed his employer the requisite top boots of Parisian leather. The duke looked down and saw his dark, richly handsome face perfectly reflected in the shine.

"I *will* concede you are the devil of a dab hand at boots, Jennings!"

Considerably mollified, the valet brightened perceptibly and began putting his mind to the manner in which the whole of my lord's extensive attire could be transferred to two middling portmanteaus. His grace did not bother to try to reason with him—Jennings, known to his master for more years than he cared to remember, could work miracles.

"Does your grace intend to be long out of town?"

"Just so long as long as my mama is *in* town!" For the first time, the duke looked up from his boots and stared directly at his valet. Something quite akin to a rather mischievous grin crossed his likable face. The impression was confirmed by a broad and most undignified wink.

Jennings threw his hands up in despair. Whenever would the duke learn what was owing to his consequence? Winking indeed! Still, he had to concede his grace had a point. The Dowager Duchess of Doncaster would arrive like a whirlwind in the night, issuing orders from dawn to dusk, meddling where she had no business to and otherwise turning his grace's well-ordered household into a state of bedlam. It had been done before and the underservants dreaded it. What was worse, she was likely to scold his lordship to death, just as though he were *not* Rhaz Carlisle, fifth Duke of Doncaster and a peer of the realm.

The valet's outraged demeanour melted somewhat. He was very fond of the fifth duke, despite his reprobate penchant for levity and his strong, stubborn, implacable will at times. True, they would rub along better if his grace heeded his words a trifle more, allowing his hair to be cut à la Titus, permitting a few gold seals to hang

ornately from his waistcoat, agreeing, perhaps, to just
a hint of scent. . . . But no! The duke was unreasoningly
firm, quite unmanageable, in fact.

Still, Jennings had to concede enormous admiration
for him—for he was no prink of fashion or jaw-me-dead
gabster. He could handle his pistols and his wine with
equal equanimity, he was as fine a huntsman as he was
shot and he had such a bruising left fist that even
Thomas Cribbs hesitated to step into the fray.

The valet, though he would die before admit it, was
inordinately proud of his employer. As he was wont to
recite to the kitchen staff until they were positively
bored to tears, his grace the fifth duke could ride to an
inch and race a curricle with consummate skill. Everyone knew that no one but the most foolhardy and green
ever challenged him to such a contest. Also—and this
was said with *much* satisfaction—his grace could stare
down encroaching fribbles enough to make them
squirm.

Unfortunately, her grace the dowager duchess,
though annoying, could not possibly be placed into
that category. Her son, when he saw her, was thus un-
failingly polite and even, to the undiscerning, discon-
certingly meek. He was obliging enough to escort her
to routs and balls and even the odd turn at Vauxhall
or the theatre. He submitted to her endless catechisms,
advice, complaints, gossip and admonishments with
bland charm, giving her to understand he appreciated
every wise word of counsel. Of course, she never noticed the stubborn tilt of his chin or the whimsical
expression in his eyes that exuded amusement rather
than concentration.

It was a peaceable enough arrangement, for his grace
never objected to having his menus overset or his residence thrown open to soirees and other such hideous
entertainments. More likely than not he would merely

amble over to his private quarters and forget the whole affair entirely. Certainly, when he was engrossed in some piece of edifying literature or playing the harpsichord he'd had installed in the library, nothing could be farther from his mind than the opulent festivities he was sponsoring—and no doubt paying for. The duchess could rail and admonish all she liked, but beyond a deceptively meek smile she could elicit nothing of consequence, *particularly* not a promise to be better behaved in the future.

It was quite provoking for the poor duchess, who delighted in meddling and managing. Matchmaking was high on her list of activities, for she positively yearned for grandchildren now that her own little nestlings had flown the coop. She connived and schemed relentlessly, but to no avail. It seemed whenever she cunningly arranged a ball so that the duke might *happen* to fall in the way of Miss So-and-so, he wriggled so skilfully from the net that the duchess was never able to discern for sure if the mischance had been by accident or design.

Just such a mischance was *now* about to occur. Jennings stifled a grin of his own and commented, with meaning, that the housekeeper had been informed of the duchess's intent. Her grace would be residing in town a fortnight before setting forth to Andover, where she was to attend the christening of her newest godchild.

"Bella's son? Remind me to send a gift."

The valet assented, knowing that the duke's generosity was legendary. Bella's son, whoever he was, would be assured a gift of extraordinary proportions. The duke allowed Jennings to help him with his coat. The superfine fitted so snugly to his lean, muscular frame that help with the buttons was welcome.

"My visit to Huntingdon will be precisely fourteen days, Jennings."

The valet completed his task, an unwary twinkle appearing in his eye. "The coincidence overwhelms me, your grace!"

The duke responded with a happy grin. It was not his habit to gossip with servants, but Jennings was such a minefield of information and so very loyal to boot that he had practically no compunction at all.

"If the duchess is attended by a bevy of young ladies of gentle breeding and excellent birth, do please ask Danvers not to hesitate to proffer my *sincere* apologies at being forced to miss them!"

"I shall not, your grace!"

Jennings entered into the joke with enthusiasm. Surveying the duke critically, he at last nodded his head in sublime satisfaction. Despite the deplorable lack of seals and jewels, he had to admit his grace looked supremely elegant and unremittingly handsome. A credit, in fact, to anyone who had the honour of valeting him.

Doncaster watched this process with a slight twitch to his mouth. "Do I pass muster, Jennings?"

"You will do, your grace." From which my lord was assured he was as fine as nine pence, for if he were not, the venerable Jennings would have had all morning to spend on the subject.

"Excellent! Inform Mistress Chawleigh to lay the covers for two tonight. Captain Argyll will be arriving from Plymouth."

"Captain Argyll, my lord! I saw that he was mentioned in dispatches. How very pleasant for you." Jennings was approving, for a nicer, less rackety young man he would be hard-pressed to find.

"Your eagle eyes miss nothing, do they?"

"No, my lord." Jennings was immodestly firm on this score.

Doncaster swallowed a laugh. "We will celebrate the

honour in the best style I know. I've ordered up some of the '79 burgundy from the cellars."

Jenning's tone was dry. "Just as well the duchess only arrives tomorrow."

The duke looked up with a smile. "Quite," was all he said.

Ancilla Camfrey shut her lips tightly and folded her arms. It was very seldom that she was ever stubborn, for despite her frittersome ways she really was very fond of her two daughters and could, by skilful management, be twisted around either of their little fingers. On this one point, however, she was adamant.

"Seraphina, you shall have a new music master just as soon as I can find one!"

Seraphina pouted. "Why, Mama? I am really quite grown, now! I am too old for the schoolroom and re-fuse—*refuse*—to be sent back!"

Ancilla saw the mutinous tears that sparkled at the back of her daughter's vivid, wide-set eyes.

"Please don't fuss, Seraphina dear. You will thank me for it I promise you! If you will only apply yourself—"

"Apply myself? I *hate* the harpsichord! I *hate* singing stupid madrigals!" I—"

"You don't hate *music*, however!" Cordelia's light voice was firm and soothing. Seraphina looked up, her sister put up her hand and smiled. "You can't cozen me into believing you don't adore Handel or Vivaldi—I've seen how you close your eyes at recitals! What is more, I'll wager my last quarter's allowance you are not indifferent to the opera."

"Delia, that is different!" Seraphina's voice was al-most a wail. "Mama wants me to have a fusty old tutor again and I won't have it! I simply won't have it!"

Miss Camfrey's perceptive eyes could see her sister

was working herself up into an unwelcome tantrum. She stood up and looked sternly into her lovely, elfin face.

"Seraphina, we are trying to spare you another humiliating debacle! You need not be a hundred percent proficient like Lady Amelia Trent—"

"She can't sing!"

"Very true, but it is not polite in you to point that out! Besides, madame, your *own* singing needs revision I am told!" Ancilla was so stern that both daughters looked at her in surprise. "I have had a dozen or so morning calls with sly old tabbies insinuating the same. I may not have been in the great chamber when Seraphina made her debut, but I am not such a slow top not to know what has occurred!"

Seraphina found herself colouring, but still managed to mumble, "Fustian!"

Miss Camfrey, seeing the telltale signs of colour adorn her sister's cheeks understood her to be coming round despite the unladylike term. She therefore raised her eyebrows significantly to her mother and left the room. Soon, Ancilla did the same, leaving Seraphina alone to recover her thoughts. If she was not reconciled to the idea of further tuition, at least she had an inkling of the need for it.

It was much later in the day, when all disharmony was long since forgotten, that Mrs. Camfrey came by the note. She was sifting idly through the mail, amused that her sister Jeeves had franked at least a half dozen sheets again, when she came by something quite unexpected among the usual assortment of bills and invitations. She stared at the gilt-edged wafer in surprise mingled with puzzlement.

"When did this arrive, Pendleton?"

"I have a notion it was this morning, ma'am. I was away but I believe it was received by one of the house-maids."

Ancilla nodded and sat down. "Thank you."

Pendleton nodded and withdrew from the room. Ancilla broke the seal clumsily, too interested in the contents to worry much about caution. The letter, as she had surmised by the seal, was from the Dowager Duchess of Doncaster. It was surprisingly brief and in no way alleviated the lines of puzzlement from Mrs. Camfrey's brow. What it *did* do, however, was send her into an agony of panic.

She rang the bell and called, most unbecomingly, across the room and into the garden, "Delia!"

The elder Miss Camfrey, happily picking a combination of jasmine and chamomile, caught her finger on a bramble berry and winced. She was far too ladylike to call back to her mother, so with a sigh she dropped her basket and scrambled down from the ladder, stopping only to remove her bonnet before making her way into the shade.

"Did you call, Mama?"

Ancilla nodded, her eyes bright. "Take a look at *this* if you will!"

Cordelia read the missive through once and set it down. Her heart had started to race in that strange, unaccountable way it had done the night of Lady Dearforth's soiree. She waited a moment to take a breath, then said, with admirable nonchalance, that they had better ask Mrs. Stevens to bake some of her halfpenny loaves and angel delights.

"I'd better send a list down to the kitchens, for no doubt we will need butter and eggs. It is fortunate I have just picked chamomile, for it will make an excellent infusion for tea."

Mrs. Camfrey stared at her daughter as if she'd run

mad. "Cordelia, dear, this is no common, garden-variety personage who invites herself to our home this afternoon! This is—"

"The Duchess of Doncaster! I know, Mama, but I cannot help thinking she would find it passing odd in us if we did not offer her some refreshments!"

"*Must* you always be so practical?"

Cordelia smiled. "I trust so, Mama, for between you and Seraphina there has to be *someone* dull enough to manage the household!"

"Dull? Pooh! You simply don't push yourself forward enough, Cordelia! When you are Lady Winthrop I hope you won't stint on what is owing to your consequence."

Miss Camfrey decided not to argue the point. She'd heard the gist time and time again. Besides, she had that familiar sinking feeling in the pit of her stomach. The thought of becoming Lady Winthrop, whilst not exactly repugnant, was depressing to her spirits nonetheless. She sighed.

Mrs. Camfrey looked at her sharply. "I hope you are not sickening for something, Cordelia dear. You have looked strangely abstracted this past week."

Well she might have! Visions of Rhaz, Lord Doncaster had been flitting all too frequently through her recalcitrant thoughts. It bothered her that she should dwell so much on their few intimate moments when she had a lifetime ahead with Lord Henry. If she could bring herself to feel a tenth as alive with him as she had with the duke, she could look towards her marriage with equanimity. As it was, comparisons were inevitable. Cordelia's imagination, never usually fanciful, was stirred. If she closed her eyes she could almost sense his presence, his intriguing eyes brimful of laughter and a trace of faint cynicism. There had been a ready understanding between them that Cordelia yearned for in her dealings with her own family and betrothed.

Now she stopped to wonder what the duchess's visit presaged. *Surely,* her meeting with Doncaster could not be connected with this imperious note. And yet, the coincidence . . . Lost in thought she did not hear Seraphina trip into the room, her long auburn hair all atangle.

"Mama! Lord Rochester wrote me the *prettiest* of poems! I told him he was a great flirt but— What *is* it?"

Seraphina noticed that her mother looked strangely excited. When she read the note handed to her, she looked puzzled and then clapped her hands in a transport of delight.

"Good heavens! She must have heard of Roving Rhaz!"

"Seraphina!" Cordelia's voice was sharp. She could not think *how* she'd come to use such a distasteful expression and, worse, pass it on to her impressionable and irrepressible younger sibling.

"Do not worry, Delia dear. I shan't call him that in front of her grace!"

"I should think not!" Ancilla's voice was stern. She took the note back again and reread it, as if to glean some secret, hidden message. "I am *still* in the dark. Why should her grace deign to make this call? To be sure we were acquainted at Miss Caxton's Seminary for Young Ladies an aeon ago, but that cannot signify. We were hardly bosom buddies and when she married Doncaster I do not believe we kept in touch. The passing *nod* of course . . ."

"Do not be such a gudgeon, Mama! She is coming, I daresay, to see *me!*" Seraphina twirled across the room in her slippered feet, gathering swaths of her muslin morning dress as she did so.

Cordelia opened her mouth to say something, then snapped it shut firmly. It might have been true, of course. His grace might have fallen head over heels in love with Seraphina the instant he set eyes on her. There was no doubt she'd been in looks the evening of the soiree. No doubting, too, the floral tributes she'd received nor the morning callers that had besieged the house night and day from that moment forward.

Cynically, Cordelia had set Seraphina's success down to a combination of her own sweet nature and a slavish desire to follow fashion. It occurred to her that Doncaster was a nonpareil, a trendsetter in all that he did. By openly supporting Seraphina, he had set his seal upon her. Her popularity after that would have been inevitable.

Still, he'd not *himself* visited the little house on Brooke Street, and above a small posy for both sisters the day after the soiree, nothing else of great moment had occurred. Yet here was the Duchess of Doncaster coming to call! Quite unaccountable unless his feelings *had* been engaged. . . . Cordelia swallowed hard. If that were so, then she wished her sister every happiness.

"I had best go prepare Mrs. Stevens for our guest. I don't doubt she will set the servants to spring cleaning with vigour. I shall cull some flowers from the hothouse and ask Anders if I may trim some of the roses. Do you think we should bring out the silver plate, Mama?"

"Undoubtedly! When *else* should we use it? The crystal, too, of course."

Cordelia nodded and opened the drapes a little farther. Her dark ringlets cascaded down her back and seemed to shine from the sunshine filtering through the window pane.

"Perhaps we can stop by Gunther's and buy some sugared candy and a marasquino jelly or a pineapple cream?" Seraphina asked this hopefully, for she *adored* sweet things.

Cordelia looked at the little ormolu clock upon the mantel. Her hands flew to her mouth and she shook her head. "We have not much time, for she stipulates two o'clock and it is already near ten!"

Horrified, Seraphina and Ancilla bent their minds to what to wear. Whilst they were still thinking, the elder Miss Camfrey made her way quietly outside. No doubt the brisk morning air would cool her hot cheeks and allow her to think.

FOUR

"Well met, Frederick!" His grace smiled engagingly at his friend and dismissed Chawleigh with a slight nod. "Come inside. I have something that will warm your bones and make you forget your troubles, I assure you!"

Captain Argyll threw his beaver across the room and it landed, to his great satisfaction, on the hat stand discreetly tucked in the corner.

"Excellent!" He beamed. "I was hoping you kept a decent cellar, for I assure you the Kings Arm's does *not!*"

"I wish you would put up with *me*. You are perfectly welcome, you know."

The Honourable Frederick made a face. "Don't fuss, Rhaz! The Arms will do until I make some sort of shift. I won't batten off you and there is an end to it."

The duke nodded. Useless to argue with Freddie, for the man had a will almost as strong as his own. One of the reasons he liked him, of course, for Frederick was the last man on earth to toad eat him or kowtow sickeningly to his lofty rank.

The duke poured from a bottle on the waiting salver and handed a glass to his friend. He watched in bemusement as the dark, velvety liquid was downed in one breathtaking gulp. "Spain has taught you some tricks, I see!"

"Devil a bit!" Captain Argyll set down his glass and seated himself quite close to the chessboard. His eyes flickered over it absently before returning, once more, to those of the duke. "Truth is, Rhaz, I'm a trifle blue devilled." He looked rueful as he made this disclosure, for he was loath to admit the extent of his depression of spirits. After returning from the Peninsula, he'd expected his family to greet him with at least *some* degree of warmth. This expectation had proven false, for the Earl of Drummond was consumed with his nuptials and felt unaccountably put out by the return of a handsome, profligate younger brother who might steal his thunder if not actually his bride.

For Captain Argyll, in peacetime circles known as Lord Frederick, was renowned for his bonny nature, insouciant sense of humour and faultless address, particularly with the female sex. It was as well he had no fortune to boast of, for otherwise he might have found himself besieged by young maidens eager for his hand. Lord Frederick, it should be noted, was *not* the marrying type.

It was a strange friendship he had struck up with Rhaz, Lord Doncaster. Where the duke was scholarly, the captain eschewed literature and Greek like the plague, calling all misguided adherents "bookish." Where the duke had been born to riches, the captain had been born in the knowledge that he was a mere second son, destined to forge his own place in the world. Rhaz loved savoury, Frederick adored sweet. Rhaz rode, Frederick walked. It was said that he had walked across half of Spain at one time and the duke, knowing him intimately, had credited the rumor. Frederick was happiest on a gentle nag of sweet disposition. Rhaz was hamstrung on anything less than a fiery Arabian or a high-stepping grey.

Perhaps it was their mutual passion for music that

had first drawn them together in a run-down tavern in Spain. For Frederick, whatever his other objections to the arts, was a musician born. He could close his eyes and imagine the most extraordinary notes tumultuously rising and falling together in a crescendo of power and harmony. Better, he could translate the thought into actuality, using whatever instrument lay to hand. Harp or lute, violin or harpsichord—it was all the same to him. He could create enchantment in an instant, using his fingers or lips as the wellspring of harmony. Whilst the duke could not play, he could listen. And listen he did, with such fierce intensity that Captain Argyll had been forced to acknowledge his presence, playing as he had never done before, because the passion of music was enhanced tenfold by its appreciation.

Whatever the reason, an unshakeable bond had been forged between the duo. Whilst they went their own separate ways in the ordinary manner of things, when they *did* meet, it was as if they'd never been apart. Captain Argyll found himself divulging to Rhaz what he had hardly acknowledged to himself: his driving ambition to earn his way in the world, heedless of title and family. He was heartily sick of listening to his elder brother's clichéd pronouncements on everything from the state of the poor to the state of his robes.

The duke's lips twitched in sympathetic understanding, for it was true that the Earl of Drummond *did* have a singularly inflated sense of his own importance. Frederick declared he was entitled to that and welcome, but he needed no part in it.

Further, he scorned to have his music performed at soirees, for *they*, he announced, were judged by rank rather than proficiency. Thinking of his own antics, the duke was inclined to agree. Little Miss Camfrey would have been allowed to sink but he, a duke, had caused her to swim. It was rankly unfair as he would have been the first to admit.

Captain Argyll continued, outlining objection after objection to the life neatly laid out for him by the earl and the dowager countess. No, he did *not* want to become a clergyman however good the living. His mouth quirked at this, for as he cheerfully remarked, he was more likely to be consigned to hell than to heaven.

Between breaths, the duke managed to stop him, recommending to him the excellent goose liver pate and cheeses set down by his housekeeper. The very thought was enough to send Frederick's spirits bouncing back. After the pair had done the kitchens ample justice, Rhaz wiped his mouth carefully and asked his friend if he had any plans beyond merely "jawing on" about what he did *not* want.

Frederick cocked his head to one side and stretched out his long, muscular legs. Though slightly shorter than Rhaz, he was nevertheless superbly built, his well-defined proportions an excellent testament to Cribb's parlour and Gentleman Jack's saloon, where he had spent many an hour in concentrated combat.

Not to *mention* the recent war, which had produced so many narrow shaves that he had become accustomed to hanging off ledges, ducking bayonets and generally exercising his fine physique in all *manner* of intriguing ways. Then there were the nights . . . but suffice it to say that Lord Frederick had a surfeit of activity, pleasurable and otherwise. Sufficient, certainly, to explain his enviably flat stomach and other near perfect dimensions.

"Quizzing me, Rhaz?"

The Duke of Doncaster smiled. "Only prodding you on, dear boy! You would not be Captain Argyll of the Seventh Fighting Dragoons if you did not have a plan!"

"True! And, yes, I do have a notion of sorts."

"Care to enlighten me?"

"I am not sure. You may think I have run quite mad!"

"There is no novelty in *that*, Frederick! You should have been safely tucked in Bedlam *years* ago!"

The captain made an unholy grimace. "My pompous windbag of a brother's sentiments *exactly*, I fear. Still, I am out and about and in high grig, too, so that is of no consequence."

"Do you intend keeping me in suspense all night or is this a novel new way of entertaining me?" The duke's voice was heavy with sarcasm. Frederick, it should be noted, was not cowed in the least. Instead, he grinned broadly and put his hands behind his head.

"A guessing game? What an excellent notion, your grace!"

The duke thoughtfully surveyed the last of the contents of his glass. Then, without warning, he dashed it against his dear, bosom buddy's shirtfront.

Frederick threw back his tousled chestnut head and chuckled. As he reached for a crisp damask napkin, his face was a medley of expressions, the chiefest of these being outraged good humour. "I hope you have a spare shirt at *least*, Rhaz! The King's Arms will never admit me looking like a regular jack o' straws!"

"Good! Stay with me."

Captain Argyll sighed and brushed a few specks off his creamy pantaloons. *They*, at least, were still immaculately clean.

"Have done, Rhaz. You know my sentiments on the matter! Besides, I have other plans."

The duke sighed ominously. "And these are?"

For the first time, the Honourable Frederick looked a trifle diffident. "I intend composing. If I *have* this talent—and I think I have—I should use it, rather than become a preaching clergyman, or worse, a complaisant country gentleman! The life of a squire does not suit, I find."

"So I should think, with that tame nag you choose to ride!"

"Betsy? There is nothing wrong with my Betsy, but that is not to the point." Brave Captain Argyll looked strangely vulnerable. The duke, seeing this, became serious.

"It is an excellent idea, Frederick, for I believe you have the gift. I will never forget coming upon you in that tavern, for the lilting melody of the panpipe still haunts me. Compose by all means—heaven knows, we need at least one genuine artist among the dross we laud today!"

Frederick was gratified, for he knew that upon such an important issue the duke could be relied upon neither to offer false coin nor prevaricate if the truth had been unpleasant.

"Thank you. My little pipes serve me well! I plan, though, to compose for harpsichord and strings. Perhaps also a lute, possibly a harp. We shall see."

"Shall I be your patron?"

Frederick coloured fiercely. "If *that* is what you think I am about, then I shall leave upon the instant! I don't take charity Rhaz Carlisle, Lord Doncaster!"

The duke's eyes gleamed. Frederick made *such* a refreshing change from the myriads of people quite prepared to toadeat him for a living. They got short shrift, of course, but sponsoring the captain would have been an unalloyed pleasure.

"Don't get on your high ropes with *me*, Freddie! You and I have come too far to argue over trifles!"

"Indeed! Then you will know I am too sensible to batten upon my friends!"

The duke sighed. "As you wish, Frederick. If *I* am not

to aid you, how will you live? Your annual stipend is a mere pittance! Shall you marry an heiress?"

The good Frederick grinned widely. "I'd as soon cut off my nose as get leg shackled! I prefer *variety*, I will have you know! That, I have to admit with relief, is *one* good thing about being a second son. I don't have to marry for heirs and I tell you, Rhaz, I shan't!"

"Touché!" Rhaz raised his hands as if sorry he asked. "What will you do then?"

"I shall become a music master. It is an easy living. I shall earn my keep by day and compose by night. I shall not have the distraction of a social calendar, so I will have ample time to think." Frederick looked defiant, as if challenging Rhaz to object. To his surprise, Rhaz did not.

"An excellent idea if you neglect to mention you are high born. I doubt too many employers would be overkeen to employ a nobleman."

"I've thought of that. They wouldn't let me loose without a chaperone, of course. Wise, too!" A mischievous dimple played across his lordship's cheeks.

"You will probably land up with some pudding-faced wench who is a musical illiterate."

"All the better! I shall earn my keep without falling captive to her charms."

"I shall hope, then, for a cross-eyed cit."

"Thank you." Frederick inclined his head solemnly. I shall be presented as plain Captain Argyll. Suits me, for I've been answering to that name the greater part of two years!"

"What about Drummond? Won't he turn up his supercilious nose at the lark?"

"Thank heavens, no! He shall know nothing about it. I wouldn't put it past him to give the game away if he did. He has followed Prinny to Bath at all events, so we should not cross company."

"I take it you have found an employer?"

Frederick nodded. "Quite providential, actually. There was an advertisement in the *Gazette* yesterday. I applied in person and appear to have found favour!"

"Excellent! And your music? How shall you go on?"

"I shall write by candlelight and forward the scores on to Mr. Beckett."

"Miss Austen's publisher?"

"The very same! He has already printed a nonsensical little madrigal of mine and has promised to review anything further that I produce. Of course, he mainly deals in literary works, but he has a knowledgeable partner in the operatic world. His decision rests with that gentleman, so the arrangement works out well."

"You seem to have it all in hand."

"I hope so, for I would hate to have to run back to Drummond!"

"You shall not."

"How can you be so certain?"

The duke eyed him quizzically and took up a chess piece. "I have heard your music."

The explanation was simple, but its impact profound. Captain Argyll laughed it off with a quick shake of his rugged shoulders but the duke knew that the nonchalance shielded a potent mixture of gratitude and pride. It would have been unbecoming in him to share this awareness, so he accepted the captain's shrug at face value and skilfully turned the topic.

"Care for a game of chess? I have been on pins to try out this set. Caught sight of it at Michener's and I believe it will serve. The pieces are excellently weighted and I have a strange fancy for the design."

Frederick leant forward and looked at the pieces carefully. The king and queen were wrought simply but elegantly, hand tooled with garlands for crowns in the classical Roman style. Each piece was slightly but subtly different, with expressions apparent in the face of each piece. Even the wood was special—sandalwood from the East and a strange new timber called "rata" from the South.

He shook his head ruefully. "Best save the set for someone who can play, Rhaz! I fear I will disgrace myself abysmally if I were to take you on!"

"For shame, Frederick! As if I càre a rap for that!"

But the captain was resolute. He did not wish to play. Rhaz sighed and set the pieces carefully back on the board. No sense in coaxing Frederick. A lesser man would yield—this second son of an earl would not.

"I insist you sing then! I am as bored as sin!"

"What?" Frederick looked shocked. "The famous Duke of Doncaster? The arbiter of fashion? The very pink of the ton?"

"Have done, Frederick, or I shall do more than merely douse you with wine!"

The good captain laughed. "I shall be awake to that suit. You shan't catch me sleeping twice, my good lord."

The duke's lips twitched and a dangerous smile played at the corners of his mouth. "Very well, Freddie! I shall take that as a due challenge. And now, I beg you, desist from teasing and do what you do best. If you are not up to singing I have purchased a tolerable violin— more's the pity, for I find that I cannot *play* the wretched instrument! Show me how it is done, or I fear I shall have to return it with a vile note to the makers. My valet threatens to find another post, for he cannot abide the scratching."

Lord Frederick Argyll chuckled and stood up. "Hand me the instrument, Rhaz! I own I feel almost sorry for it!"

The duke obediently fetched the old golden brown violin. As Frederick took the bow and tuned it up reverentially, his grace allowed his thoughts to wander.

Miss Cordelia Camfrey again. He sighed and tried to dismiss the memory of her low, well-modulated voice and speaking grey eyes. The soft curve of her lips as she trustingly appealed to him was particularly difficult to summarily remove from his thoughts. He was taken with her—every muscle of his strong, sinuous frame told him that as if his mind was not already apprised of the notion. What he could not understand was *why* he was so attracted. She was nothing *like* any of the young eligibles his eager, misguided, thoroughly doting mother seemed to imagine might appeal. Nor was she like any of his somewhat *less* insipid ladybirds. . . . He drew himself up short. Cordelia was not to be compared to that category. What, then? What was it about her that allured him so and wreaked such havoc upon his equilibrium?

Her beauty, though substantial, was *worlds* away from the stunning guinea-gold hair and azure eyes he found he preferred. Even her *sister's* curling auburn tendrils were more likely to please than the long, jet black strands that escaped their pins and just outlined the nape of her neck with soft, fluffy tendrils. Though slender, she was nonetheless too rounded in parts to quite match to his taste for willowy slim women in languishing, statuesque poses. He thought a little harder. Honesty? Yes, there was that undoubtedly. He admired her for it. His sampling of womankind in the past did not lead him to have too much in the way of expectation in this regard. His mother, certainly, was a prime example of the guile and conniving he found typical to the female sex. In the most benevolent way, of course, she was scheming and tirelessly underhand. He smiled as he thought on his latest ploy to foil her. She would no doubt be *quite* overset by his absence from town.

"Head in the clouds, Rhaz?" The instrument was tuned but the duke had not noticed. Frederick rested the bow on a chair and fingered the violin idly, a small signet flashing red on his clean, well-kept hands.

"Possibly." There was a slight drawl to the duke's words that alerted Frederick to something out of the ordinary.

"Dare I guess the direction of your musings?"

"You may, though I take leave to inform you you may be far out!"

"I'll take the chance!" Frederick looked deep into one of the single flames that flickered from ice-white candles scattered strategically about the room. He stared for a moment; then a slow smile crossed his strong, sun-soothed features. "I see a woman."

Rhaz snorted. "You *always* see a woman!"

Frederick set the violin down and leaned closer towards the flame. He scowled at his best friend. "Hush! Desist from all disparaging sounds! I see . . ."

"I'll tell you what *I* see! A muttonheaded, shimble-shamble—"

"Be quiet! I see dark hair and the faint whisper of a smile, delicate cream . . ."

Rhaz closed his eyes. The description was dangerously close to the truth and all his senses began to reel.

"Stop it, I say!"

Chestnut curls bobbed up cheekily. "Am I close then?"

Rhaz would not give Freddy the satisfaction. Besides, he had no wish to have Cordelia's identity guessed at, or bandied, even playfully, about town.

"No! You are far out actually! If you must know, my tastes have taken a turn for . . . for . . ." He searched his mind for something his tastes might have taken a turn for. Seraphina's fulsome beauty popped conveniently into his thoughts. "Auburn!" he called out in relief.

Frederick looked at him suspiciously. Rhaz was behaving rather strangely and that was a fact. If he had not known the duke better he would have thought . . . He shrugged his shoulders. If that was the way the wind lay with his grace, he would tease him no more.

With a faint, dismissive smile on his features he merely cocked an interested brow and took up the violin, glimmering like burnished gold in the candlelight.

The remainder of the evening was transformed from the merely pleasant to the utterly memorable. When the last strains of the violin's "Ode to Starlight" faded gently into the air, the duke opened his eyes and nodded. There would be no need to frank Lord Frederick. If he was not feted as the greatest composer of the decade, the duke would be sadly off the mark.

It would have been a comfort to Lord Frederick to know that the duke was rarely, if ever, far wrong.

FIVE

Pendleton took a deep breath and swallowed the excitement welling up in his throat. It was not every day he was obliged to announce nobility. It was one in the eye for his archrival Pinkerton, who was perennially puffed up because his mistress was sister to an earl. An earl? Hah! Today Pendleton was to announce no less a personage than a duchess.

He fingered his livery, checking carefully to see that the frogged lapels were all in order. Silver on blue. He was rather proud of the uniform, for it gave him a certain air. Higgins, of course, looked too lanky for the garb and Darrows seemed always to appear as if he had been dragged backwards across a meadow by a very angry bull. He would take good care to see that Darrows was ensconced in the servant's quarters when her grace made her arrival.

Thank heavens that nodcock groom at least knew his business. The duchess's cattle would be safe with him so long as he was not required to do too much in the way of headwork.

Pendleton looked at the time. Gone quarter past already and no sign of the heavy wheels upon the stone paving outside. He felt a trifle anxious and considered removing his coat. If only Mrs. Stevens had not stoked the fire so hot! Still, she had been in a frenzy of baking,

the little angel cakes only now sitting neatly on a rack
cooling. Together with the jam tarts, gingerbread, raspberry water ice and wafer-thin sandwiches, it would be
a regular feast, it would.

The sound of hooves brought Pendleton out of his
reverie. Instantly, he was bellowing orders at two of the
underservants and admonishing Darrows not to set a
foot above stairs. Then, with a stately and orderly pace,
he made his way out to the front door. He had a long
wait, for the carriage was stabled before the duchess
alighted, her broad body laden with such essentials as
a sturdy walking stick, a tippet, a fan, a reticule of tre-
mendous proportions and something very like an over-
sized redingote of purple hue.

Pendleton was much impressed with the peacock
feathers that flowed majestically from her turban. They
appeared most suitable to her consequence and invited
stares from servants as far beyond his realm as number
five, Conduit Street. Since this particular was likely to
add to his own consequence, he was more than satisfied,
despite being directed to carry several of her numerous
belongings.

By the time her grace was announced, tea was already
neatly laid out and the Camfrey girls becomingly arranged on sofas of pale blue. Cordelia managed to con-
tain her curiosity by counting all the stitches in a
tapestry just above Ancilla's head. Seraphina, sad to say,
was not as restrained. Almost as soon as she had made
her curtsy to the duchess, she was plying her with questions. She was not so bold as to ask directly after Rhaz,
but the duchess would have been a fool not to understand the direction her thoughts were taking.

Strangely, she did not depress Seraphina's attentions,
but rather scrutinised her closely and even rapped her,
at one stage, with the stick of her fan. Seraphina's stifled
yelp of pain almost caused Cordelia to giggle. Fortu-

nately, she overcame the urge and thus appeared to be very pretty behaved, though rather prim.

Ancilla was almost as curious as her younger daughter. After exchanging pleasantries with the duchess, she recommended her to the angel cakes and confessed her surprise at the visit.

The duchess chuckled a hearty, earthy kind of a laugh and wagged her finger in Ancilla's face. "I don't *doubt* you are surprised, Ancilla! It is an age at least since we spoke. You were a rackety young thing at Miss Caxton's and I *do* believe you have not changed since then!"

Ancilla, never inclined to believe she was forty, blushed slightly and, to Cordelia's amazement, started stammering like a schoolgirl. The duchess waved her hand airily and bade her not to take anything she said into account, for she knew she was a managing old soul and sincerely had no wish to offend.

The unexpected kindness struck Cordelia, who had certainly conceived the duchess to be an old tartar, incapable of the sort of civility to which Ancilla had become accustomed. The ice somewhat broken in this airy fashion, tea was poured and the conversation steered to less dangerous waters. No doubt her grace would state her object by and by.

Every so often she would rummage in her reticule and draw out her lorgnette, which she would affix to her eyes and use to stare at Seraphina in particular. The younger Miss Camfrey took not the least offence, for she knew she was in excessive good looks, her ravishing auburn hair coiled in the very height of fashion. She was wearing a canary morning dress of striped organdie, the bodice cut low in an artful square. A tiny chemisette of gold fichu preserved her modesty, but all the same, her charms were apparent and for the gentleman, at least, most appealing.

Cordelia, too, was in looks, but hers were of the gentler nature. She wore a turquoise muslin overdress with an apron front, high waisted in the fashionable mode and trimmed with a single ribband of snowy white. Her kid slippers exactly matched that of the ribband, but no one was to know this, for they were demurely tucked beneath the folds of her skirts. Seraphina, on the other hand, appeared to have little compunction in allowing her dainty buckled pumps to be displayed. Despite a heavy frown from Cordelia, she amiably allowed her stockinged ankles to make their shocking appearance from time to time. The duchess seemed not to mind, for she surveyed the ankles with impunity and emitted a rasping sort of laugh that appeared to denote satisfaction of sorts.

"Prime enough piece, ain't she?" she remarked. Ancilla, divining her grace was referring to her youngest and dearest, nodded emphatically and declared she was, despite her obvious lack of ability at the pianoforte and other gentler accomplishments.

At this, her grace chortled and afforded Ancilla a sharp stare. "Some men don't care a *button* for such poppycock! By all accounts my *son* don't seem to care a tuppence ha'penny for such fandangled nonsense!"

At last, then, the duchess was coming round to the subject of her visit. The very thought of Rhaz and his appreciative eyes stirred the older Miss Camfrey deeply, but she did not show it, for above clutching the little handle of her teacup overhard, her face remained impassive.

Seraphina's eyes sparkled as she nodded vigorously. "Indeed, ma'am, I believe that may be true, for your son, you know, rescued me from a most *shocking* coil! He seemed not to mind overmuch that my song was off-key and my register sadly flat! I declare if he had not come to my aid the other evening, I would have been quite undone!"

At this, the duchess nodded her head sagely, stating that most likely she would have been ruined, for a young lady without accomplishments was hardly worth a sou on the marriage mart. Seraphina was inclined to take her up on this, but sank back into her chair, suddenly silenced. Cordelia hoped the duchess's hasty words would have the unexpected outcome of making Seraphina more reconciled to the arrival of her music master.

Just as she conceived those thoughts, Pendleton interrupted with an apologetic frown upon his face. It appeared that Captain Argyll had arrived, but without forewarning there was nothing prepared in the servant's quarters. He had mentioned something about the King's Arms, but . . .

"Nonsense, Pendleton! Admit him at once! His possessions may be deposited in the guest chamber above stairs." Ancilla turned to the duchess. "I would dislike it excessively if he were forced to kick his heels in the foyer. I interviewed the man yesterday and can vouch that he has breeding, at least, if not birth!"

The duchess raised her eyebrows a fraction and helped herself to a sugared bun. Mrs. Camfrey looked suddenly uncertain. "That is, if you do not mind . . . ?"

"Mind?" Her grace looked querulous. "It is *your* home, Ancilla! If you wish to admit upper servants to your drawing rooms there is nothing to be said against it!" Deceptively amiable, the barb on the duchess's tongue was quite lost on Ancilla, who smiled happily and reiterated her orders to Pendleton.

Seraphina's face instantly turned mutinous, but under the watchful stare of the duchess, she could hardly vent her spleen. She determined at once that she would be gracious but aloof. If the music master saw immediately that she was not a mere chit out of the schoolroom, he might revise his treatment of her.

Seraphina, indeed, hoped that he would instantly hand in his notice, for it was one thing to engage to tutor a schoolroom miss, quite another to tackle a young lady of the first stare. Seraphina knew she was that, for she had been offered numerous rides in the park and particular attentions by gentlemen of quite superior rank. The experience was quite heady for one of her youth and innocence. Cordelia just hoped that the novelty would not turn her head, because for all her frothiness she was very good-natured and an excellent little sister.

They had not long to wait, for Captain Argyll had been deposited not in the foyer, as Ancilla suspected, but in the blue salon just adjacent to the more formal receiving room. He entered briskly and with a good-humoured smile made his bow. Ancilla made the introductions, the duchess condescending to slightly nod, the only evidence of this being a slight bending in one of the plumes on her turbaned head.

Captain Argyll looked a little shocked to see her. This instantly served to restore a modicum of her good humour, since she naturally assumed he was suitably awed and honoured by her presence. Of course, it was no such thing. Captain Argyll was merely stunned to see his best friend's mother grace what he had thought a rather shabby and provincial residence. Indeed, the duchess's presence alarmed him somewhat, for if his pupil moved in the first circles, his secret would be harder to keep. He just prayed Mrs. Camfrey would not take it into her head to travel to Bath. If she did, he would be undone indeed.

None of these thoughts showed on his face as he gravely acknowledged Cordelia, then Seraphina in turn. Whilst the elder Miss Camfrey curtsied prettily and murmured something quite suitable to the occasion, Seraphina was struck dumb. Cordelia had been anxious that her sister would say something outrageous to offend. Instead, it was nothing of the kind. She was gaping like a fish and needed to be prompted before making a rather harum-scarum curtsy and blushing quite delightfully.

For Seraphina, lively—mischievous, naughty Seraphina—had just made a most unsuitable discovery. In less than a second she had fallen for her music master and all the activity in the room faded into nothingness as her eyes met and held quite the most beautiful man she had ever seen.

If Captain Argyll felt a similar stirring, nothing in his demeanour suggested it. He gravely took Seraphina's gloved fingers in his and promised to do his best by her. She made no objection to this rather high-handed pronouncement, but rather gazed soulfully into his eyes and suggested they adjourn at once to the music room.

Ancilla's eyes met Cordelia's over their heads. Her expression was so outrageously smug that the elder daughter nearly choked. She wouldn't have put it past Ancilla to choose a music master so charming that Seraphina would not make the faintest protest at having to practice her lessons. Ancilla's way was always the most flighty, but in the strangest manner she invariably achieved what she wanted.

The duchess looked slightly disapproving, commenting that, whilst Seraphina undoubtedly needed to hone her musical skills, the haste seemed unwarranted. The younger Miss Camfrey had the grace to blush and Cordelia rushed to the rescue, stating that both sisters had been certain the duchess would want to be private with their mama and so had arranged for other afternoon activities. At this, her grace inclined her head regally and acknowledged that this was so. She *did* wish to speak alone with Ancilla.

Captain Argyll's clear blue eyes meekly met those of

the duchess and Mrs. Camfrey. He allowed himself to be steered out by both sisters without so much as a backwards glance.

Her grace produced her lorgnette once again and stared out past him. A puzzled frown furrowed her forehead as she tapped her stick against the floor. "I have the oddest notion I have seen that boy before!"

Ancilla shook her head. "Impossible, your grace! I personally inspected his references and they state quite positively he has been out of England gone on ten years now. He has been situated in Spain, Italy and India I believe."

Since the references had been hastily scrawled by the captain himself, he had found it necessary to deal in half-truths, sketchily outlining a life abroad that *could* have been true, had he not been otherwise engaged in doing service to king and country. Of course, the Iberian War had kept him on the Peninsula for close on two years, so the Spanish part of the fabrication was semiveracious at least. The duchess remained unconvinced, but she shook her head at the memory that was patently eluding her.

"Yes, well, we are not here to discuss music masters I suppose!"

Ancilla desisted from asking what they *were* here to discuss. Of late she had learned patience and her grace would probably not take kindly to prompting. She therefore assented with a half smile and poured a cup of the chamomile.

"I don't doubt your thoughts are heading in exactly the same direction as mine!" The duchess burst out with this remark so fiercely that Ancilla nearly dropped her cup.

"Pray enlighten me, your grace! I do not know—"

"Fustian! Any mama awake to her suit would be casting her eye in Rhaz's direction. What *I* say is—"

"Beg pardon?" Ancilla still appeared bewildered.

The thought dawned on the duchess that she had genuinely not thought of coupling her daughter with the duke. After the amazement came amusement. She chortled rather rudely and reached for her reticule, from which she extracted a large, hand-embossed handkerchief emblazoned with the crest of Carlisle.

"You really are such a widgeon, Ancilla! Any other mama would have *grasped* at the chance of catching my son but I do believe the thought simply has not crossed your mind!"

"Indeed it has not! As a matter of fact I should tell your grace that Cordelia has just accepted a most eligible offer. She is to become Lady Winthrop, you know." Her tone held an element of pride that was quite lost on the duchess.

"Tush! That is all very fine, but I do not speak of Cordelia! I speak of Seraphina of the auburn hair! I quite see why Rhaz was taken with her, for she is undoubtedly a beauty even if she is a little too flighty for my tastes!"

Ordinarily Ancilla would have rushed to her daughter's defence. She was too flabbergasted, however, to do more than set down her teacup and gaze at the duchess with wide, puzzled eyes. An attachment? You must be mistaken, your grace! I daresay they have not met above twice!"

"That may be so but their meeting certainly created a stir by all accounts!"

Ancilla began to see the light. "I collect you refer to the disastrous soiree when my little fledgling was invited to sing? I may be an abominable parent but you yourself have seen I've done everything I can to rectify the situation. Captain Argyll has been retained for the quarter at least!"

"Ancilla, I do believe you have not two thoughts in

your head! Forget about Seraphina's deplorable skills!
You should be more interested, by far, in the fact that
my son paid her so huge an attention! It can only mean
one thing, I assure you! He was attracted and I intend
helping you to snare him!"

If Mrs. Camfrey had been speechless before, she was
struck dumb now. Fortunately, the duchess did not
seem to notice, for she was caught up in a long-winded
monologue by which Ancilla was given to understand
that dowry was of no consequence, for Rhaz was "as
rich as Croesus" and did not need an heiress to bolster
up depleted fortunes. More salient to the duchess was
whether Seraphina was wellborn—and she had satisfied
herself on this score—and well-bred. This she seemed
to be, though a "trifle high-spirited." Still, as the duchess mourned, they did not make offspring the way they
used to and beggars could not be choosers. By all accounts Seraphina was a dutiful daughter if not quite
biddable. When the duchess stopped for air, Ancilla
opened her mouth to speak but was again forestalled
by a rush of words. It appeared that the duchess considered Rhaz's commitment to the single state "reprehensible" and she intended rectifying the position.
When she finally folded her arms and looked inquir-
ingly at Ancilla, it was all Mrs. Camfrey could do not to
stifle a laugh.

"Your grace, I do not believe one duet can be considered an attachment!"

The duchess eyed her fiercely. "No? You do not know
Rhaz! He would not trifle with single ladies and set up
their expectations unless he has intentions!"

"But he did not set up Seraphina's expectations!"

"No? Then he *should* have!"

All of a sudden Ancilla doubted. It was true Seraphina
had been in high grig when the note from the duchess
had arrived. True, too, that she had worn the duke's

posy the instant it was delivered. . . . She looked doubtfully at the colourful dowager duchess. She looked so
positive that all her troubling doubts were removed. If
Seraphina was attached to the duke and he to her, nothing could be so eligible. A social coup, in fact, though
Ancilla did not care the snap of her finger for such
things. Still, she loved Seraphina and if there was ought
she could do . . .

The duchess breathed a sigh of satisfaction. Ancilla
might be a blockhead at times, but she *was* the sister
of a marquis, and though she had married beneath her,
her bloodlines were unimpeachable.

The duchess leant forward eagerly and Ancilla politely ignored the creaking of her stays.

"Now *listen,* Ancilla . . ."

By the time her grace had said her piece, Mrs. Camfrey was left in no doubt as to her role. In a matter of
moments the duchess had turned her pleasant, well-ordered life topsy-turvy and upside down. In the *scurviest*
of ways she was to connive and contrive with the bossy
old so and so to steer Seraphina into the duke's sphere
of influence.

Her grace was too cunning to invite Seraphina to a
mere house party. Rhaz had foiled her intentions before
by his annoying manner of slipping out of town just at
the times she most wanted him to stay. No, there would
be no muddles and sudden urgent, pressing engagements this time. If her grace wanted to be certain of
throwing Seraphina her errant son's way, there could
be only one suitable time to invite the Camfreys.

A pity it was still two months away, but there, addlepated Ancilla would probably need that time simply
to prepare. She must point out to her the necessity for
riding habits and chic, understated gowns of shimmering lace. . . . She caught herself up and smiled. No, two

months was not so very long, after all. Better a well-laid plan . . .

"You shall stay with us for Christmas. Doncaster Place, Rhaz's chief residence, is not seventy miles from London. I shall have two carriages sent round for your baggage and your servants—"

"Christmas!" Ancilla put her hands to her cheeks. She had thought to spend it quietly *en famille,* not in some draughty mausoleum that was probably the handsome ducal edifice of the fifth Duke of Doncaster. Besides, without his personal invitation . . .

"Stuff and nonsense, Ancilla! Rhaz shall do exactly as I say! He is a most biddable son, you know!"

Ancilla refrained from asking why it was then necessary for her grace to go to such extraordinary lengths to secure his compliance in this scheme which she was not sure she could quite approve. Instead, she mildly mentioned that perhaps an afternoon tea or a simple evening whist party might suffice.

The duchess looked her scorn as she pulled out an immense filigree fan studded with rubies and wrought, in immeasurable places, with gold. Ancilla wondered wherever she could have procured such a hideous thing and whether it served any useful purpose whatsoever, for it looked so heavy that it surely could not function quite as it ought.

Happily, the duchess was oblivious to her disparaging musings and began a lengthy discourse on quite why Christmas was the most opportune moment to foist two young ladies, a flighty mama, three abigails, a manservant, a groom, a music master and nigh on ten portmanteaus on the fifth duke's noble attention.

By the time she had finished, the duchess had glibly announced a whole *host* of entertainments that left Ancilla bereft for speech. The crowning glory came when her grace announced, with great satisfaction, that

Seraphina would have a chance to prove the superiority of her music master when she was allotted pride of place in the traditional Christmas pageant held on the Carlisle estate.

Ancilla was stretching out for the smelling salts with an unusually faltering hand when the duchess unstopped some of her own and rather indelicately wafted it under the poor woman's nose. The vile concoction was enough to revive anyone and Ancilla recovered sufficiently to push the bottle away and indignantly remark that she felt very ill used.

The duchess humphed, commented that this was *precisely* the type of behaviour one would expect from a peabrain and proceeded to rattle off a million and one reasons why the connection was desirable and why Christmas was by far the best time to accomplish it.

She *assured* the beleaguered Ancilla that no more than a few gentle prods would be required to extract a proposal of marriage from her exasperating son's lips. Ancilla did not share her classmate's optimism.

Still, in the face of the duchess's overpowering glare, she acquiesced mildly and held her peace.

SIX

The music room was more a library cum sitting room, with several instruments scattered about in rather haphazard a manner. Frederick's eagle eyes noted a harpsichord and cello in the far corner and a little spinet somewhere in the muddle of some volumes stacked up high. These last, he noted, were probably more used than the instruments, for they abounded in bookmarks and revealed none of the deplorable dust that seemed to have settled upon the two larger pieces. In an instant he detected several scores in the mahogany-and-glass cabinet on his left. More were lying upon the music stand, but whether they had recently been consulted was hard to say.

Seraphina unwittingly answered this question, for seeing the direction of his eyes—which were vivid blue, verging on violet, she quickly announced that it had been an age since she'd practiced, but Cordelia was tolerably well versed in the art. Since her accents bordered on disgust, the captain was given to infer she thought her sister's virtue quite incomprehensible.

Cordelia laughed pleasantly, her soft, bell-like tones a strong contrast to her sister's more striking tenor. She declaimed, giving Captain Argyll to understand that, while she enjoyed tinkling on the harpsichord and was reasonably able to produce a melody, she was by no means proficient. The captain then handsomely invited her to join his lessons to which Cordelia laughed and promised that perhaps she would. Seraphina felt suddenly rather possessive of her music master and strangely loath to share him, though she loved her sibling dearly. Fortunately for them both, the elder Miss Camfrey recalled a pressing engagement for four and bid herself excused.

Alone with her captain—for she thought of him as that—Seraphina's high spirits surfaced to the fore. Though she deemed practicing "vile," she peeked at him through abundantly adorable lashed eyes and murmured that she was ready to learn.

The captain almost laughed aloud. The chit was obviously self-willed and spoiled, but he felt she would suit. He had expected to be bored to tears with his charge, but now he felt that she might present something of an unexpected challenge. Heaven knew, she was angelic to look at and angelic by name. He wondered if the appellation of "Seraph" suited her, but thought not.

He was singularly undeceived by her meekness on meeting him. She was a cheeky little devil if ever he saw one. Still, that made for an interesting life and there was nothing good Lord Frederick liked more than that. He thought with amusement on Rhaz's hope for him. Anything less like a "cross-eyed cit" was hard to come by.

Certainly, in her morning dress of canary lemon with ringlets of auburn spilling out from abundant coils, she could hardly be described as a dowd by even the most exacting of critics. Frederick's experienced eye roved downward to the more obvious of her charms. An innocent, but enticing nonetheless. He brought himself up sternly when he noticed his pupil colouring. He was here to teach and teach he damn well would.

The fierce thought was soon tempered by a more cautious adjoinder. He *would* teach, but in his own inimitable way. Stuffy music rooms bored him to tears. He suspected Miss Seraphina suffered from the same complaint.

"When would you wish to start, Miss Seraphina?"

"Now if you wish! I promise to try with those detestable scales but I warn you, sir, you shall regret it, for more clumsy, muddlesome fingers you would not credit!"

"Then I shall not press you, Miss Camfrey! There is nothing I loathe more than cowhandedness when it comes to music. We shall take a stroll through the gardens rather."

Seraphina was so taken aback she quite forgot how pleased she should have been at escaping the misery of scales. Instead, she scowled in a most unbecoming manner and announced she was not in the habit of being called cowhanded.

"No?"

The captain's one-syllable response brought the blood rushing to Seraphina's cheeks, for behind the syllable lay a wealth of meaning. Seraphina could tell he meant that, if she had not previously been so described, she *should* have been.

Useless to tell him that she was being hailed as a diamond of the first water from all sources. A music master would not be privy to high society and so he would not understand its significance. Besides, being boastful would hardly recommend her to him. There would be only one thing he could be interested in and that, maddeningly, was the one thing Seraphina fell far short of: music, music, detestable music! True, she adored listening to some of the baroque composers, but listening was worlds from performing and performing, as she knew, was something that she simply could not do.

She was at an impasse and Frederick, watching her

struggle with her thoughts, knew it. He stood with his back to the window. His shoulder-length chestnut hair was caught in a velvet riband at the back of his head, slightly old-fashioned, but then, he had never been an arbiter of taste like his good friend Rhaz.

He had taken care not to dress above his station, so his coat, while an excellent fit, was not of the first stare and his cravat would have reduced any self-respecting valet to tears. Though crisp and ice white, it was nevertheless tied in a deplorably simple knot, threaded through shirt points of such a constrained height that any dandy seeing him would have chortled himself into fits.

Still, there could be no denying the perfectly smooth outline of his buckskin knee breeches, nor the athletic muscles that they encased. Seraphina, glancing downward, found herself dwelling on intriguing parts no lady strictly ought to. In fairness, it was hardly her fault, for the breeches were such a snug fit she would have had to be blind not to be drawn to the very region that they so artlessly covered.

A slow curve crept across Captain Argyll's slightly pink, bow-shaped lips. He placed his gloved hands upon his head and regarded Miss Camfrey with a twinkle. "Do I pass scrutiny?"

Seraphina was shaken from her reverie. What a detestable man! He was positively gloating at her, as if he had read her thoughts! She turned her nose up coldly. "I have no notion of what you mean, captain!"

To her chagrin, the infuriating man merely chuckled and pointed out the window. "What lies out there?"

"A forest does!" Seraphina's words were abrupt to a fault. She could not imagine why the man should wish to know, since he had been engaged for the sole purpose of tying her remorselessly to the stuffy old room.

"Excellent! I have a mind to a walk!" The captain's

tone was bracing and brooked no argument. Seraphina's eyes widened in surprise. "A walk? I thought we were to begin our lesson!"

"We are!" The captain grinned and an engaging twinkle lit his eye. "Music is an intonation of nature. Its echoes, its crests, its waves and its silences are all an aural reflection of that which we see. To understand it, one has to live it, breath it, sense it. A music room is sadly flat when one can have the wind at one's back and soft, verdant green clover at one's feet."

Seraphina could hardly make sense of his words, but his eyes were so magnetic and his voice so beguiling that she thought she could follow him anywhere forever. The forest seemed but a small distance to traverse if it would be with him.

"Shall I get my parasol?"

The sensible words made him laugh. He shook his head. "Not a parasol. They are too clumsy and inevitably get muddied! A chip straw bonnet will do and I would exchange those delicious slippers for half boots at least!"

Seraphina looked down and noticed that he was regarding her feet with interest. She wondered if he had remarked her delicate ankles, but with a sigh thought not. More likely he was pondering how long it would take her to unthread her exquisitely laced roman ribbons and edge her toes into something odiously more serviceable. Still, the thought of escaping the house when she had thought she would be a prisoner to it gladdened her heart considerably. With a lighthearted hop and a skip and a merry, twirling entrechat that caused her captain to laugh aloud she announced that she would be back shortly.

"No more than five minutes, mind!" She scowled, not entirely convinced the captain would wait if she kept him dallying. As she shut the music room door behind her, she lifted her skirts in an unholy flurry of activity and literally dashed up the stairs. It was fortunate that there was no one about to see her, for her unladylike haste would have put even the lackadaisical Ancilla to the blush.

Miss Camfrey's maid was partaking of an excellent luncheon of ham and cooked turnips below stairs, so even *she* did not witness the interesting spectacle of Seraphina's dash from slippers to half boots, from organdie to muslin, lemon to aqua and finally to a dashing cherry-striped affair with a wrap over the front and an overdress of light, ethereal pink. She had—or so she believed—just sufficient time to stare into the looking glass and pinch her cheeks so that they attained a healthful glow before dashing downstairs again, preparatory to making a sedate entrance into the music room.

She might have saved herself the trouble, for when she opened the internal door it was only to find the scores slightly scattered from the wind and the curtain billowing from an open exit. She glanced at the wall clock and was disconcerted to find that nearly half an hour had elapsed from the time she had promised the good captain five minutes.

Angrily—for if she wasn't caught up in anger she might have felt stupid and a little guilty—she trod out into the garden and across the avenue of well-tended oaks towards the open forest on the far side.

She was glad of the chip straw, for the sun was still high in the sky and it was unseasonably hot. The half boots, however, were another matter, for they felt leaden and airless on her feet. She looked about her as far as the eye could see, but there was not a sign of her missing tutor. She did not know whether to be glad or sorry, for whilst she was still loath to begin lessons with a man so callous as to hold her to her word—what,

after all, was a mere twenty minutes here or there?—
she'd been strangely excited by the attention he would
doubtless pay her in the tuition.

Maddening, maddening, maddening!

She kicked a pebble and it flew out of sight, dropping
gently into the rivulet that ran through the estate. Apart
from the odd call of a wild finch, she could hear nothing of any moment. For all she knew, Captain Argyll
had given up his purpose and returned to his quarters.
With a rather cross shrug, Seraphina sat down by the
water and removed her boots. She was rather old to
paddle, but since there was no one to see her and she
was, after all, on her own estate, she did not consider
this of any account.

The water was refreshingly cold, and when splashed
on her face it offered a wonderful respite from the
noonday sun. Idly she wondered about the interview
taking place within. The Dowager Duchess of Doncaster
had seemed hopelessly puffed up in her own consequence—rather disappointing, in fact, when she had
met a personage as elegant and civil as her son. For an
instant, Seraphina thought of Rhaz, Lord Doncaster.
Undoubtedly he was of the first stare, his modish evening garb proclaiming Weston or Scott at the very least.
His dark eyes had been infinitely kind as he took her
hand and helped her through the deplorable madrigal
she'd been tricked into performing. When she thought
of that loathsome Lila chit, her eyes narrowed, then
relaxed.

She would think of something pleasanter, like the
possibility of an offer from the duke. This morning she
had been in transports at the prospect, but then this
morning she had not met Captain Argyll. Confound
the man! She had no *notion* of his first name and he
was entirely ineligible besides being arrogant and insuf-
ferably superior.

Still, she had never been more aware of a man in her life and the sensation was driving her mad with annoyance. His clear eyes proclaimed he knew *exactly* what she was thinking, which was mortifying besides putting her beyond the pale.

As she dreamily stared into the water, she was arrested by a sound unqualified in its purity. The lilting notes floated to her as if on air. High pitched, they nonetheless had a singular clarity and a conjugation of notes that were at once as unfamiliar as they were sweet. Seraphina felt her heart beat faster as she realised the music was not some ethereal figment of an overactive imagination, but the perfect, true and concordant notes of the stranger she had met earlier on in the day.

It was true that she knew nothing about Captain Argyll other than that he was pleasing to the eye and passing expert at the finer arts. What she learned of him now, through his music, told her much more. A lot that she learned she was not yet ready to understand. So, shaking her boots out hurriedly, she stood up and made for the trees. It did not take long to find him, for the gentle notes of the panpipe filled the air and acted as a guide far more discerning than the clearest map.

Captain Argyll, when she found him, was deposited at the banks of the river, his coat carelessly flung to one side and his mane of chestnut hair reprehensibly loose at his neck. The riband, Seraphina fleetingly noticed, was still tied at the nape, but what use it was to man or beast was questionable, since his abundant locks seemed destined to be free.

The melody was so fraught with soft tenderness and strange counterpoints that Seraphina was terrified lest she disturb him. She watched, for a moment, as his hands curved lightly and effortlessly over the pipes. His strong jaw and aquiline profile seemed at odds with his gentle theme, but Seraphina had to admit that, odd or not, the part fitted the whole and the whole the parts as nothing she could have imagined. She was just reflecting on this philosophy when her unshod toe caught on a particularly nasty variety of stinging nettle.

Her yelp of pain caused the music to cease instantly as the captain looked up to find his audience—he had suspected her presence long before her sudden cry—looking annoyed and somewhat conscious.

"I have stubbed my toe!"

"So you *should* have! Did I not tell you to don half boots?"

"*Ordered* me more like!" Seraphina scowled, but her heart sang, for in truth she was delighted to have exchanged the tedium of the house for the exhilaration of this confrontation.

"You shall have to get used to that, I am afraid! Military manners!"

"You are not at *all* like my other tutors." Seraphina regarded him suspiciously. The captain did not seem put out by this cryptic comment; rather he smiled his lazy, quite imperturbable grin.

"I should hope not! My own tutors were enough to make me run a mile! God forbid I should be added to their ranks!" Captain Argyll cursed himself for a fool and hoped that Seraphina did not notice his slip. A mere tutor would not have had tutors himself.

Fortunately, she did not seem to notice, for she was too pleased at the *content* of his remarks to be concerned with the particulars. She therefore nodded rather happily and unbent a little. If the captain did not intend being stuffy, she could be more than reconciled to his services. "What was that you were playing, just now?"

"The music? Some unknown composer—I forget his name. Did you like it?" Seraphina nodded. She was surprised at the intensity of her liking but was too vulnerable, at that moment, to share it.

The captain, however, was astute enough to sense something of her agitation and divine its cause. He smiled to himself. Though Seraphina had not so much as touched an instrument or hummed a bar that day, he felt that her first lesson had progressed very well indeed.

SEVEN

The guest room was decorated prettily in the pastel shades Mrs. Camfrey delighted in. The captain reflected with resigned humour that the chamber was more fitting for a woman than a man, for it sported no less than three looking glasses and several rather pretty china dolls. Still, as far as comfort went, he could make no complaint, for the room certainly offered a much more charming prospect than the camp bed and makeshift shelters he had become accustomed to over the years of the Iberian campaign.

He noticed with satisfaction that Pendleton had ordered his trunks sent up. These were now placed neatly beside a Queen Anne writing table. A pitcher of water and a washtub had been placed at the south side of the room. He walked over to them and immediately washed his hands and splashed a little water on his face. Then, throwing off his coat, cravat and shirt, he let them tumble in a forgotten heap upon the floor.

My lord was too anxious to see whether his writing implements and instruments were intact to take note of trifles. He carefully opened the first of the bandboxes and closed it almost immediately. They contained all manner of clothing that no doubt he would never need or want in his new calling.

His valet, used to working in an earl's household, simply could *not* be convinced to desist from packing fine lawn shirts and endless neckerchiefs of Eastern silk. Had he realised, Frederick would have unloaded it all at the King's Arms, but since he had not chosen to open that particular portmanteau, he now found himself blessed with the whole wretched lot.

The second box pleased him better. It contained his carefully wrapped lute, a marvellously old violin and an excellent quill pen and ink. Several smaller items of clothing had been included as well. Frederick reflected glumly that, until he was in a position to purchase better, these would have to serve as his work clothes. Heaven only knew, they had seen service! It was almost with fondness that Frederick thought on the bitter battles, the hardships and the sheer ingenuity that had got him through Spain almost without a scratch.

The haunting melody Seraphina had heard floated through his head once more. He added a small arpeggio to the opening bar, then carried the theme through to the sixth and seventh before allowing a small diminuendo to hush the lilting rhythm and cause a tension in the counterpoints to follow. He had used panpipes earlier, but strictly speaking, the fullness of the harmony would gain substance if plucked on the sweet strings of a harp.

He nodded and began to write, bold strokes confidently crossing page after page. My lord's extraordinary gift—that of perfect pitch—served him well. He was unhesitating in his inscription. When he finished, he lit several of the tapers that had been set out for him, for the house had sunk into a quiet darkness. He wondered fleetingly where Seraphina lay and whether she, too, was awake, pacing her chamber in the half-light. In the ordinary scheme of things it would be uncommonly easy to set up a dalliance with the youngest daughter of the household. Her eyes invited it, bewitching and innocent at one and the same time.

The captain tried not to think of her lips or other assets, for he had a long night ahead of him and he found the contemplation strangely disturbing. Doubtless his restiveness was caused by not having had a woman recently. Fortunately, *that* could soon be remedied. He chuckled upon this uplifting thought and wondered whether Harriet Smith was as charming as ever—*and* as abundant with her favours. Doubtless she was.

A sad smile suddenly crossed his utterly beguiling features. Occasionally—usually in the quiet shadows between waking and sleep—he indulged in what he considered "maudlin fancies." This was that annoying, elusive time when he found himself wishing for something that quite possibly did not exist. The themes of his composition floated through his mind, adding poignancy to the thoughts that kept recurring, unbidden and unwanted.

He reached for the quill and added another small flame to the candelabra. By morning, he was satisfied.

*Glittering, shimmering, sparkling, these are the fragments of
my mind reflecting on you.
You transform the darkness the deep molten shadows
with a heart that is brilliantly true.
Romance is a rainbow, a spectrum of
colour that's vividly lustrous on a sparkling wet day,
but love is much deeper, much more than pure sunshine it's
starlight
when all else is grey.
Mirror for mirror your thoughts are like
echoes
of my thoughts, my psyche, my conscience, my soul.
I love you, adore you*

I need you, my heart mate,
for two parts make more than a whole.
Romance is magic when mingled
as our love and laughter and friendship shall always be.
There'll never be moments of dark or despairing while your light
shines deep within me.

The morning mail carried two letters from the captain. One was addressed to Mr. Beckett of Islington Publishing House, London, and the other was rather cryptically addressed to Mr. R. Carlisle of Huntingdon. Neither address raised any brows, nor was the coincidence of his grace the Duke of Doncaster's hunting box lying just west of Huntingdon in any way remarked upon.

Cordelia hastily penned her own missives, carefully crossing every line so that one sheet, not two, would be charged for. Seraphina had no such qualms and was therefore busily occupied in committing to paper *tomes* for her good friend Miss Sarah Appleby of Knightsbridge. Since much of this related to the stunning person of "her captain," the note was necessarily long and brought a strange blush to her cheeks when she found the maddening man but two steps behind her. She covered up the wafers hastily, but not before she saw one of those annoying, slow and irresistible smiles cross his face. She was still debating whether the insufferable man had caught a glimpse or not when her mama looked up from her *own* letters and addressed him.

"You do not dine with us, Captain Argyll?" Ancilla's voice held a slight interrogative, for when the captain did not appear for breakfast she was concerned that he might have found himself relegated to the kitchens. She was determined that every civility be accorded to him. She would have been *mortified* if he was made to feel like a mere upper servant, for, though strictly speaking that was what he was, she nevertheless could not bring herself to think of him in that light.

The captain nodded briefly. "I had an excellent breakfast in my chamber. Thank you."

It did not suit him to be socialising with the Camfrey sisters. For one thing, he wished to concentrate on his work; for another, he did not want to risk being recognised by some of the morning callers who might imminently appear to pay their addresses. He did not wish to dwell on the other reason, for he refused of think of it himself. If he wished to put a distance between himself and a certain Miss Seraphina Camfrey, that, too, was entirely his own business.

"You shall dine with us this evening, I hope!"

"Thank you, ma'am! That is very kind of you, but I prefer to eat above stairs."

Seraphina opened her mouth to tell him what utter poppycock he was talking when she recalled the disturbing effect he had on her person every time he entered the room. If her nerves were not to be permanently jangled, the arrangement might turn out to be a good thing. Still, she could not resist a wistful glance in the excellent captain's direction. The first thing she encountered was the firmness of his jaw. That was followed by the delicious spectacle of his lips and further by the sardonic twinkle behind his sea blue eyes. Seraphina could swear he could read every thought in her head. She determined to veil her wayward thoughts to confound the man.

"Quite right, too! Mama, you must not forget we are in London! It would look very odd in us to be entertaining the servants!"

"Since when do you care about town gossip?" Cordelia was mortified by her sister's remarks. She cast a look at the captain, hoping to discern whether he'd been offended by her sister's unmannerly outburst. He was carefully putting the damask serviette to his lips, so any attempt to read his thoughts was foiled. If there was the hint of an appreciative twinkle behind his intense, dark-lashed eyes, Cordelia did not have time to notice. The uncomfortable silence was broken by Seraphina, who was half prepared to cut out her unruly tongue and half prepared to add fuel to the fire by making some *other* disparaging remark. Really, if the man could at least have the decency to look offended, she need not put herself to the trouble of thinking of another way to offend. His odious appearance of unqualified ease was most unnerving.

"When would you wish to commence lessons, Miss Seraphina?" The tone was respectful, but Seraphina had the annoying suspicion that tone and intent did not necessarily go hand in hand.

"Oh, I think I will give today a miss, Captain Argyll!" She waved her hand in an airy dismissal. "I have *so* much to do I hardly think I shall have *time* for the services of a music master!"

She wanted to hurt him and she succeeded. For an instant, Frederick wondered why the chit was so venomous. It was either, he thought, because she genuinely loathed him or it was some sort of protective device. But protective against what? After an instant's thought, he grinned. If Seraphina of the auburn hair found him a threat to her peace of mind, he made no complaint. Honour decreed that he not dally with her in her own home, but inclination veered decidedly on the reverse side. He would have to tread carefully, for he was in dangerous waters. Still, a dull life had never been to his taste.

He carefully set down his cup and nodded briskly. "Very well, Miss Seraphina. You are dismissed. Miss Cordelia, I shall be honoured if you would have me teach. I noticed your music sheets the other day. If you would like to practice them, I shall endeavour to be of material assistance."

Cordelia, a little ashamed of Seraphina's inexplicable rudeness, took the captain up eagerly. No doubt he was feeling a trifle strange in a household where he was employed to teach and found no opportunity of doing so. "I would love to! Thank you!"

The captain smiled at her goodwill and resumed his coffee. Seraphina looked daggers at her sister, then slumped a little against her chair. She would look silly begging to be included. There was nothing for it, she supposed, but to dredge up a few errands and be on her way. In her wildest dreams she would not have *imagined* how much she would wish she could stay.

Ancilla looked up from her letters thoughtfully. She might have been an errant mama in many ways, but she knew better than to try to force the issue of the music lesson with Seraphina. Better, indeed, that she be allowed to play truant—and yes, Ancilla suspected, allowed to regret it. She therefore mildly remarked that, if Seraphina was not to be indoors today, it would be greatly appreciated if she could acquire the receipts for boiled cockles and cold turbot from Miss Haversham, an aging spinster on the corner of Melden Terrace.

"What is wrong with our turbot, Mama?"

"Nothing. Only Miss Haversham has the knack of the most *scrumptious* cooking! I took over some dressed venison and a small perigord pie the other day and the old dear insisted I stay for tea. I was greatly surprised at the quality of her table, for she lives alone and is certainly not in her first glow of youth!"

"No, indeed! What did you have?"

"Among other things, the most superb cockles and turbot lightly smothered in a delectable lobster and anchovy butter sauce. There was horseradish on the side and something else, but I am not perfectly certain what.

Miss Haversham very kindly promised to inscribe the recipe for me. So if you will, Seraphina, I'd be much obliged."

Seraphina nodded. For all her foibles she was extremely good-hearted and recognised at once what Ancilla delicately avoided saying. Miss Haversham needed company and it would be a kindness to make her feel useful.

"I'll take her some of the barley water Mrs. Stevens has just boiled up."

Ancilla nodded approvingly. "Leave out the liquorice root, then, for the poor woman suffers from indigestion. A little more lemon might act as a restorative."

Seraphina nodded. "I shall add more sugar, too. Shall I go past the lending library?"

"If you do, try and procure a couple of Minerva Press books. I could do with a little light entertainment!"

"Mama!" Cordelia dimpled. "Are you not too old for romantic nonsense?"

"It will be a sad day when I am!" came back the quick rejoinder. "By the by, Cordelia, I hope you don't intend becoming all stuffy when you are Lady Winthrop!"

"Stuffy? Why should I be so?"

"Lord Henry appears to disapprove of my choice of literature! I was just settling down with a nice, juicy Gothic when he recommended me to Plutarch or some such person."

"Plutarch? Never! Lord Henry does not have the *wit* to—"

Cordelia bit her tongue. It was unforgivable to criticise her betrothed to herself, let alone in company. She glanced up to see if her slip had been noticed. Ancilla appeared satisfactorily bland, but the captain's eyes met hers sympathetically and she felt the colour rise to her beautiful, high-boned cheeks. Seraphina was looking, not at her, but at the captain. Something in the intensity of her gaze stirred Cordelia. A most remarkable thought flashed through her mind only to be summarily dismissed. Seraphina's hopes lay with Rhaz, Duke of Doncaster. She had almost proclaimed as much. A small lump appeared in Cordelia's throat. She scolded herself for being ridiculous and turned to her mother once more.

"What I mean, Mama, is that his lordship was probably recommending you to quite some other person! Are you sure it was Plutarch?"

"No, but it sounded deadly dull at all events!"

There was no answer to this, for Cordelia could only think her mama very likely right. Her betrothed, though singularly unimaginative, tended to regard himself as an authority on most subjects. He would look down on a Gothic because that was the correct thing to do. Similarly, though he would blanch at the thought of *reading* what was in his extensive library, he would have ensured he had all the classics and most of the Greek and Roman works at least. All properly leather bound and placed upon his shelves according to height and colour, no doubt! She pinched herself for this uncharitable thought. Lord Henry had been sincere and kind enough to make her an offer. She must never allow herself to sneer at him, however silently. For the tenth time that day she wondered whether she could, in all kindness, jilt him. She sighed and thought not. Even if Seraphina *did* contract a spectacular marriage with the duke, it would be grossly unfair of her to insult him and make him a laughingstock before all society.

No, best make the most of things and try, at least, to accord him respect if not total comprehension. Rhaz's black eyes mocked her in her imagination. *He* would not cry compromise, she was sure. If he . . . But, no, her thoughts were running on far too dangerously. Perhaps the imminent lesson with the captain would do her some good. Surely, the serenity of the harpsichord might serve to soothe her tumultuous passions. Perhaps she would sing, too. Very likely the discipline of honing her voice and concentrating on scales would reduce her pulses and force her to a steadiness that Lord Henry would approve of if he only took a moment from his thoroughbreds to think on it.

She stood up. "I am ready when you are, Captain Argyll!"

He smiled into her perfect features and wondered why on earth his heart did not flutter as it did when addressed by her wayward sister. Still, he *liked* what he saw of the clear, steady grey eyes and the soft expression that lit her face when she spoke. He wondered at the faint wistfulness he detected behind her dark, sultry lashes, but he was far too polite to inquire. Instead, he stood up and made a small, slightly deferential bow to the ladies. Whilst he took care not to be high-handed, he was also loath, in his new role, to be too subservient. The attitude he adopted must have been most satisfactory, for Ancilla smiled benignly on him and bade him a very good morning. Cordelia followed him through the door with only a small, quick backwards glance at her sister. It was no joy to her that her piquant face looked miserable.

EIGHT

Rhaz, Lord Doncaster, thundered across the turf at breakneck speed. The dewy leaves and faint flashes of cornflower and yellow left but a hasty, ill-formed impression on his faraway mind. For a moment he felt himself transported not to the far side of his bounteous estate, but to the formal rigours of the ballroom, with its bright gilt drapes and fashionable red silks. Candelabras of brilliant crystal seemed more real to him than the scent of horseflesh and leather that crept into his nostrils and jostled to find space in his thoughts.

As his mount slowed to a trot and finally edged towards the inviting water, my lord's eyes closed, shuttered against the morning sun and the tumultuous images that kept surfacing, unbidden, into his consciousness. He set his gun down and swung his legs over the stallion, murmuring soothing words of praise. Such kindness was typical of the duke—second nature rather than concerted effort.

It would certainly have taken more than a little concerted effort to forget a certain Miss Cordelia Camfrey, whose laughing silver grey eyes were becoming a source of discomfort to the duke. And her deep, rich ebony hair . . . He sighed. So nonsensical to be fretting over a woman, and one that he had met just once, at that. Still, he'd felt an intangible connection that did not stop at mere admiration. For the hundredth time he cursed himself for a fool for not taking advantage of those smiling wide lips when he'd had a chance. A curious thought crossed his mind yet again and he shrugged it off crossly.

No, it was *not* time he consider marrying. Nor was it likely that he would honour the line with a connection so far beneath him. Lastly, of course, there was the small matter of her tardiness. Quite simply, he had been a laggard. The sad result of this circumstance was that the lady in question was already—very definitely—engaged.

His grace sighed as he plucked an elderberry from a wild bush and flung the fruit as far as he could into the river. He'd made inquiries and nothing that had been presented to him thus far served to dispel the gloomy knowledge that Lord Henry Winthrop was a pompous windbag with nothing more pressing on his brain than the hocks of his carriage mounts.

The duke stared wryly into space and wondered what such a likable young lady was doing accepting the hand of such an unlikely suitor. The answer was not very far away, and it made the furrows on my lord's brow deepen considerably. The moment he had stared into Miss Cordelia Camfrey's honest eyes he had been struck by the strength of her character. It was disappointing to feel she was marrying for money, but he could think of no other explanation likely to serve, except rank and title. Either way, the thought left a bitter taste in Rhaz's very masculine mouth as he turned his horse around and made for the house.

"Helena, I *do* wish you would stop being such an addlepated jaw me dead! I do believe you are more interested in the stables than you are in my comfort!"

Whilst cousin Helena made haste to deny this accusation, Rhaz could not help feeling the truth was well founded. Helena Moresby—his cousin by marriage and chatelaine of the large country seat he was pleased to think of as a home away from home—was ineffably a woman of the countryside, more interested in the horses than their master. At times, Rhaz was grateful for this singular lack of attention from her. He was used to being fawned upon by any number of people and being treated as second fiddle to any bug-bearing, lice-infested, flea-faring stallion was just the sort of irony that his quick, incisive brain enjoyed.

Still, he could do without the ceaseless prattle and inevitable scolding as he handed the reins over to his head groom and asked for the time. Lady Helena pointed shortly to a clock and bade him not sit on the well-stacked bales of hay, for his riding clothes were wet and like to dampen the stable straw. At first, Rhaz thought she was quizzing him and his fine, mettlesome jaw moulded into a quick grin. The gesture was not met with humour, but rather by a grunt and a stern adjuration to do as he was bade.

Grumbling somewhat at this summary treatment in his own home, Rhaz checked that the horse was adequately hosed and housed, then made his way up to the great doors of the country retreat. His cousin followed in his footsteps, lamenting roundly that he had not purchased *half* the animals she would have liked him to have done at Tattersall's latest auction.

My lord did not trust himself to reply. Tattersall's had been nothing short of a dead bore. The only animal of interest—a midnight stallion of promising origin—was indisputably short in the hocks. Its owner, a florid man with a belly that protruded from faded buckskins, had looked unaccountably put out by his grace's churlish refusal to sport his blunt. But refuse he had and unwittingly forged for himself another vapidly jealous enemy.

Such things ceased to bother Rhaz, who was now inured to the self-seeking pettiness that seemed to be the cloying outcome of rank and fortune.

Instead, as he headed towards his conservatory, he bent his mind to a way he might honourably rid himself of his guest. Lady Helena Moresby was a good-hearted soul but a sad trial to one who wished to be left to his own devices. He wished to be free, without fear of unintentional rudeness, to make his own purchases. He thought fretfully that he should not have to apologise for being astute enough to resist being humbugged into buying high steppers short on their paces. Rather gloomily he reflected that Lady Helena was almost as bad, by all accounts, as the good Lord Henry.

He smiled at her politely and murmured that he would like to take the morning to look over his accounts. When she had gone, he stared at the sun filtering through the delicately curved windowpanes of his conservatory roof. Though he was pleased with the way Nash had used the revolutionary new curved iron glazing bar to good effect, his thoughts were by no means on the elegant domed glass above his head. True, the odd splash of sunlight reminded him, unaccountably, of sparkling silver grey eyes, but he forced himself to look beyond this intruding image. Something short of unkindly *evicting* poor, well-meaning Helena had to be done about her. Suddenly he stopped in his tracks. He dragged his reflections two steps back and cocked his head to one side. Helena as trying, sap skulled and equine mad as Lord Henry? The strangest germ of a notion began to reveal itself in his intelligent, well-ordered and intolerably handsome head.

Miss Haversham peered at Seraphina with semiblind eyes. Her hands trembled slightly as she selected a book from her heavy, mahogany shelves. "If it is not too much trouble, dear. . . ."

"Not at all!" Seraphina moved across the room to help. As her eyes flickered over the title she sighed: *Mrs. Parsons Guide to Good Husbandry and Household Harmony: A Treatise on Etiquette and Other Matters Relating to the Home.* It would, she considered, be a long morning.

Miss Haversham fussed over her and rang the little tea bell by her side. It was not long before a tray of refreshments was wheeled in and Seraphina bidden urgently to partake. Seraphina's thoughts were far away as she smiled politely and bit into a coconut-and-treacle macaroon. She wondered about how her sister was doing and, more, the types of teaching methods the good Captain Argyll employed.

When she finally took up the tome, there was such a decided flush upon her cheeks that it was well that her hostess's eyesight was not all that it used to be. Seraphina should have been suitably edified by the instructive text, but sad to say, she was not. As the hands slowly crawled across the newfangled pendulum clock that was Miss Haversham's pride and joy, the young Miss Camfrey was devising plots and stratagems to ensnare her tutor. Reprehensible, of course, but understandable in a lady just out of the schoolroom and in the first, fresh, diverting and infinitely delectable throes of love. The Duke of Doncaster, it should be noted, was just a fuzzy, inconsequential mist of memory to her.

Her grace the duchess, had she but divined the errant direction of Seraphina's thoughts, would have choked upon her teacup. Rhaz Carlisle, the fifth duke, teetered only on the brink of Seraphina's consciousness. In truth, as her thoughts delightfully wondered, he was— had he but known it—almost banished over the precipice of her psyche. He would have chuckled to learn of this fact, for my lord enjoyed, more than most, an ironical turn of mind.

Still, it was as well he did *not* know of it, just as it was fitting for the dowager duchess's meddlesome plans that *she* was not aware of the novel trail of the younger Miss Camfrey's musings.

Seraphina plotted and schemed as she mouthed aloud the sanctimonious pronouncements of Mrs. Parsons and her guide to a harmonious household. Ordinarily she would have laughed aloud at the receipt for thinning hair that Mrs. Parsons seemed to think would sooth any balding spouse. It required fresh honey to be poured into a still along with precisely a dozen handfuls of vines and a vast quantity of rosemary drops. The sap from this was to be allowed to drop until it turned sour. Mrs. Parsons evidently considered it beneficial to turn sweet to nasty—a fitting testament to the priggish style and self-righteous preachings of the remainder of the vile volume. With relief, Seraphina noticed Miss Haversham nodding off. When the older woman's chin had finally drooped into her chest, she closed the offending piece of literature and tiptoed from the room. She was politely escorted down the hallway and out the honey-coloured Bath-stone building. The light outside was blinding, but a welcome relief from the dim, chintz-curtained room within. Seraphina's maid—a saucy little snippet of a thing—seemed equally delighted to make her escape.

On the spur of the moment, Miss Camfrey decided to waive away the little gig that awaited her patiently outside. Instead, she took a left turn down the long, winding cobbles of Melden Terrace and turned right into town. From there, it was but a hop, skip and jump past Hookham's—she had forgotten entirely to step in for Ancilla's Minerva Press volumes—and a short walk to Pritchard's, the music shop. What she bought there must remain a secret, but it was a thoughtful, determined and slightly mischievous Seraphina who wended her slow way home.

"You have an excellent tone, Miss Cordelia!"

"Good luck rather than dedication, I am afraid, Captain! I really ought to apply myself more."

"Would you care to join in our lessons?"

Cordelia's mouth twitched. "The ones you *hope* to give, Captain?"

He laughed, but there was a firmness about his jaw that did not fool the perceptive Miss Camfrey. "The ones I *intend* to give!"

The sudden glint in his eye made Cordelia almost sorry for the outrageously absent Seraphina. The captain looked just the type to brook no nonsense. Probably just what Seraphina needed, on reflection, though Cordelia was only too happy she did not need to attend the inevitable fiery sessions. "Perhaps now and again I shall, Captain, but I am perfectly positive Seraphina would prefer to study by herself."

The captain looked sceptical and raised such comical brows that Cordelia allowed a chuckle to escape her. "Truly, sir! When she applies herself I am convinced she will be as butter in your hands."

The captain permitted himself a luxurious image of this that would probably have brought a blush to both sisters' cheeks. He said nothing, however, but neatly stacked the scores in a rosewood cabinet trimmed with a medley of rare zebra and tulip wood. When he commented on the cabinet, Cordelia's eyes lit up. It seemed it was one of the few reminders she had of her dear papa. It was he who had installed the music room and procured all the furnishings including the little spinet and the harp that remained, as yet, untouched.

The captain noticed Cordelia stifling the sparkle of unbidden tears and became silent. Her eyes sparkled silver and for an instant he was struck by the ethereal quality of her beauty: jet black hair against creamy skin and dreamy pink lips that put the most exquisite of autumn blooms to shame. Still, his heart beat steadily and he experienced none of the flutter of sapphire and auburn that Seraphina's strange mix of colouring wrought inside him.

He checked the time on a tiny fob he pulled from his modest waistcoat of serviceable green merino. Time, he thought, that his errant pupil returned. If she did not, he would take a walk through the woods and whistle some of the dark refrains that seemed to jostle through his mind. Dark as in mysterious and haunting rather than as in purely sinister. He could hear deep bass wrestling with the lighter, sweeter, more velvety tones of cello and lute. There could be no doubt that the renegade Miss Seraphina was contributing to the urgent notes that seemed to press against his temple in an attempt at passing through the boundaries of intangible to real.

Cordelia could see his thoughts were far away as she nodded quietly in his direction and shut the door behind her.

"Good morning, Miss Seraphina! Too beautiful a morning to waste indoors, is it not?"

"I thought you were coming to find me and scold!"

"Should I have been?" His keen eyes raked her up and down and she had the goodness to blush.

"Possibly! I loathe and detest lessons, you see!"

"I think I do, for you have very neatly managed to avoid me for all of one week now."

"I did not think you had noticed."

"Foolish girl! When I am paid to teach you? Come, come!"

Seraphina bit back a moment's disappointment that *this* was the reason he had missed her. Frederick, of course, would never give her the satisfaction of knowing *quite* how she had cut up his piece. He had toyed with the idea, often enough, of either kissing her or spanking her, but since neither of these actions would have been appropriate to the role for which he had been paid, he'd determined at last to give her a little leash. In this, he was rewarded, for Seraphina had suffered many agonies for her stubbornness and was now more than happy that he had sought her out at last.

"Where are we going?" Frederick stepped up amiably next to her.

"I was collecting wild figs and pinecones for Cordelia's syrups. They are famous around here, you know!"

"I did not, but I am not surprised. She appears very capable. Here, let me take that."

Without warning, he seized the basket she was carrying and spun it round to his left, so that they were now ambling amiably side by side towards the forest.

Seraphina felt her breathing quicken and became very aware of his hand dangling only inches away from her dimity day dress and almost touching her. Indeed, when she briefly stumbled over a pebble their hands *did* make contact and the sensation was memorable to both parties.

Frederick, however, refused to take advantage of the circumstances. He was very aware that Seraphina, despite her high spirits, was only a very green girl, highly impressionable and still patently an innocent. Though these facts alone made his muscles involuntarily tighten, he chose, rather painfully, to ignore the urge that came as naturally to him as breathing. The self-control he inflicted upon himself made the walk necessarily rather quiet, but neither minded, for Seraphina's wrath seemed to have yielded to a softer and infinitely pleasanter type of companionship.

At length, they stopped. Both had been so lost in their thoughts that neither had picked so much as one pinecone, never mind uncovered any of the wild figs that grew abundantly in the forest. The uncommonly hot day seemed to remember its season and slowly turn to autumn, as a wind swept through the trees, rustling the pretty red leaves and shaking a good many off upon the ground and through Seraphina's shining auburn hair.

Despite his good resolutions, Frederick could not help but comment that Seraphina looked like a wood sprite, her deep auburn hair a perfect match to the autumn colours that surrounded them. She blushed prettily, her mouth opening in surprise at her first compliment from the man who had begun to haunt her dreams.

When he indicated to a gnarled wood stump, wide and weather-beaten, she sat down smiling, but her heart was beating loud and she was perfectly certain he could hear.

Frederick gathered up a moss-covered stick that lay buried at their feet. Tapping it against a nearby rock, he beat a rhythm that was steady and predictable. He raised his brows and whistled. When Seraphina asked him what he was doing, he asked her what tempo he was beating. The march was easy to recognise, just as he'd hoped. Pleased with this game, Seraphina clapped her hands and asked for more. Frederick was astonished by her perspicacity, for he moved quickly through rhythms until she was recognising complicated septets without much thought. Finally, with slight devilry in his eyes, he beat out a simple 3/3 time. She wrinkled up her nose.

"A waltz?"

"Indeed, Miss Camfrey! And I was hoping you would do me the honour." He bowed mischievously and despite Seraphina's hesitant mutterings that the dance was "fast" and she had not yet acquired permission from the patronesses of Almack's, it was not long before she was in his arms, his soft, sensuous whistling burning deep ripples of awareness into her ears and, as it seemed to her, her very being.

Frederick longed to allow matters to progress, but he was a gentleman and Seraphina was entrusted to his care. So he took the moment to teach her a little about artistic composition and just why the waltz required such an unusual rhythm.

Flushed, Seraphina concentrated hard, and from the few salient questions she asked, Frederick understood that his task was not as daunting or as hopeless as he had first conceived. A little originality in her lessons and the fair Seraphina would blossom. He looked at her wistfully and wondered which beau would eventually whisk her away.

It was in these circumstances, then, that Miss Seraphina began her lifelong love affair with music. I could say *more* than just music, perhaps, but for the moment I will desist. The workings of Miss Camfrey's heart were still tangled up in youthful expectations and confusions. She expected to be duchess—the idea of being wife to a simple music master was unthinkable. If the prospect nevertheless imposed itself upon her dreams, none, save herself, could know.

Rhaz's lips widened into a deep curve as he set his seal upon the wafer-thin parchment. If this did not send the good Lord Henry posthaste down to Huntingdon, nothing would. He offered as bait a couple of tidy roans and the chance of sending some prize mares to stud. The Duke of Doncaster's Arabian stallions were legendary among the ton. Lord Winthrop would be foolish beyond belief if he did not take up such an unexpected and rare opportunity.

Next, he tore open the envelope that awaited him in his study—the conservatory had become unseasonably hot—and he settled down on one of the comfortable chaise longues scattered tastefully about.

He almost laughed out loud at Frederick's comical descriptions of his charges and the beautiful wayward daughter he would, for his sins and penance, be forced to teach. Rhaz chuckled deeply, for the thought of his friend hamstrung with regard to any amorous pursuit was a great joke. He scanned farther and nodded more seriously at Freddie's projections for the future. If he could scribble off an entire score in an evening, it would not be long before the young Lord Frederick would be famous.

Just to make certain, the duke took up his pen and began to write once more. *This* missive he thought very carefully about sending, for he was generally loath to meddle in any affairs but his own. Still, if Mr. Beckett had any doubts, or the unnamed partner became suddenly short of funds or inclination, the noble seal of Carlisle never did any harm. Frederick would undoubtedly succeed on his own merits but if Rhaz was of a mind to smooth things along, it was his prerogative, surely, as a friend.

The estate book loomed large on the table. For the next several hours, his grace found himself closeted with it. This might sound more gloomy than it actually was, for Rhaz held a deep interest in innovative agriculture and sponsored several ingenious plans to modernise the estate's farming techniques. The saving in labour was put to good use, for he had a vinery planted, the

crop for which he widely distributed among his tenants,
a handy incentive to implementation of his profitable
and newfangled plans.

He was pleased to note that, for the first time, the
estate was doubling its turnover, allowing him to order
every chimney swept and a winter's worth of firewood
delivered to the dependents of Huntingdon. This still
left him with more than he had projected spare, but
this was of small consequence to the duke, who had so
large a fortune that estate revenues were a mere pittance in the grand scheme of things.

Careful calculation revealed it had been a record
breeding year for grouse and pheasant. Accordingly, in
the spirit of Christmas coming, he pardoned two noto-
rious poachers whom the gamekeeper had incarcerated
pending sentence and ordered a free lunch for all. This
benevolence was in addition to the usual midwinter
Christmas fare traditionally served up on the estate. To
create a balance in his woods and fields, he specified
grouse, partridge and selected fowl to be chief upon
the menu. If a couple of jugged hares and potted wood-
cocks also found their way into the festivities, my lord
was bounteous enough to turn a blind eye.

Of course, when word of this benevolence reached
London, he knew he would be pronounced "Mad
Rhaz" or "Bad Rhaz" or some such thing, for peers of
the realm were notoriously clutch fisted and wary of
the populace getting above themselves. None of these
things particularly concerned his grace, however. Whilst
he was perfectly prepared, when circumstance arose, to
do the pretty and follow the wiles of the ton, when matters of personal conscience were involved, the fifth duke
forged his own path and damned the consequences.

He would have been surprised to know how closely
a certain Miss Cordelia Camfrey followed these self-
same principles. Half the pomades, barley, nasturtium,

herbs, chamomile and sage she nurtured were stilled
or dried and pounded into potations not for herself,
but for the dozens of urchins she refused to turn from
her door.

No matter how hard times were with the Camfreys,
or how frugal she endeavoured to be, Cordelia never
allowed the needs of the sick and the poor to be over-
looked where she could help it. Now that they were a
little more removed at the dower house, beggarly visits
were more infrequent, so she'd taken to sending baskets
of remedies down to the local parishes.

Still, as Rhaz gazed thoughtfully out of the window,
he knew nothing of this. What he did, know, however,
was that the memory of Miss Camfrey refused to be
shaken from his mind. He found this at once self-indul-
gent and annoying, for he had never before had trouble
dismissing thoughts—even outrageous ones—from his
head.

It was not just her beauty and honesty, though these
were powerful factors. What was it then? A magnetism
that tightened every one of his singularly lithe muscles
and made his patience in not immediately courting her
strained to the limits. *Damn* Lord Henry and damn him
again! He wondered how soon he could lure him to
Huntingdon and whether his bizarre, shadowy wisp of
a scheme would wash. He thought not. He sighed and
buried his head back in the accounts.

For all the gossip and talk, Rhaz, Lord Carlisle, was
no scoundrel. If Cordelia was not free, he would endeavour to forget.

NINE

Seraphina sat thoughtfully upon her bed. She was careful not to let the candle's small flame catch upon the airy chintz bed hangings that hung lavishly from their posts. She was glad that despite Cordelia's protests she had bought the more expensive shade, for the draperies offered a pleasing luminescence to the room and made her feel very snug indeed.

Carefully, she unwrapped the small parcel from Pritchard's and opened it carefully. It was a score. Mr. Pritchard had personally selected it for her when she'd explained the types of notes that appealed and hummed but a few bars of the haunting melody Captain Argyll had so effortlessly piped by the waterside.

This score, of course, was different, but in its own way Seraphina thought it captured some of the essence of melody and tone that had so appealed that day. She set the crisp paper down carefully, afraid that she might knock the taper over in her interest. Her heart beat a little, for she felt rather silly and was not quite certain that she would be able to accomplish what she hoped to.

She glanced at the notes and despaired, for the arpeggios were daunting, and in truth, it was a long time since she had practiced anything at all. With a sigh she tried to read only the treble, and from this, she managed to painstakingly elicit a tune of extraordinary lightness and depth. She read again, but soon reading was not enough, for the effort of imagining the notes was too great for one as unskilled as herself.

She swung her legs off the bed and threw a frothy robe about her shoulders. Then, her feet still unslippered and her hair all atangle, she picked up the taper and the score and tiptoed out of the room. Her toe stubbed against the cocoa-coloured door—the exact shade of her walls—and she allowed herself a faint, heartfelt yelp of pain. No one appeared to stir, however, so she closed the door carefully with the hand that held the score and took the cantilevered stairs two at a time until she reached the pink marble landing. The house seemed strange and dark and unexpectedly cold, though several yellowing tapers sporadically lit the way in simple chandeliers. Most, though, were melted down by now, so Seraphina knew the hour was late indeed.

She found the music room by dint of a little guesswork, for the tapers stopped at the landing. Pushing the door open, she accustomed her eyes to the dark until the light of her own flame revealed candles laid neatly by. She lit several of these—Cordelia would have disapproved, she was sure—and sat down at the harp. Slowly, surely, she fingered the central tune of the melody, though the crotchets did not flow and every small piece of plucking seemed daunting in magnitude.

The sweet notes came alive as her stiff fingers relaxed and she remembered, at last, to tune her much maligned instrument. This process was by nature painstaking, for she had always considered tuning a bore and consequently never paid much attention to the finer points. She was determined, however, and this counted for much, for she achieved a tolerable degree of harmony and by the faint light of dawn had at least managed to pluck all the central notes of the melody.

Tired fingers set down the score as she rubbed her eyes and realised that the night was fading and the early bustle of the scullery maids was likely to begin. One last time, she took the harp between her knees and began to play. She closed her eyes as the lilting notes floated into her ears. By now, the tune was as smooth as silk, though unechoed by the more intricate chords or edified by subtle, lilting arpeggios. Still, the music remained warm, haunting and sensuous, and it caused a delicious sense of well-being to waft through her senses.

When she opened her eyes, a familiar form leaned against the doorframe. The first thing that Seraphina noticed was that he was wearing little beyond buckskins and slippers. His muscular torso gleamed in the flame light and Seraphina thought she had never seen anything more beautiful to behold. Her eyes moved up to his face, where the firm thrust of his jaw was clearly visible through the soft, unbound locks of chestnut that tantalisingly brushed against his cheeks.

She had no time in the half second she'd taken all this in to look any farther. Her heart was stammering painfully in her chest as he rushed forward and ripped the score out of her hands. His lips curled ominously and there was none of the lazy blue laughter in his magnetic eyes. Instead, they were sea blue stormy and fury was etched on every feature.

"I hope you are satisfied, Miss Seraphina dear, to have made a mockery out of me! And there, I thought you were such an innocent."

Seraphina was bewildered beyond belief, all her joy in the discovery of music, in the painful steps to rediscover her ability to *create* that music, dashed.

Frederick was advancing on her, but not in the heavenly way of her childish dreams. His look was black and his scowl prodigious as he edged towards her, his powerful, semiclad body a menace rather than a delight.

"I have no notion what you mean!"

"Do you not?" Frederick was disbelieving as he drew closer and ripped the precious score in two. He had no notion of how Seraphina could be playing his music, or where she could have come by the notes. All he knew was that she *could* play and that she must, somehow, have tumbled to his identity. The thought was painful, for though he'd looked upon her indulgently as wilful, he'd not formerly regarded her as underhanded.

The shock of hearing his own melody lilting from the music room had quite discomposed him. Up all night, caught between his writing, his composing and his wayward, strictly untutorlike thoughts with regard to Seraphina, he'd paced up and down the hallways, finally deciding to nip outside for a breath of fresh air. Though the front doors were always firmly barred at night, he'd remembered the French doors leading out from the morning salon. Doubtless they'd be left unlocked, for they led out only to the topiaries and herb gardens and could not be accessed from outside.

His heart had nigh on stopped when the familiar theme wafted into his consciousness. Though greatly simplified, there could be no mistaking that the score was his. He was mystified, for Mr. Beckett had only just organised the printing and the music was still too new to be circulating generally. Heedless of the unsuitability of his attire—unusually so, for he had removed his undershirt and not even *remotely* thought of a gown—he had marched over to the music room, his thoughts abuzz with confusion, curiosity and a gnawing, heart-stopping concern.

The sight of Seraphina playing his music was, for an instant, the fulfilment of every fantasy he could ever have dreamed of. Her luscious, long auburn locks fell about her in a veritable swath of beauty and the concentration on her face added depth to her character.

Not that he was thinking much about character, for the creamy expanses of her shoulders were clearly visible and her frothy nightdress was not designed, evidently, for use outside her bedchamber. Indeed, it seemed a waste of perfectly good fichu and gauze, for the amount that it revealed made its function rather superfluous. Frederick felt his breathing deepen and in that split second knew that he had never in his life wanted a woman as much as he wanted Seraphina.

The bitter thought that she had deceived him, that she could play with feeling better than most, though she was still diffident and a trifle stiff, shocked him. He forgot that she was ignoring the arpeggios, the bass, the intricate little fingerings he'd prescribed. He forgot, too, that her time was slow and her plucking a trifle inconsistent. What he saw was Seraphina at the harp playing music she could not possibly have come by through chance. *That* meant she knew exactly who he was and was making a May game of him, but for what reason he had not yet divined. All this came to him in a flash. As Seraphina backed away, he moved towards her with growing determination and anger.

"Captain Argyll! You are mad!"

"Mad? Not mad, but stupid! I thought you were the most confoundedly lovely, heart-stoppingly beautiful little hoyden and I find, instead, that you are merely a hoyden."

"What can you mean? You are hurting me, Captain!"

In truth, Frederick did not even *notice* how hard he was gripping her arm. When she complained, he released her, but the fury pent up inside did not abate. Tears were in Seraphina's eyes as she suddenly realised her own immodesty. She looked down at herself and felt naked, wholly vulnerable and insensibly ashamed. She tried to cover herself with her hands, but the gesture was futile.

Frederick, noting the gesture, felt some of the storm abate.

"Here." He handed her an Indian silk that had been left by Cordelia the day before.

Seraphina sniffed and murmured her thanks, still confused but heartened by this small gesture of kindness.

"I am not a brute, you know, though I have the devil of a temper!"

Seraphina nodded. "I *knew* I should not touch that silly instrument! Music and I just do not belong together and there is an end to it! I am sorry my playing offended you so much, Captain! I shall speak to my mama tomorrow. I am certain when I explain to her the futility of this whole thing she will release you from your duties on full pay. If not, I will endeavour to pay you myself, though my pin money, I fear, is sadly depleted. Next quarter, though . . ." Her lips trembled and she bravely brushed away a tear as her other hand fiercely draped the silk closed.

Frederick felt the most ridiculous urge to hold her in his arms and comfort her. And what was that the brat was saying about pin money? He resisted his strong, masculine urge with an effort, but reviewed her last few sentences in a less jaundiced light. Doubt and hope pricked at his consciousness in equal quantities.

Could it be . . . ? Was it possible that the chit truly did not know who he was or that the score was his? Was it possible that she lacked skill but not talent, that she had picked up his themes unconsciously and not through the art of careful revision and studious practice? If so, it would make Miss Seraphina the notoriously unaccomplished into Miss Seraphina the purely understimulated. Impossible, yet he determined to find out the truth, for his whole life, he suddenly acknowledged with clarity, might hinge upon the answer.

"Come sit here." His tone was gentle and Seraphina

found herself obeying unquestioningly. The room was becoming lighter and the sounds of footsteps upon the stairs and morning murmurs could just be detected in the stillness. Frederick looked over at the mantelpiece and checked the time. Early still. The kitchen servants would be preparing for the day, lighting up the great fires and possibly tammying, but the housemaids would not be in yet, neither, he quickly assessed, would the footmen. There was time, but not a great deal. Just to be perfectly certain, he strode over to the door and locked it, firmly removing the key and tossing it over to Seraphina.

"Now. Tell me how you came by that piece if you please! And no gammoning me! I did not become captain of the seventh dragoons without first cutting my eyeteeth. If you tell me any tarradiddles I shall have you over my knee in a twinkling and it shall be no more than you deserve, I promise you!"

Seraphina, despite her misery, her despair and her strange, overpowering satisfaction at being closeted in the same room with this handsome, stern and altogether *fascinating* gentleman, nevertheless was not so cowed as to let this threat pass without comment.

"You wouldn't dare!" Her sparkling eyes defied him.

"Would I not?"

His eyes held hers and Seraphina knew that all the defiance in the world was useless. The wretch was as capable of carrying out his threat to spank her as he was of whistling a tune. Since Seraphina had first hand knowledge of his aptitude at *this,* she squirmed a little at the thought of his aptitude at the other.

Frederick watched the thoughts flitting through her mind and grinned. Let the chit worry. If it served to keep her strictly truthful, he was unrepentant. "Well?"

"I came by it at Pritchard's. I was hoping to surprise you, though heaven knows why I should have bothered."

He eyed her closely. The chit was telling the truth. By some extraordinary coincidence . . . "Why that particular piece?"

"Mr. Pritchard suggested it. He said though it was new it was fast becoming the rage and I should try it, especially as I . . ."

"As you what?"

She coloured delightfully, loath to explain that she had hummed several bars from the haunting melody she'd memorised by the waters that beautiful, sunny day. It seemed an age ago. "What consequence is it?" Her fiery eyes lit up once more. "There can be nothing that objectionable about the piece I purchased! Why, only the other day you piped a piece that had *just* the same quality, melody and mellifluous counterpoints! You cannot deny it, sir! What is more, if I happen to enjoy such perfection of sound, it is entirely my own business! Do stop badgering and permit me to return to my chamber! I should never have left it!"

Frederick experienced a moment of heart-stopping joy. The little widgeon had not tumbled to his identity. She was not mocking him and the coincidence that lay between them was serendipity born of a mutual flare for harmony. Above all, she loved his work and his work, as he had always known, was a mirror of his soul. *That* was why he had objected so violently when he'd thought it abused and that was why he now, more than ever, felt himself bonded with this woman, for better, for worse, forever and longer.

He did not tell her those thoughts. He only moved towards her and raised her from her seat. Wonderingly, she noticed that the blazing lights of anger had been replaced by something infinitely more wondrous—the glistening crystal of tenderness and something unreadable far behind.

"I owe you an apology, Miss Seraphina!"

"And I you, Captain! For I should never have attempted so intricate a piece. I am sure my clumsy fingers mangled what is meant to be the most delicate harmony I have ever heard. In the future, I shall be satisfied to listen only."

"Not if *I* have the smallest say in it! I was not angry at your playing, Seraphina. Only angry at . . . I shall not say what. I thought I was mistaken in you but I find I was not. You remain the most adorable, unutterably . . . But hush! I must not say such things. For the moment, let us cry friends, shall we? When we take up our lessons at a more appropriate hour—in more civilised garb"—he looked at her with regret—"it shall be on the basis that you have within you a fundamental understanding of rhythm and form. You are not musically inept, merely musically illiterate. I shall teach you and that state of affairs shall not longer lie between us."

Seraphina nodded. She would like, she knew, nothing more. As he held out his hand for the key, she placed it in his and their flesh touched for an instant. The connection, to her, was like lightning. By the tightening of his jaw, she knew he felt the same and an exultant flush flowed through her being. On tiptoes, she raised her head and planted a light, impudent kiss upon his mouth. Then she unlocked the door and crept upstairs, heartened that the bustle in the kitchens below had not yet reached this quiet corner of the house.

Frederick stood a long time, his hand upon his lips, before he glanced down the corridor, waited for a sprightly maid to turn into the crisp linen room and bolted up the stairs.

TEN

It was some time later that Cordelia paced up and down the sparsely furnished morning chamber. A brisk ride in the autumn sunshine had proven a welcome diversion for her rather sombre reflections. She was to become Lady Winthrop and the sooner she accustomed herself to the idea the better.

One last time that morning, she dutifully endeavoured to shut away the ubiquitous memory of his grace's scorching glance upon her back and his soft, infinitely tender smile as he'd regarded her lips. Oh, how she wished . . . She cancelled the thought with determination. If the noble duke was destined for her sister, there was nothing more to be said or thought.

"Good day, Miss Camfrey! I have the most *quizzing* of news!"

Cordelia whirled around to find herself facing her future spouse. Her tousled hair had fallen from their pins and she felt a crimson flush rise up to her cheeks. "Lord Winthrop! I was not expecting you!"

"No, indeed! I should think not, since it was not long since that I escorted you to the park. You must think me a *very* overzealous fellow!"

Cordelia refrained from tartly replying that she felt nothing of the kind, for Lord Winthrop's idea of an outing to the park was simply one where he stopped the curricle under the shade of a handy tree and took the time to comment, in tones ranging from revulsion to envy, on all the horseflesh that passed before his critical eyes.

Miss Camfrey was convinced that if she wore a chequered spencer, her shift and nothing more than a parasol, my lord would not notice. Not, that is, unless, like Lady Godiva, she was mounted on a noteworthy stallion and felt the need to try her paces at a dash rather than the requisite sedate trot.

Still, my lord was good-hearted and that counted for something. Especially as he was looking at her now, with animation lighting his eyes and an indefinable eagerness etched across his features. Miss Camfrey scolded herself for wishing that he might take a sharp blade and trim some of the wilder excesses of his bushy red beard.

Even in so admonishing herself, she sighed. It was no use. Lord Winthrop could shave until his skin was as pink as a baby's—it would not make him any more personable. She cursed Rhaz again and again, for making her think shameful thoughts and draw comparisons where they were neither fair nor warranted. In a sudden, guilty desire to please Lord Henry, she smiled and bade him sit.

He looked dubious for a moment, as if unexpectedly trapped. Social visits were anathema to him, and though he did his duty by his affianced, additional burdens seemed the outside of enough. Still, he gingerly edged himself into one of the few quality seats Cordelia had not had the heart to sell.

She rang the bell for some fresh lemonade and raspberry cordial, which seemed to cheer him somewhat.

"Have you a little of that spiced orange Madeira cake over? I found it rather soothing on the palate."

"I shall ask Mrs. Stevens. At all events, if it is to your taste, I shall send the receipt on to your housekeeper."

"Old Fuss Bellows?" His Lordship snorted. "Like as not, she'd burn it to a cinder. She is a dab hand with a mutton broth or a buttered lobster, but sweets are beyond her, I'm afraid!"

Cordelia wondered fleetingly why his lordship referred to his servant as "Fuss Bellows." Too tired to ponder the matter over long, she nodded.

Before she could introduce a topic more dear to her heart, however, Lord Henry continued. "I am delighted you are so talented, Miss Camfrey! I look forward to your housekeeping skills with pleasure. Rutherford has too long been a bachelor establishment at the mercy of—"

"Old Fuss Bellows!" Rather in spite of herself, Cordelia's humour rose to the fore.

It was quite lost on Lord Henry, however, who nodded vigorously and murmured, "Quite!" in tones of heartfelt meaning.

A stillness fell on the room and Cordelia had the uneasy sensation that she ought to say something. "Lord . . ."

"Miss Camfrey . . ."

A collision of words. Cordelia smiled ruefully and suggested that Lord Winthrop speak first. He nodded as if that was his due, but rather benignly indicated that since his news was of some great moment, she, in this instance, might like to discourse first.

Cordelia schooled her features not to protest at this pompous presumption of self-importance. Instead, she thanked him mildly and then fell silent, staring at the Kidderminster carpet as if it might give her some inspiration. The orange Madeira cake materialised, and with it came some clarity to Cordelia's thoughts. Henry's

mouth was full when the words came spilling out, slowly
at first, then all in a tumble.

"Lord Henry, I wish you to know that I am very sensible of the offer you have made me and extremely,
extremely grateful for your—"

"Tush, my dear! It is nothing. You will make a fine
substitute for Old Fuss Bellows, though I trust you will
leave her be in the matter of catsups, snipes and quails."
He looked an interrogative, and if Cordelia did not feel
so wretched, she would have been hard-pressed not to
laugh. Lord Henry's stomach was second only to his
horses.

"I am perfectly certain she needs no intervention
whatsoever, Lord Henry, but we stray from the point!"

He nodded, though he muttered something to himself about half-baked plum pies, poorly soaked trifles
and execrable sillabubs.

Wisely, Cordelia ignored these grumbles and allowed
her words to take on a life of their own. "I have to be
perfectly honest with you, your lordship. I accepted
your suit for material reasons only. I think you know
that, but I am not perfectly certain that—"

"Material reasons?" He looked bewildered; then light
seemed to dawn. "Oh! You mean, I collect, that you
were interested in my wealth! Perfectly proper I should
say for any female circumstanced as you are!"

"Then you do not mind that—"

"Mind? Why should I mind? You are a pretty enough
female"—he looked at her doubtfully—"though I daresay you could put on a pound or two." He waggled his
finger in the air. "But it is not as if you cannot ride or
would be taken for a flat."

Cordelia was not precisely sure what this meant, but
she understood the drift of the rather unflattering series of compliments that followed. It seemed that since
she was not likely to either convert his stables into a

ballroom or to serve up burnt perigord pie—a matter he had *dreaded* in taking a wife—she was, in his eyes, perfectly acceptable. The matter of love simply did not seem to enter into his thinking. Taking up the delicate subject—Cordelia wanted to marry him in perfect honesty if nothing else—she coloured deeply and inquired what his lordship expected of her.

At first, he did not seem to understand the direction of her thoughts. When he did, he cleared his throat rather doubtfully, hemmed and hawed for perhaps some seconds—it seemed like aeons—and muttered something about an heir.

Cordelia nodded intently, though for the first time she seriously began contemplating what this process might entail. The thought of Lord Henry . . . She subdued a faint shiver. Henry Winthrop was a kind man, if not blessed overmuch with wit or joie de vivre. He seemed to find the subject equally embarrassing, for he glossed over it quickly and murmured that naturally after their first two children . . .

Cordelia looked at him in puzzlement. "Yes?" She prompted. He coughed and looked rather as though he wished himself safely back at his stables or Tattersall's at least.

Finally, he kicked the tassels of the poor, beleaguered Kidderminster and plunged headlong into the sentence that so eluded him. "Naturally if you wish a separate establishment and further marital freedoms—"

Gradually it dawned on Cordelia that he must mean "extramarital." She blushed again, but fortunately Henry was so caught up in his *own* tangle that he remained quite oblivious. When he'd finished, the room was pregnant with silence. Cordelia was bereft of words, satisfied that she was not marrying Lord Winthrop under false pretences. He did not seem to have even the remotest need for the love, companionship and passion that, up until now, Cordelia had thought the natural adjuncts to wedded state.

This lack of sensibility on Henry's part should have relieved her mind most frightfully. Her ready acceptance of his suit had been weighing on her conscience for some time. Now, however, just when she was free to make the connection without guilt, she baulked at the notion and, ironically, at Henry's complete lack of romance. *Silly nonsense!* she chided herself and settled down to hear what Lord Winthrop was so anxious to impart.

Strange to say, it had no bearing on what had just occurred—or indeed, insofar as Cordelia could see, on anything much to the purpose at all. Before she knew what she was about, he began a long, hideously monotonous monologue regarding, if Cordelia understood it right—and she was not perfectly certain that she did—the ancestry of his finest mares and the vindication of their bloodlines.

About fifteen minutes through the speech—minutely interspersed with descriptions of fetlocks and height and hocks and paces—Cordelia's eyes were drawn to the clock on the mantel. She wondered if anyone was likely to rescue her—Seraphina perhaps—but she thought not.

Just as she was focusing her thoughts once more on Lord Henry's sudden and strange animation, she felt a choking at her throat and the same heart-stopping sensation she'd first experienced when Rhaz, Lord Carlisle and the fifth Duke of Doncaster, first cast his burning dark eyes upon her. Those self-same eyes were now fixed upon her as Pendleton—*completely* in his element—announced the gentleman who very properly stood two paces behind him.

Cordelia was too surprised to do anything more than stand up shakily. Lord Henry, however, became unac-

countably and overwhelmingly gushing, ushering his
grace in with a great sweep of his hand and many utterances and gesticulations that no one—least of all the
nobleman in question—could make any sense of.

Light dawned in his grace's eyes when Winthrop pronounced him a positive rum one and came dangerously
close to slapping his back. His lordship, it appeared,
had received his grace's very kind invitation to review
the stables at Huntingdon.

What, he asked with candour, were the stallions like
at stud? Cordelia was caught between cringing and
laughing outright. She chose neither, for the duke
caught her eye and the laughter came out as something
between a gasp and a choke. Evidently he shared her
badly stifled amusement, for his mouth twitched
treacherously and his eyes seemed to twinkle as they
glanced a certain young lady's way.

His answer was suitably serious, however, as he turned
to Cordelia's betrothed and set his mind to being
charming. Poor Henry did not have a hope, for at the
expiration of a mere thirty seconds he found himself
quite in the duke's thrall, stuttering with excitement at
the thought of possibly coupling his bloodstock with
those of the famous Carlisle Arabians. From this, Cordelia inferred they were talking horses.

Her heart still beating wildly, she helped herself to a
piece of preserved ginger from the Madeira cake tray,
indicated to Rhaz to do the same and settled herself
down once more. I use the term "settled" in the broad-
est of senses, for the pulses that raced through her tem-
ples could hardly be so described. From time to time,
she felt Rhaz's deep, dark eyes upon her. When she
trusted herself to look up, they smiled almost into her
soul. The interview was agony, for she did not know
why he had come nor yet how she could let him leave.

It struck her how remiss it was of Pendleton to have

admitted him, for there was no sign of Ancilla, and
Seraphina, too, was nowhere at hand. It had been a
stretch to admit Winthrop, but then, she was his affianced—some degree of license could pertain and the
door had always remained firmly three inches ajar. With
Rhaz, however, it was unaccountably different. Pendleton must have been so overawed at his presence that
mere considerations of nicety must have completely
flown out of his head.

Still, one could hardly suppose Rhaz to pose any
threat to her virtue, not with Lord Henry standing between them, raving on and on about . . . What the devil
was he raving on about?

"Aramiss and Drixon!" He finished his sentence with
a triumphant nod and turned towards Cordelia. "Isn't
that famous news, my dear?"

Miss Camfrey had not the faintest idea what he was
talking about, so she nodded her head emphatically
and agreed. After all, Lord Henry might be slow upon
certain subjects, but when it came to horses, whatever
he said was bound to be correct.

To her surprise, his grace stepped forward and took
her hand in his. Turning to Lord Henry, he inquired
whether he minded, and finding that he did not, he
led her hand up to his lips and scorched it with the
mark of his mouth. Cordelia felt herself reeling from
the dizzying sensations that played havoc with her mind.

All traces of laughter left his grace the duke's eyes as
he held her hand a fraction longer than was strictly
appropriate. A moment later, he had dropped her
hand, but still it felt warm, as though encased in the
strong, masculine fingers of his own.

"You do me much honour, Miss Camfrey! I shall have
a coach sent round for the purpose."

"Beg pardon?" Cordelia was still dazed. She certainly
had no notion of what he spoke.

"A barouche, Miss Camfrey!" Henry's words echoed those of Doncaster. "You shall need one, for I daresay mine will be a trifle small for a party."

"A party?"

"Indeed, yes! I must say, it is very handsome of you, your grace!" Lord Winthrop beamed happily.

Rhaz was not so sure. The excellent notion he had conceived to rid himself at one and the same time of both Lord Henry Winthrop and his equally horse-mad, shatter-brained cousin Helena Moresby appeared to be a double-edged sword.

He'd offered Henry the chance of reviewing his stables and sending his mares to stud simply to draw him out of Cordelia's sphere and into that of Helena's. What he had *not* anticipated was that the shortsighted Lord Henry should think that he'd intended a lengthy stay or that he would assume Cordelia to be interested enough to want to accompany him. Of course, once he had made that assumption, it was necessary to invite both Ancilla and Seraphina, for it would have been shocking, indeed, for Cordelia to make up the party without chaperonage.

The duke did not particularly mind having Huntingdon descended upon by unexpected guests, but he was not sure how easy it would be to restrain his desires in the face of daily contact with the delectable Cordelia. *Especially* as she had quite specifically placed her trust in him to treat their growing attraction as a mutual friendship only. He sighed inwardly, for despite the fact that she was wearing last season's riding habit, it could not be denied that the vivid emerald looked stunning against her dark hair and that her wide, bright eyes glowed from her recent exercise.

The visit would be a sore trial to him. Still, none of these doubts were allowed to show on his dark, wonderfully well-proportioned countenance. If his eyes wandered a trifle to Cordelia's lips, no one noticed but she, and her heart was hammering too loudly in her breast to make any objection.

"The younger Miss Camfrey and your delightful mama shall naturally accompany you, Miss Cordelia."

Cordelia's spirits lowered immeasurably. Of course! This was merely the duke's elaborate way of furthering his acquaintance with Seraphina. Tears stung at the back of her eyes but she willed them away.

"Thank you, my grace! I am sure both will be quite honoured by the invitation, but I must tell you it is probable we shall not be able to take you up on your very kind offer."

Lord Winthrop nearly fell out of his seat. "Dash it all, Cordelia! It is not every day that Drixon and Aramiss have a chance to be coupled with two prize-winning Arabians!"

"I daresay not." Cordelia tried not to allow the tartness in her tone to become perceptible. "Seraphina, however, is inundated with invitations. Besides"—she looked uncertainly at the duke, unsure whether to confide minor household matters to him—"Seraphina's music master has only been employed for this quarter. It would be a sad waste of his services if we were suddenly to withdraw to the country."

"Bring him with!"

"Beg pardon?"

The duke repeated himself firmly. "Bring him with. I have any *number* of instruments lying about that might serve the purpose."

"Yes, but . . ."

Lord Winthrop decided to take a firm hand. "Miss Cordelia," he uttered firmly. "since you are a mere female and bound to get all in a tither about these things, leave them, I implore you, to me. There can be no more important circumstance than getting the horses to stud"—he cast a knowing glance at Rhaz—"as I am perfectly certain his grace will agree. Therefore, my dear, I shall just have to cast aside your objections and, by the right of my superior lineage, sex and masculine intelligence, outrule your gentle heart on this matter."

Cordelia glared at him. Her heart did not feel particularly gentle as the amused Duke of Doncaster could quite plainly see. Just as she was about to take issue with Winthrop's sweeping dismissal of her sex, she caught Rhaz's sudden, unexpected wink. His hand was over his mouth to stifle hoops of sudden, unbidden laughter. Shakily, he nodded, and as solemnly as he could, announced that since all females were *indeed* so feeble, it was fitting that he lend them strength and decision.

Cordelia, looking over Winthrop's thin, balding and slightly reddish head, witnessed the rather edifying sight of the fifth duke nigh on choke in amusement. In response, her lips twitched slightly and she felt a familiar glimmer of humour overtake her annoyance.

Just as Lord Winthrop was nodding solemnly and vowing what a pillar of strength the fifth duke must prove to all womankind, she choked, spluttered and allowed the tears to spill readily from her eyes. Such hilarity was alien to Winthrop, who looked first at Rhaz, then back again at Cordelia.

"Pardon me for missing the jest," he muttered pompously. Extracting no answer beside an unbecoming crack of renewed hilarity, the second Lord Winthrop jammed his beaver upon his head, made a quick bow to his intended and departed as abruptly as he had arrived.

ELEVEN

"I trust the trip is in order? If I had known the disruption my invitation would cause, I might never have given it."

"It was kindhearted in you, your grace! You must know Lord Winthrop values his stable above all else."

"Then he is a fool!"

The duke took Cordelia's hand in his and looked intently into the black of her long, tangled lashes. He could not see her eyes, for the sudden flutter she felt at his touch caused her to cast them down towards the tip of her sensible half boots.

"Your grace—"

"I wish you would call me Rhaz. We are friends, are we not?"

"We hardly know each other!"

"I feel I am sufficiently long in the tooth to discern a friend in a matter of moments. Do you not share similar sentiments, Miss Cordelia?"

She did, but her tone was muffled as she acknowledged it. She hardly trusted herself to speak, so strange were the feelings that flowed between them and the doubt and uncertainties that crested and peaked like an untameable sea between them.

Friendship. He spoke of that so easily, yet there was something more between them. Cordelia could feel it

flutter through her senses and wondered if she were
the only one affected in this dizzying manner. She concluded rather soulfully that she must be, for the duke
remained rock steady to her touch and even acted as a
support to her as she rocked, strangely off balance.

Lord Winthrop had left in such haste that the door's
three inches had narrowed, slightly, to two. The duke
had great difficulty in maintaining the correct distance
between them, especially since, when she finally *did*
look up from her contemplation of her boots, her face
was more lovely than he remembered.

Gently, he took her hands in his and narrowed the
distance between them farther. The pulse in her neck
must have encouraged him, for before he could set reason to disorder, his lips were upon hers and he felt the
trembling, feather-light touch of her arms about his
back. Cordelia closed her eyes and marvelled at the
firm warmth of his grace's lips as they took possession
of her senses.

His scent was of musk and a strange, elusive fragrance
reminiscent of pinecones and firs. His hair, pitch
against the skintight lawn shirt and elegant cravat, fell
slightly from his shoulders and brushed against her
skin. Silky as she had imagined . . . His face, whilst clean
shaven, nevertheless harboured a dark shadow faintly
discernible to the touch. Daring, she allowed her hands
to explore as he uttered a short oath and searched her
bright eyes for the truth and honesty he knew he would
find.

When he did, his mouth again moved towards hers
and Cordelia could feel a strange well of warmth per-
vade her body. She had never before experienced such
an electrifying effect upon her person. Rhaz, too,
seemed similarly affected, for his strong hands trembled, sending the prism from his single, elegant emer-

ald refracting into a million small lights across the
room.

This delightful situation might have progressed to
new and interesting heights had it not been for a cheery
step upon the marbled corridor just outside. The duke,
mindful of Cordelia's reputation and rather chagrined
at his own loss of control—his heart's desire was, after
all, betrothed—gently put her from him and straight-
ened his cravat. Though his eyes were speaking with
tenderness, Cordelia did not see them, for Seraphina
hurtled in and announced how delighted she was the
duke had taken the trouble of calling.

In the same way that Winthrop had imagined that his
grace's visit pertained to himself alone, Seraphina made
a similar mistake. She assumed without blinking that the
duke's call originated solely from the desire to reac-
quaint himself with her. Perhaps, to be fair, this muddle-
headed notion had developed after a singular talk with
Ancilla, who had summoned her almost immediately after the duchess's departure. Whatever the reason, the
thought did not cross her mind that it might be *Cordelia*
his grace wished to see. If it had, much of the misunderstanding that was to follow might have been averted. Still,
it is seldom possible to apply hindsight to current situations, and for the moment, Seraphina was flattered beyond anything to have so huge a success at the outset of
her first town season.

Her feelings for Frederick were as yet so young, so
strange and so entirely novel that they had not yet crys-
tallised into devotion. If anything, she was confused, for
he was a mere music master and therefore beyond her
sphere in terms of marriage. Despite her roguish kiss
and the insensible flutterings of her own heart, she accepted that Captain Argyll intended, as he said, friendship only. Accordingly, she fluttered her eyelashes like

a fledgling flirt and set out to be as charming and as alluring as ever she could.

She would have been chagrined to notice the duke's indulgent smile or the sideways glance of amusement he cast her elder sister. Cordelia might have been comforted, too, if she had noticed his expression. Unfortunately she did not. She was still trying to control her breathing and recapture her pulses from the electrifying effects of the moments before.

When she'd finally achieved this, she stole a glance at the duke, but he was so occupied in indulgently pandering to Seraphina's high spirits that the speaking moment was lost. Seraphina, brightly decked in a morning gown of crisp green lawn, looked sparkling. Cordelia swallowed a faint lump in her throat and quietly resumed her seat. All the lustre of the day was dulled for her, as she watched the heart-stoppingly handsome profile of her heart's desire. Strong and dark, he was truly an incomparable. Cordelia's fingers unthinkingly fluttered to her mouth, where his kiss was impressed upon her forever.

To the duke—Roving Rhaz—too late she remembered his amorous appellation—Cordelia must have seemed an inviting manner in which to pass the time. She blushed crimson at her own lack of reserve and at the fact that she had not roundly slapped his face in the manner in which he deserved. Yet he had looked so gentle, so infinitely tender . . .

Seraphina's chatter intruded into her thoughts but she found she could no more concentrate than collect her wits enough to order up tea. Fortunately, Pendleton was not so backwards in his attentions, nor, indeed, was Mrs. Stevens. By the time the delectable cake tray had made its entrance, Cordelia had recovered her poise enough to smile benignly at her sister and offhandedly at the duke. She vowed he would never know how close he'd been to melting all her defences and eliciting a declaration of love from her lips.

Love . . . Cordelia turned the word over in her mind despairingly. Since she was always strictly honest in her dealings with herself, she had to admit that, eligible or not, possible or not, honourable or not, she was head over heels for Rhaz, the noble fifth Duke of Doncaster.

Seraphina was still strategically batting her eyelashes and regaling the duke with snippets of her newly acquired town bronze. If she did not feel quite the same pangs of attraction and yearning that she did for her common music master, the lustre of Rhaz's rank and name was still firmly printed on her impressionable mind. It was clear that Ancilla expected a declaration from the duke and Seraphina quite thrilled at the prospect, for there could be no greater matrimonial catch, this season or any other.

Of course, his wide-set eyes and strong, aquiline nose seemed a trifle formidable and if she preferred the tantalising fall of chestnut locks to the stark, more regal à la Titus mode, that was her prerogative entirely. It was possible, she thought in confusion, to find *two* men appealing and Captain Argyll, after all, far from being as eligible was, she had to admit with an inward sigh, entirely *ineligible*.

Still, there could be no doubt that while the duke was all that one could wish for, his ironical gaze was disconcerting and she could not help the feeling that he was indulging her as a benevolent parent would a small child. She peeped up at him suspiciously, but there was not a hint of a smile lurking on his fine, wide lips as he nodded seriously and agreed that there could be no better read than Miss Burney's *Evelina*.

At first, Seraphina accused him of hoaxing her, but he murmured rather endearingly that this was not the case. When next he spouted several incidents very closely pertaining to the text, she was convinced. Rhaz chuckled inwardly and thanked the heavens his mama was such an inveterate reader of Gothic romances and other tales of high drama but dubious literary merit.

His twinkling eyes caught Cordelia's and she responded with an unwilling, but answering, smile. He was prepared to bet more than a few sovereigns that Cordelia's literary taste more nearly matched his own. He was quite tempted to tax her on it, but desisted, since Seraphina had taken up a new tack and it would have been unbecoming in him to interrupt. Still, while his mouth still tingled with their shared caress, he hoped and assumed that there was sufficient understanding between them to make words unnecessary. The matter of Lord Winthrop would be resolved—he was sure of that.

When Ancilla poked her head around the door and hurried both sisters up with an apologetic shake of her head at Doncaster, he took his leave with good grace. He would have been astonished to know that tears filled Cordelia's eyes as she vowed not to see him again. Or not alone, at all events.

"Shall you have your lessons in the afternoon, Miss Seraphina? I understand you are engaged until midday today. Perhaps some time after luncheon might suit?" The words were everything that they should be of a music master, but something in the tone made Seraphina quiver in anticipation. Captain Argyll had just knocked briskly on the door of the breakfast room and made an unannounced entrance.

"This morning will be excellent, Captain! I have played truant quite long enough and for that, Mama, I most heartily beg your pardon." Seraphina looked across at Ancilla and made a small grimace. "I am sorry

I took such a pet! I just loathe being made to feel like a small child at lessons."

Ancilla nodded. "That is perfectly understandable, my dear. You have your wings to flutter and it must seem irksome to you. I know *I* would find such an obligation a dead bore! Still, we cannot have a repeat of Lady Dearforth's soiree. I doubt either your pride or reputation could withstand such a thing twice."

Seraphina looked contrite, but an irrepressible twinkle lurked behind her lovely eyes. She shot a quick glance at the captain, who was standing quite correctly at ease with his long, slim fingers behind his back. Since he had not yet been outside, his fingers were not gloved and Seraphina had the sudden urge to kiss each one. She wondered what her sister and dear mama might think and tried to stifle the ready laughter that rose to her wide, quite generous lips.

"Indeed not! Horrors! And to that end I intend to devote today *entirely* to my studies. If that is all right with you, Captain?" She shot him a sidelong glance of pure mischief.

He chuckled inwardly at the child's audacity and made a stiff, servantlike bow. "I am entirely at your service, Miss Camfrey!"

"Seraphina, shall you not have dozens of morning callers buzzing about you like butterflies?"

"Doubtless I shall, but you may tell them I am engaged in morning calls of my own!"

"Very well then." The resignation in Cordelia's tone was palpable. She looked up with a slight, exasperated dimple surfacing about her mouth. "I suppose *I* shall have to entertain them?"

"You are a *dear*, Cordelia!"

Ancilla smiled serenely. "Then that is settled! I am going to pop over to Hookham's."

Seraphina gasped. "I am so sorry, Mama! I quite forgot to get your books!"

"I noticed. Never mind, Seraphina. I managed to finish that horrid, prosy piece by Sir Francis Bacon. Now I feel quite virtuous and may happily procure a couple of Gothics without feeling the smallest qualm!"

Seraphina crossed over and gave her startled mother a quick hug. "Excellent. You *do* deserve them. I am sorry I forgot."

"It is a trifle. You work at your accomplishments and I shall be more than mollified."

Seraphina nodded. "Shall we remove to the music room, Captain, or is the day too fine?"

She challenged him laughingly with her clear sky blue eyes.

"The music room will be an excellent start, Miss Seraphina." His tone was slightly repressive. He did not want Ancilla to decide a chaperone was suddenly a necessary accoutrement to the lessons. Though he would admit it to no one but himself, he was looking forward to the day with immense anticipation. If the naughty chit did not behave herself, however, the whole day might be spoiled.

Fortunately, Seraphina nodded demurely and did not press the point about the woods. Ancilla appeared to notice nothing amiss, for she gently opened the *Morning Post* and waved her youngest daughter away with a graceful little gesture of her hand.

Cordelia set down the last of her chocolate. It was a grim day ahead of her, for she was to consult with Cook about the meals for the following week and she knew it was going to be a battle since no one but she truly understood the deplorable state of their financial affairs. Between trying to cajole Cook into preparing bream instead of buttered lobster and one side dish instead of the usual three or four, she would have her work cut out for her. Then there were several matters pertaining to the household that she needed to discuss with Mrs. Stevens and Lord Winthrop was due to arrive some time after one to escort her to an edifying lecture on the evils of modern society and man's propensity to sin.

If she was not a thoroughly well-bred young lady, she would have stuck her tongue out at the very least. Instead, she sighed quietly to herself and flashed a quick, loving smile at Ancilla. "I almost look *forward* to the gaiety of Seraphina's morning callers!"

"If you were not betrothed yourself I am sure you would have your *own* fair share of admirers!" Ancilla looked her daughter over critically. She was quietly blossoming into something quite out of the ordinary way. Not a beauty in the conventional sense, but peculiarly striking nonetheless. *Such* a pity she did not take during her seasons. The young gentlemen must either have been blind or bewildered by her lively intelligence.

For an instant, she pondered whether Cordelia would be *happy* as Lady Winthrop. His lordship was *such* a dead bore. Still, the match was a social coup for Cordelia and certainly preferable to the life of a spinster. She *must* be happy with the notion. Putting aside her momentary concern—Ancilla *loathed* dwelling on the unpleasant— she smiled at her firstborn and bade her sternly to have a happy day.

Cordelia nodded. Impossible, of course, when she could do nothing but dream of . . . of . . . She blushed even to *think* what she dreamed of and with whom. Silly creature! Impossible dreams always came to naught and made the dreamer miserable. As always, she would make the day as useful and as provident as she could.

"Do not worry your head about *me,* Mama! I shall have a well-spent morning, I assure you. You may select a novel for me, too, though if you will! I am in the mood for something frivolous! Perhaps *Pride and Prejudice* again—it is every bit as excellent as *Sense and Sensibility* was."

Ancilla sniffed. "Nothing *happens* in them, Cordelia! It is just about ordinary people like you and me! I warrant Miss Austen has not inserted a single ghost, a *single* mysterious treasure chest or even a hideous creaking coat of armour! No blood or shrieking banshees in the mists, no evil—"

"Stop it, Mama! You are making me laugh!"

"I am serious, Cordelia! But I must say, a little laughter suits you. If you want to read dreary Miss Austen I am sure I shall not stop you."

"Thank you. I deem that awfully kind in you I am sure. And now, if you will excuse me."

Ancilla nodded and Cordelia crossed the hall and made her brisk way down the cantilevered steps and across the hall to another, narrower flight, which would ultimately lead her down to the kitchens.

"Miss Seraphina, I take leave to tell you you are a scamp! I have a good mind not to instruct you at all this morning."

Seraphina turned an innocent face upon the man she was rapidly coming to esteem very highly indeed. He might have relented a little, but for the naughty pout that just touched her lips and caused him to want to kiss her very thoroughly for the rest of the morning and well into the afternoon. Setting aside the thought firmly, my lord—or the captain, as he was known to the household—reviewed his pupil rather firmly and warned her that he intended to be a hard taskmaster.

Seraphina blithely nodded and announced she'd expected nothing else from a man with as authoritarian an air as himself.

"I shall, however, be good," she promised as she bestowed poor Frederick with the kind of smile that threatened to undo all of his resolutions.

"Very well, Miss Seraphina. I have an excellent notion of your aptitude on the harpsichord and your ready sensitivity to tempo and themes. You have a gift, for where most people need to be taught, you appear to have an innate sense of rhythm."

Seraphina hung on his words, for though she had received fulsome compliments in her life, none meant as much as these careful, unadorned words.

Frederick continued. "I am actually at a loss to know what went so dismally wrong at your famous soiree! I would have thought you would acquit yourself tolerably well even *without* practice. *Not,*" he uttered in stern accents, "that I am in any way condoning a lack of regular practice." There was a small pause. "I am merely slightly baffled and, yes, admittedly curious as to the *cause* of your failure." He did not mince his words. "What did you sing?"

Seraphina coloured at the memory. " 'Lost is my quiet forever.' " His grace the Duke of Doncaster came to my aid towards the end. I was never so mortified.

"Rhaz?" The name was out before the captain could stop himself. How *very* unlike the duke! He made a mental note to quiz him on it in the future.

Fortunately, Seraphina was still so embarrassed by the memory that she did not think it at all peculiar that a nameless music master should be acquainted, on firstname terms, with an illustrious nobleman of Rhaz's rank. She merely nodded and admitted that the evening had been "quite hellish" until she'd been rescued.

The captain nodded decisively. "We shall have to remedy that then. I do not think we have the sheet music for the Purcell, but I think I can find something similar."

He rummaged among the papers and came up with a sheet. "Excellent! You may sing this—it is in the same scale—and I shall accompany you. Then we shall see what can be done about making you a singer!"

His smile was so encouraging, Seraphina forgot her nervousness and took up the sheet. She cleared her throat and began. The captain listened with rapt attention as she sang the first few bars. Since he did not interrupt her, she gathered up her confidence and continued, faltering a little over some of the more *testing* notes, but nonetheless finishing the piece with relative ease.

There was a moment's silence when she had finished. Seraphina looked uncertainly at the captain, wondering what thoughts were flitting through his mind. Whatever she imagined, it was certainly not that he would look at her, tousle her glorious hair with *unmannerly* intimacy, then throw his head back and laugh.

Indignation rose stronger and stronger in Seraphina's breast as Frederick took a handkerchief from his pocket, wiped his eyes and planted a delightful, earth-shattering kiss upon her nose. The impudence! Seraphina seethed, but her nerves positively *jangled* from the unexpected caress.

At length, the twinkle dimmed from her thoroughly unsettling tutor's eyes. He took her hands in his and rather solemnly announced that he feared her singing skills were sadly beyond redemption.

"I shall have to reduce my fees, Miss Seraphina! I cannot in all honesty promise to tutor your singing voice, though the rest of your musical skills yield unsuspected promise."

He noted with sudden compassion how her beautiful, misty, sky blue eyes were suddenly dewy and he could all but detect a sniff. "Here." He handed her the hand-'kerchief. "Dry your eyes, my little angel. You may not be a singer, but you are a musician born. Any old person can sing. Few can achieve the heights with harmony as I suspect you can. We will work and you will learn. I shall not reduce my fees, for rather than turning out yet another insipid young miss vaguely accomplished at humming out a tune, I am going to make a musician. There, there! If you cry you shall break my heart."

His words were so compassionate, so truthful and so unutterably soothing that Seraphina no longer felt humiliation. He was not mocking her. If she knew no better, she could swear he was doing the reverse.

She consigned the handkerchief to the occasional table and sat down. For once, her lovely, animated face was solemn.

"Captain Argyll," she said, "I really would like to learn."

TWELVE

Ancilla noted with pleasure that Seraphina no longer demurred about practising her music or closeting herself with her tutor the best part of every morning. Despite the social whirl and long rounds of balls, soirees and theatre outings, Seraphina's spirits never seemed to flag, and while most of the household was still abed, she would be stolidly practicing and playing and heaven knew what. At least, she no longer had a fit of the sullens at the mere mention of her music master.

Perhaps she was sobered by the prospect of becoming duchess to the handsome, awe-inspiring Rhaz. She must have decided that accomplishments would be a boon, after all. Whatever the reason, it was not uncommon now to pass the music room and hear strains of Purcell, Bach and Handel waft through the house. Other melodies, too, beautiful and poignant, but to Ancilla's limited knowledge unidentifiable. These, of course, were Frederick's own pieces, for he found in Miss Seraphina a soul mate and the pleasure of playing for her was unparalleled even by the pleasure of writing them.

Mr. Beckett had received his scribblings with gratifying eagerness and the works of Lord Frederick were fast gaining critical acclaim by anyone at all fashionable among the ton. Since Frederick, however, had removed himself from that set, he was not to know the impact

he was making. Nor, in fact, did he particularly care,
save for the overlarge purse that was posted his way with
an entreaty from the normally reserved Mr. Becket for
more. So the time passed, with Frederick writing by
night and teaching by day. He did not know which aspect of his day he enjoyed more and it was a testament
to Miss Seraphina's bounteous charms that he suspected it was the former.

Certainly, if Seraphina was not a virtuous young lady
and he not an impeccable gentleman in all matters of
the heart, he suspected that, had Miss Camfrey elected
to distract him from his evening composition, he would
not have taken it amiss.

Still, there were times when he was thoughtful, for
Seraphina obviously still regarded him as a superior servant albeit attractive beyond belief. He watched her
comings and goings with amusement tinged with resignation, for as society's latest success, she was inundated
with morning callers, invitations to picnics (when it was
fine), the opera, Drury Lane and the inevitable Almack's.

These outings she quite obviously relished, being in
the throes of the first-season syndrome and not yet so-
phisticated enough to assume the mantle of boredom
and languid ennui that was generally fashionably
adopted by more seasoned members of the ton.
Frederick could afford to be indulgent, for he was not
mean-spirited enough to deny her her first pangs and
pleasures of growing up. Understanding her soul, he
felt certain that in the end she would be drawn to him
like a moth to the flame, recognising in their mutual
tranquillity a serenity that could not be gleaned from
the dizzying heights and aspirations of the social whirl.
He was prepared to wait for Seraphina to come to this
self-knowledge herself, for forcing an issue of such magnitude could serve no good and was likely to drive a

wedge between their ever growing joy in each other's company.

A week before the proposed trip to Huntingdon, Frederick gently instructed Seraphina on the best manner in which to manipulate the seven pedals at her feet. He watched as she concentrated fiercely and thought that he had never seen a lovelier sight than the faint lines that creased her brow as she practiced and the magnificent tendril that hung down her face like burnished gold reddened from a rosy sun. He longed to reach out and touch them, but instead contented himself with the surprise he had in store.

"Miss Seraphina, I took the liberty of inquiring of Pendleton what engagements you were likely to attend this evening."

She allowed her fingers to arpeggio gracefully across the strings, delighting in the newfound skill that sent silvery notes humming through the room. Frederick nodded approvingly and waited for her response.

"Captain Argyll, tonight is the one night I have free! Cordelia is to attend a soiree with Lord Winthrop, but since I do not know his relations, I have not received an invitation. Cordelia said she could procure one for me, but I suspect it will be stuffy and deadly dull—you know what Winthrop is like, so one can only *speculate* on his relations!—so I beseeched her—indeed I *entreated* her—not to!" She ended her sentence on a slightly mischievous giggle. "I suspect poor Cordelia envied me, for she did not press the point as I had feared, but rather murmured that an evening at home would be charming."

"I hope you do not share her sentiments?"

"That an evening at home would be charming?" She sparkled at him and he was hard-pressed not to kiss the living daylights out of her. "I think it will be *splendid!*"

"I am sorry to hear that, Miss Camfrey, for now I shall

have to dispense with *these.*" He pulled from his unfashionably capacious pocket tickets to the little frequented
Sandown Concert House, just short of Pall Mall.

Seraphina looked at them suspiciously. "What are
those, Captain?"

"These are tickets to see a performance of Gluck's
Orpheus. It was written principally for the harp, so I
thought you might find it edifying. There is also to be
a short performance of Johann Baptist Krumpholtz's
harp concerto—number one, I think, though I am not
perfectly certain on that score."

"I don't believe I have heard either."

"Possibly not, for they are relatively modern. Still, I
believe you will find them intriguing."

Seraphina's eyes shone. "I am certain I shall! Thank
you, thank you, Captain!"

Frederick longed to hear his own name upon her
lips. It was on the tip of his tongue to beg her to desist
from all formality when he thought better of it. It would
not do to be on first-name terms with a music master,
and until he had established himself, he had no desire
for his identity as an eligible peer to be revealed. So he
smiled in a heart-stopping fashion and contented himself instead with the immeasurable joy of lifting
Seraphina off her feet, swirling her high in the air and
setting her down upon the Kidderminster with unbridled aplomb.

"You could break your back!"

"I have carried much heavier, I assure you."

Seraphina cast a quick look at his iron-hard muscles
and believed him. Her slight flush pleased Frederick,
who believed that she was not entirely unreceptive to
his charms. He waited for her breathing to subside a
little before settling down in the padded mahogany
armchair with its scrolled arms and twisted back rail.
In truth, the comforts offered by its elegant red velvet

upholstery were wasted on him, for his thoughts were firmly situated with the young lady who was taking the opposite seat.

"When do we leave?"

"We? Miss Seraphina, for shame! You cannot think I would invite you to a concert unchaperoned? The tickets, since Miss Cordelia is otherwise engaged, are for yourself and *Mrs.* Camfrey."

Seraphina's face fell so endearingly that Frederick was caught between a chuckle and exultation, for the chit surely could not be indifferent to him if such was her reaction on the minor disappointment.

"Mama will not care for such an entertainment! She has told me *heaps* of times that concerts are deadly dull!"

"What a singularly uninformed parent! Perhaps I should educate *her*, too."

"Oh, Captain, stop funning! Please escort me! It won't be half so"—she was going to say thrilling but wisely found another word—"educational."

He shook his head and was so implacable on the matter that Seraphina grabbed a candlestick and was about to throw it wildly in his direction when Ancilla appeared.

"Seraphina! Set that down at once!" Her tone was uncharacteristically peremptory and her bright-eyed fledgling, so surprised, obeyed almost immediately.

"I am so sorry, Captain. I had forgotten, when I employed you, what a sore trial Seraphina can be. Don't scowl, child. If you wish to go on in society, you must learn to control your temper."

Seraphina, her moods as changeable as the wind, drew her mother impulsively into the room and very prettily begged Frederick's pardon before explaining what utter "fustian and tommy rot" he'd been talking.

After she'd hurtled headlong into a list of all her griev-

ances followed by several breathfuls on why Frederick
would be the perfect escort, she peeked up at her mama
and used age-old tricks to beguile her into being twisted
round her little finger.

Very thoroughly done and the observant Frederick
would either have applauded or spanked her for the
excellent performance.

At the end of it, however, Ancilla's lips twitched and
she gravely asked her daughter a few simple questions.

"Do I infer that I do not pass muster as a suitable
companion for you, Seraphina?"

"You would be impossible, Mama! You are always so
fidgety at recitals. Besides, Captain Argyll—"

"Refuses to escort you unchaperoned." His clipped
voice interpolated in no uncertain tone.

Ancilla looked at him thoughtfully and made her decision. "Captain Argyll, if you have better things to do
with your evening I shall understand perfectly, for
Seraphina is undoubtedly a handful and—"

"You *know* that is not the case, madame." Frederick's
voice was respectful but firm.

"In that case, may I not prevail upon you, Captain?
In the ordinary way of things I agree it is most prudent
to arrange a chaperone but the concert is for this evening and I am unfortunately promised to Lady Lewen-
thal. Cannot *you* escort this naughty little puss? I fear,
if you refuse, she'll be up to all sorts of shocking tricks
and then we *shall* be in the basket!"

"Oh please, Captain!"

Frederick still looked unconvinced, but after both females had made their case, cast beseeching eyes at him
and practically insinuated that Seraphina could be in
no danger from him due to his particular station in life,
he allowed himself to be beguiled. This was not due to
any weakness on his part, but because more than anything else in the world he *himself* wished for this time.

He rationalised the perverse breach of social conduct by reasoning that none among the haute ton would attend such a function when two major luminaries were having pre-Christmas balls on the same night. Further, as a male, he would offer more fitting protection to Seraphina, for Pall Mall at night was often less savoury than might be wished for. As an aside, he realised he did not know much about Sandown Concert House, save that it was housing these performances. It might be prudent, then, to attend, in the event of the venue for some reason proving unsuitable.

Lastly, if they *were* to be seen by anyone of Seraphina's acquaintance, the excursion could be explained away as a mere extension of formal lessons. There could be nothing amorous read into the connection of a young lady of good ton and a mere music master of lowly origin.

If he had been a fortune hunter or a . . . But, no, then he would have needed to be a peer of the realm at least and none save he and the duke knew that this, *precisely,* was what he was. With careful planning, Seraphina might attend her concert and not be compromised.

He nodded and sighed, but the unexpected joy that surged through his being could not altogether be ascribed to an overpowering desire to hear *Orpheus.* When the smile lurking in his soul finally made it to his lips, both ladies appeared equally delighted, for Ancilla was loath to forgo her engagement but too kind a mama to have made Seraphina miss out on her treat.

Seraphina was glowing and Ancilla gave her a quick hug, commenting that it was as well she attended, for as a duchess she would be expected to sponsor all *manner* of dreary events. Seraphina took her up on the word "dreary" but Captain Argyll stood stock-still, stunned as if all the wind had been knocked out of his powerful body.

He did not think it politic to question Ancilla too closely on her meaning, but he had to admit that, never once, in all Seraphina's undoubted whirl of gaiety, did he imagine or even consider that she might become betrothed. And to a duke, no less! He cast his mind over all the eligible—and ineligible—dukes that he knew of and came to the mystifying conclusion that none served the purpose. Mayhap he had forgotten some noble strand—he would have to consult Rhaz, who would naturally know such things.

Rhaz! His heart stopped. The fifth Duke of Doncaster was clearly the most likely candidate, although everything in Frederick's being cried out against the possibility. Impossible, impossible, impossible! For one, they had often joked how their tastes ran to opposites— Frederick sweet, Rhaz savoury; Frederick mild, Rhaz spicy; Frederick walking, Rhaz riding . . . The list could go on forever.

Further, Rhaz was the most confirmed bachelor on the planet saving, of course, he himself. And yet . . . Had Rhaz not spoken of some new paragon? Frederick wished he had not indulged in quite so much of the duke's high-quality wines, for the life of him he could not remember what the fifth duke had hinted at that evening. His heart sank as he recalled Seraphina's fleeting reference to him the day they had had their first true music lesson.

Both ladies were now looking at him in puzzlement, so he inferred that he must have missed something. Seraphina appeared as beautiful to him as ever, but now, unaccountably, more distant. He was surprised to find that despite the relative chill of the evening, for winter seemed on its way at last, his brow was hot and he had the sudden urge to loosen his already deplorably undertied cravat.

"Beg pardon!"

"Head in the clouds, Captain?" Seraphina smiled sweetly but there was a naughty chuckle at the back of her throat.

Frederick flashed her a grin that did not pass undetected by a thoughtful Ancilla. Still, when she repeated her unanswered question Frederick's mind turned immediately to the problem.

"*You* take the carriage, Mrs. Camfrey! I would not *dream* of depriving you of your conveyance." He thought regretfully of his own well-sprung chaise stabled at Drummond and firmly put the notion out of his mind. "If Miss Camfrey is willing, I shall call up a hack."

Ancilla nodded doubtfully. Cordelia would baulk at the expense, no doubt, but she could see no other way.

"I shall reimburse you, Captain, of course. Also, if I may, for the price of the tickets . . ."

Frederick's eyes flashed and he drew himself up a little taller, if possible. In the few seconds that elapsed, he forgot *entirely* that he was meant to be a penniless tutor forging a way for himself. His tone was authoritative and slightly tinged with a drawl as he turned on Ancilla and shook his head firmly. "You insult me, Mrs. Camfrey!"

Ancilla shook her head in confusion. "Indeed, Captain, I never meant—"

"Then no more shall be said on the matter or the whole enterprise shall be shelved." Frederick's voice was stern and his fine lips were drawn up in an uncompromisingly straight line.

Seraphina looked on him in horror but Ancilla, after raising her brows slightly, shrugged and smiled.

"Then I shall have to thank you, Captain!"

He looked slightly mollified and bowed. "Believe me when I say the pleasure is entirely mine, Mrs. Camfrey!"

She nodded, but long after the duo had returned to their lessons she looked after them consideringly. The strangest suspicion had entered her head. . . .

Orpheus was better than Seraphina might have imagined. She watched as a bewitching lady with round, dimpled arms gave life to the performance, her feet tapping at the seven pedals with splendid ease. Her dress was cut uncomfortably low and upon her head were sparkling gems of red and green, entwined in a heavy coronet of gilded silver. Her cheeks, to Seraphina's obvious delight and Frederick's stern disapproval, were well tinged with paint. There could be no question that the young lady in question was not quite respectable, but what did it matter? She played like an angel and Seraphina was transported.

By the light of several glittering candles liberally placed around her instrument, she played at first solo and then as a tinkling refrain in concert with the orchestra.

When her eyes could be dragged from the performance, Seraphina noticed that she was possibly alone in her appreciation of the music. Several young bucks were undoubtedly appreciative, but the direction of their glances caused her to blush crimson and cast her eyes up to Frederick, who was looking grimmer and grimmer by the moment. A few calls to the stage and several of the gentlemen threw hats in the air, or roses, or . . . yes, Seraphina could see it clearly: baubles and trinkets that glittered like stars in the candlelight.

Several times the player almost stumbled on the chords or missed her beat, but she plucked bravely on, even managing a roguish glance now and then when some *particularly* candid comment was audible above her efforts.

Seraphina, however, grew crosser and crosser, her enjoyment of the evening quite spoiled by the incivility and lack of attention—or *appropriate* attention—that the young lady was receiving. She noticed that Frederick had drawn her closer, and whilst this offered no end of distraction in itself, a particularly loud comment from the gentleman behind her caused her to turn around and hiss, "Be silent, sir, if you please!"

What a commotion such a simple comment caused! Seraphina was not to know that the auburn wisps of her hair were a veritable temptation to even the most self-controlled of men, that the demure gown of white silk studded in pearls and offering a faint hint, through translucent gauze fichu, of unspeakable delights, could act as such a powerful stimulant to the already bright-eyed audience.

She was soon to learn, however, for the roar of the audience formerly focused on the gifted harpist now turned upon her. Frederick noticed her quiver and tremble, her brow uncustomarily suffused in an embarrassed flush. He could have *kicked* himself for taking her to such a place, albeit in honest ignorance.

He leaned towards her and bade her edge her way out of the building. The silvery strains of the harp were complemented by cello and flute, but Seraphina had stopped listening. She stood up and Frederick draped the heavy folds of his greatcoat around her. She had been surprised at its elegance, for the masterful work of Scott was evident in the understated capes that hung in perfect precision from the shoulders. When she'd taxed Frederick on it, however, he had looked vaguely uncomfortable and turned the subject, so the matter of the greatcoat still lay between them. Or rather, on Seraphina, wholly obscuring the magnificence of her gown. She had so much wanted to look her best for the evening, and here she was, miserably being bundled out of the theatre in a greatcoat three times too large for her slender, waiflike body.

"Miss Seraphina, my heartfelt apologies! It was abominable of me to have subjected you to such . . . such . . ." Frederick glared but was at a loss for words.

"You were not to know, Captain! Besides, I *did* enjoy the music! The lady was passing accomplished, was she not?"

Lord Frederick would, in former times, have heartily agreed. He might even have blithely set her up as one of his ladybirds, for the creature was indeed as talented as she was . . . He glossed over this thought, for Seraphina was staring at him with wide, innocent and damnably fascinated eyes.

So he snorted instead and muttered that the lady's accomplishments were not of the brand he had anticipated. Seraphina, not so green as everyone thought, did not press him to explain, for his meaning would have been obvious even to a sapskull like Winthrop. She coloured a little and pulled the greatcoat closer against both the biting cold—surely snow was in the air?—and as protection, for her light gown was surely not made for walking up and down the streets of Pall Mall in the dark.

Frederick suppressed another curse, for the unsuitableness of their situation was not lost on him. He had arranged a hackney coach for the expiration of their concert, but since they had left the theatre early, there was little alternative but to walk, for waiting was unthinkable and there was not a single hack about for hire in the less fashionable Pellington Street off Pall Mall. Of course, when they approached the centre . . . But no! What a half-wit he was! If Seraphina was recognised with him, she would be ruined!

Much better by far to turn around and head towards the Thames. The walk would be longer but the chances of curious eyes far less. Better yet, Rhaz's town residence . . . But no! The Dowager Duchess of Doncaster was probably still haunting the place. She would fall into fits if he were to arrive with Seraphina. Especially, he thought rather dourly, if Seraphina was *indeed* intended for Rhaz.

No, he would take her quickly down to the wharf, where there was always a hack for hire. From there it would be but a short distance back to Melden Terrace. He prayed that no one would pay too much attention to the caped figure at his side. She was shapeless in his greatcoat, but her features remained magnificent nonetheless and that hair could be the death of them. Too beautiful by far!

He turned the startled Seraphina swiftly round and began pacing away from the city centre. He took good care to keep to the roadside, second nature by breeding but also by good sense. If a carriage should happen to rumble by it would be *he* that they first saw, rather than the fair Seraphina.

He tucked her arm firmly in his, for he felt very protective all of a sudden and, despite all his years on the Peninsula, more than slightly vulnerable. His step matched Seraphina's so exactly that he was certain that they were two people in perfect concert. He smiled a little to himself at this whimsicality. A concert of the soul. He wondered if Seraphina felt it. He looked at her and her eyes were shining so brilliantly he had to conclude she did. The walk—despite its odious necessity—would remain in his memory always.

THIRTEEN

The new gas lamps flickered a dim yellow for fifty yards or more before stopping as abruptly as they had started, several paces back from the entrance to the narrow, cobbled street that would wind its way down to the river. Frederick hoped that its very narrowness would serve to deter unwieldy coaches. In this way, their unchaperoned amble was less likely to raise brows. Still, the streets were now dark, the moonless sky verging on pitch-black, and he wondered whether he should, after all, have kept to more reputable thoroughfares.

Seraphina had no such qualms. The evening, to her, was magical. The strains of the harp still lingered in her ears, and though the spectacle had not been quite what she had expected or what, in fact, she ought to have witnessed, it did not detract from her enjoyment one jot. Further, the unprecedented chance of having her tutor all to herself in such heady circumstances was quite intoxicating. She peeped up at him from beneath her abundant auburn lashes. All she could see was his shoulder and sleeve, but that sight was in itself pleasurable, since the good captain obviously had no need or use for padding or artifice.

His dress was more debonair than usual, strictly military in style—deep, shadowy blue with silver epaulettes and matching buttons. Beneath his waistcoat she could detect an elegant gold seal and fob, though she blushed to look more closely. His pantaloons were a perfect fit and therefore quite unmentionable to a lady of good upbringing. Nevertheless, there was no law precluding her noticing and notice she did. Perhaps Frederick felt her stare upon him, for his grip tightened and the glance he threw her was not wholly servile like in nature.

Seraphina smiled up at him and he felt the breath knocked out of his very experienced, entirely masculine body. He was dizzied at the effect Seraphina had, given the fact that he was himself no greenhorn among the fairer sex. She was more beautiful than anyone he had ever encountered, but the attraction was more substantial than that. She understood his music and therefore his soul stripped bare. He understood her wiles and her mischief—had he not those self-same impulses deep within himself? And the attraction—that was no wishful imagining! He would wager all his quarterly earnings and more that she was as compelled as he.

The stars twinkled in the deep, dark sea of sky. Their lustre was reflected in Seraphina's eyes as she looked at him, missing a step as she did so. He helped her correct her balance, pulling closed the greatcoat that had opened during the stumble. He trembled a little at the sight that greeted him. Pure white on delicate cream, her pearls shimmering and dancing like a veritable constellation of heavenly stars.

"Angel, my angel," he breathed before setting her to rights.

"Beg pardon?" The words were forced from Seraphina, who felt so breathless she thought she might well fall into a faint of sheer pleasure.

The captain shook his head and smiled. "Do you stargaze, Miss Seraphina?" He wished to steer her onto safer subjects and recover the distance that suddenly seemed to have been dangerously bridged.

"Stargaze? You mean with a telescope?"

Frederick nodded, watching her with interest. Most women would have assumed he meant vaguely looking up at a velvety sky and noticing the orbs of light that reflected back from the heavens in a meaningless cascade of twinkling illumination.

"Never, Captain!" Her tone was wistful, so Frederick decided to probe further as their feet brought them ever closer to their destination.

"Do you wish to?"

She nodded. "I was a sloth at the boring old globes, but I have to admit I have an interest in the heavens."

"Perhaps because of your name."

"Beg pardon?"

" Seraph. Angel."

The words, from his lips, were an intimate caress. Seraphina tried to hold his gaze but could not. The moment passed when he chuckled softly and asked her why she was such a sloth.

She coloured ruefully. "Detestable governesses! They forever prosed on about the terrestrial and celestial orbs just precisely when I wished to play truant in the meadows!"

"You must have been a devil to teach!"

"You know firsthand, Captain!"

He nodded gravely, then reduced her quick remorse with a merry grin that she only just detected in the heady darkness. She tightened her arm on his sleeve and they walked on in companionable silence. This was first broken by Seraphina, who was curious as to the personality and habits of the handsome stranger who was rapidly capturing her heart.

"Do you stargaze, Captain?"

He nodded. "In Spain, the skies were pitch-dark and

frequently, whilst we were waiting for a battle to be fought or nursing our wounds, we would look up from our truckle beds or even just the haystacks or plain earth we were lying on and gaze intently. Somewhere along the way I procured a little telescope and interested myself in the pure science of the thing."

"Science? I have never regarded the sky in that light."

Frederick smiled. "Most don't, my dear, but astronomy is rapidly progressing, and for those fortunate enough to catch nightly glimpses of Saturn, the excitement is palpable."

"I can imagine! Saturn, if I recall, is the farthest planet known to man."

"Now that is where you are mistaken!"

Seraphina blushed for her ignorance and wished she had paid more attention to the rambling of the hated Miss Werstead. The captain, however, more aware of the bouncy young thing at his side than any of the town-bronzed, ripely seductive vixens he'd ever had truck with, noticed her dejection and shook his head.

"This time the fault is not yours, Seraphina! I daresay all the celestial globes have it wrong!"

"How so, Captain?"

"A passing acquaintance of mine—fellow named Herschel—has furthered the world's body of knowledge in an extraordinary way."

"In what manner?" Seraphina's eyes lighted up with interest. Captain Argyll's knowledge, it seemed, extended a lot further than the sphere of music. She was fascinated to explore him—and his wisdom—further.

"Do not look at me so, Miss Seraphina! You disturb my senses."

She coloured and Frederick's wide, sensuous mouth snapped shut. He had said too much! Far more than what was within the bounds of gallantry. But there, he was not, in his current role, even *meant* to be gallant!

Seraphina could well take up his comment and label it an impertinence or worse.

She did not. Her feet, delicately slippered in a delectably unsuitable confection for the walk they were currently engaged in, slowed almost to a halt but did not stop. Instead, they ambled seductively alongside him as if loath to reach the quay that was their final destination. Her deep sapphire eyes were almost luminous, for his own had suitably adjusted to the dark and were now glancing sideways at hers with unusual intensity.

"Sir William Herschel discovered, some years ago, that the sun has one *more* planet slowly orbiting the dark space we choose to call our heavens."

"Truly? Beyond Saturn?"

He nodded firmly. "Beyond Saturn, Seraphina. He thought it a comet, at first, but we now know that what he saw was our farthest planet. He called it after His Majesty, but it is now more commonly known as Uranus. King George appointed him king's astronomer and he has discovered more still since then. Uranus is orbited by two moons and he has recently uncovered two new moons circling our old friend Saturn. Since he is still stargazing, who knows what next he will uncover? His son Frederick is at it, too, I might add. He has found that so many of our stars are actually *double* stars, orbiting each other. Sometimes I hope, with my small scope, to rival them. Another planet perhaps?" He looked at her rather ruefully. "Unlikely, but not impossible! Sir William discovered Uranus with a ten-inch scope. Mine is a mere four, but still I gaze with excited anticipation most clear, dark nights. Odd, is it not?"

"Wonderful! You are a man of so many facets! I never dreamed . . ." Seraphina fell into an embarrassed silence but his lordship was too astute to miss her meaning. His tone was therefore gentle as he pointed out two hackney coaches waiting for hire at the edge of the icy, lapping waters of London's largest river.

He was just raising his hand to indicate that he required one of its services when a queer little man in a striped waistcoat and perilously purple pants puffed up to the quay. He took out his quizzing glass and muttered something to Frederick about his prime little piece. Frederick found himself in an instant's quandary. Sir Archibald Huffington was one of those seedy people forever hanging on to the fringes of the ton. He was tolerated for his eccentricity, his enormous wealth and the sad fact that half of London was in his debt in one way or another. The man had a vicious tongue and an even more vicious temper. Several slightly nastier things were whispered about him in select circles, but since nothing was ever proven, Sir Huffington was permitted to remain.

Now the vile man was ogling Seraphina in the most *odious* way and offering Frederick an advance to take "the goods off him." Seraphina opened her pretty little mouth to formulate the most *scathing* of replies, but Frederick stopped her with a peremptory gesture. If Sir Archibald heard her speak, he would know he was mistaken in his first surmise. He would know Seraphina was quality born, and as sure as the sun rose every day in the sky, he would make ample use of that knowledge, either by blackmail or by the spread of the delectable gossip that was yet *another* reason why the old tabbies tolerated him.

Frederick knew that neither scenario would suit. He therefore looked Sir Archibald in the eye, lifted his fist and planted such a facer across the surprised man's face that even as he landed in a paltry, snivelling heap at their feet, his expression was so ludicrous as to make Seraphina chuckle. The hackney coach riders, just making out the debacle in the faint mists that were rising up from the waters, saw fit to applaud and Frederick cast an indulgent grin their way.

But what was to become of Sir Archibald? Left to his own devices, he would undoubtedly either call Frederick out—for in his bold, military-style evening dress he had recognised him as the gentleman he was—or he would piece together who *Seraphina* was and make his angel's life a living hell. Accordingly, Frederick, ever a muscular man of action, ordered Seraphina to turn her back.

She refused so indignantly that he thought better of arguing with her in a public street and shrugged his fine shoulders in resignation. So long as the chit had the sense to keep herself covered in the folds of his greatcoat, he wished to waste no more time. Besides, he reluctantly admired her spunk. Any other gently bred female would surely have taken the opportunity of swooning at this point.

Accordingly, he reached over to the spluttering, dazzled and bruised Sir Archibald and placed his hands in the man's capacious pockets. When he produced a decanter of Burgundy from the lined pocket inside of his garb, he nodded his head in satisfaction. Then the rumours were true! He did not feel any surprise. Sir Archibald's addiction to salubrious liquids had been hinted at often enough—he had just never really stopped to care.

Sir Archibald was making a pathetic attempt at reviving himself. His eyes swivelled from Frederick to Seraphina, and in that cunning glance, Frederick knew for certain he had no choice. Unhesitatingly he unstopped the bottle and placed it firmly to Sir Archibald's lips. The man protested, for an instant, then gave himself up to the intoxicating aroma that assailed his nostrils. A little more gently then, Frederick proceeded to pour the entire contents down his gullet until all that could be seen of the man was purple pantaloons across a cobbled street. Seraphina stared at Frederick and shivered.

She had no idea he could be so forceful—such a gentle man he had always seemed to be. Then she remembered the firmness of his jaw and the quiet, authoritarian tone he used only when she was making a *particularly* foolish cake of herself. Captain Argyll was acting entirely in character, and though his actions were dubious and possibly debatable, Seraphina applauded him loudly in her head.

The clapping was echoed on the wharf, for the two curious hackney coach drivers had drawn ever closer at this unusual interlude in their evening. They were used to common brawls, of course, but the two men—well, certainly the victor—were clearly gentleman. When Frederick rather shortly ordered one of them to bundle the "sadly inebriated gentleman" into a hack, the larger of the two grinned broadly and admitted he would be "much obliged" especially as the order was accompanied by a quite satisfactory coin of inducement.

Frederick racked his brain for the man's unfashionable address. Somewhere near Kensington, if he recalled. One of the older buildings . . . Lord Caxton had once spent several months in that vicinity on a repairing lease. He closed his eyes, concentrating. At last, his efforts were rewarded. Remembering, he mouthed out the place and bade the hack farewell. The second driver's eyes now turned to Seraphina and for an instant Frederick debated the necessity of coshing him over the head as well. The man took one startled glance his way and became quite humbly servile, even offering to open the doors of the chaise for her.

Frederick declined the kind offer, but his jaw relaxed into a quick grin. There would be no trouble with this man and he hoped above hope a quite dramatic scandal had been averted. Of course, he would have offered at *once* for Seraphina's hand had damage actually occurred, but as he silently smiled to himself, he preferred to do things in his own time, in his own unique way. He looked at Seraphina and it felt as though his heart would burst in his chest. So lively, such animation, so much potential bottled up beneath the ladylike veneer. He never imagined what a joy it would be to teach her, to unleash some of that potential . . . His breathing grew deeper as he allowed himself to reflect on further potential he might explore with her. His eyes caught hers and he felt, rather than knew, that she was thinking similarly reflective, slightly wanton thoughts. It would be nothing to reach out and stroke that mass of burnished copper . . . to tease her mercilessly with his lips, just a hairbreadth away . . . His fingers unfurled and the pulses in Seraphina's slim wrists and neck were raging. Fortunately, her gloves and her coat preserved her modesty, for if Frederick had seen that rush of desires he would, quite truly, Sir Archibald or not, have been compromised.

Instead, Frederick saw parted lips and high colour, the first flush of youth. The sight both inflamed and cooled his ardour, for Seraphina was a lady, gently born and, despite her mischievous inclinations, utterly innocent. So he sighed and searched around in his head for some dampening thought. The image came easily: dark and handsome and intolerably painful. Rhaz, the fifth Duke of Doncaster and his very best friend. His brow furrowed painfully as he realised that the fruition of his dreams was not meant to be. Rhaz had branded Seraphina with his first claim. Cruel fate! If he had had a notion, even an inkling! But no! He would never know, for on this matter Frederick determined to be silent. If the sentiments were reciprocal, he would stand back for the sake of his great love and his friendship.

Seraphina looked at him quizzically. It was all he could do not to allow her to tumble into his arms and be madly, wildly kissed. He was a gentleman, though, so despite his inner turmoil, he maintained a polite and proper distance. Miss Camfrey's heart slowly stilled as she found him very thoughtful for her comfort and impossibly charming in manner, but nevertheless unexpectedly silent. An unease had descended upon them that made the dark, starlit evening sadly dimmer.

When Sir Archibald Huffington was duly delivered to his residence, it took both the hackney cab driver and the sadly underpaid manservant to ease him out of the coach and into the house. Their efforts were not made any easier by the baronet's strange predilection for song, nor by his very loud insistence that he was perfectly sober and could manage for himself.

Several candles were lit in the houses alongside of him, a surefire indication that yet again his nocturnal carousing had wakened the genteel neighbours. The hackney coach driver, awake to every suit and in a *particularly* charitable frame of mind given the glittering coin rattling round in his pocket, felt he should earn his keep. Consequently, in a *very* loud voice, he told the under butler that the "gennelman" had been extracted from the King's Head, a well-known taproom at least five miles south of the scene of the crime. If Sir Archibald had any interesting snippets to relate with regard to the well-turned wench, his credibility would be sorely tried, since gossip spread like wildfire among servants. It would not be long before every house in London knew that poor Sir Archibald had been carousing again.

The hackney coach driver smiled grimly as he jumped up onto his perch and took the reins once more. It was not often he had the chance to cast one in the eye to the gentry folk, but tonight he'd done just that. With a little whistle between his teeth, he urged the horses on.

If the King's Head had not *exactly* transacted business with the purple-breeched dandy he'd just dumped on the doorstep, they would nevertheless not miss out. Harry Turkington was about to descend upon them with a half crown's largesse in his pocket. Ah, it was a wonderful night! He *click-clicked* with his tongue and the horses obediently changed to a trot.

FOURTEEN

"Do hurry up, Delia dear!" Seraphina skipped into the luxurious chaise and flung herself against the squabs. "Isn't this heavenly? I declare there's enough space for us all to stretch out with perfect decorum!"

"And since when has decorum been a prime consideration with you, Seraphina my love?" Cordelia dimpled wickedly, her spirits high though she could not, for the life of her, understand why. Perhaps it was the crisp chill of the morning or the prospect of an interesting ride through the picturesque green countryside. Whatever the cause of her animation, she was certain that it was *not* the fact that she was now occupying the duke's own seat, preparatory to a visit to that gentleman's vast country estate.

"I cannot see why Captain Argyll has to sit up with the outriders! Can he not take his place inside?"

Ancilla lowered her head to climb in and caught the last of Seraphina's remarks. "We've been through all this, Seraphina! Captain Argyll is an excellent shot and we can rest secure in that notion." She refrained from saying that she thought that, if Seraphina wished to further her chances of becoming a duchess, it would be wise not to pursue too active an acquaintance with the good captain. For though his manners were ineffably those of a gentleman, he appeared to hold Miss Camfrey in a thrall that Ancilla deemed slightly concerning, given that he was employed only as a common music master. She held her peace though, knowing her youngest daughter too well to force the point.

"The duke has been most thoughtful and has provided hot bricks for our comfort. He has also attended to a picnic hamper so we should not starve before arriving at our destination."

"What, ho?" Lord Henry, rather out of breath, climbed the few small steps and waved away the Camfreys' gardener cum groom.

"Lord Winthrop, we thought you were making your own way to Huntingdon?" Ancilla's voice was light, but the dismayed glance she cast Seraphina's way was heartfelt. Cordelia, too, felt a strange sinking of the spirits as her betrothed fussily set himself down and called out orders from the open windows of the splendid well-sprung barouche.

"I was of a mind to, Mrs. Camfrey, until I bethought me of a better plan! Since the duke is sending two carriages over, both of them sporting excellent stallions, I felt it would be a shame—not to mention discourteous—not to avail myself of the opportunity of viewing their mettle firsthand. This looks a fairly well-matched team, I might add. I shall inform his grace." He looked up with a bland, satisfied smile and remarked benignly that all the ladies were in fine looks. Having dispensed with all his social obligations, he then took a small peek into the hamper and selected for himself a smidgen of carved Westphalian ham, a sliver of pheasant and several helpings of an excellent duck-and-gooseberry tart. Seraphina was hard-pressed not to giggle, but Cordelia frowned at her warningly, so the morning passed without any hurt feelings or further social disasters.

Unfortunately, the afternoon was not as serenely spent. Cordelia found herself wrapped up in a pleasant daydream that had little to do with the man seated opposite her and much to do with a certain, unattainable, striking and magnetic man that seemed to occupy far too much of her thoughts for comfort. She could still feel his strong caress, his burning eyes and his amused empathy from every single encounter she had had with him. Winthrop, sensing her abstraction, attributed it to a maidenly embarrassment at his own splendid presence. Accordingly, he good-naturedly, misguidedly and *excruciatingly* pompously set about drawing Cordelia out of the cocoon she had so carefully woven for herself.

In between odd excursions into the bountiful picnic hamper—Cordelia was now feeling decidedly queasy at the sight—he decided to discourse with her on the horses they were about to view at Huntingdon until even Ancilla was forced to roll her eyes heavenwards and comment that perhaps Cordelia looked tired.

"Tired? Never! Our Miss Camfrey is never peaky! Too much rumgumption and all that! For myself, I have hardly had a day's tiredness in all my life! Brisk walking and plenty of exercise, I always say! Now Dr. Foggarty, he would tell you . . ."

And so it went on until all three female passengers were longing to make their escape. Seraphina kept peering wistfully out of the window, but Captain Argyll was always too far forward to be seen. She sighed and wished something exciting would happen to relieve them of the tedium.

She did not have long to wait. Captain Argyll crossed to their window as the late autumn leaves fluttered to the ground and the mild sunshine was dimming to shadows. He pointed to a crossroad and indicated they were nearing Huntingdon, one of the duke's extensive domains. While it was not his principal seat, most of the hills and meadows that stretched farther than the eye could see formed part of the estate. Cordelia was interested to note how neat everything looked, how the cottagers seemed as robust and as spanking clean as their tidy, thatched homes. The road stretched tantalisingly to the east.

The elder Miss Camfrey could not help feeling a spark of anticipation. Somewhere to the east, his grace was strolling, riding, awaiting their arrival perhaps. She reflected on his brilliant smile, how his cravat would be elegantly but not ostentatiously tied, how his— But no! Such thoughts were unbecoming in her. She flushed and did not notice the teasing interplay between Frederick and Seraphina. Ancilla did though. She sighed, for Captain Argyll was so charming, such a perfect gentleman, so very much everything she could wish for in a son. . . . He had the taming of Seraphina, too. It was difficult to turn a blind eye to the sparkle that instantly appeared in striking coincidence with the captain's presence. Almost, she could swear, there was an attachment . . . Yet that was ridiculous! Captain Argyll was nothing more than a penniless employee. It was unthinkable. Yet such gracious manners . . . She sighed. If only *he* had been the duke! And Cordelia? Despite Winthrop's assertions to the contrary, she *was* looking peaky! What was going on with her girls?

Suddenly, Ancilla was forced to cast this thought aside, as a gunshot caused the carriage to swerve unsteadily across the path and onto the soft, velvety grass verge. The first was closely followed by a second, and as the team in the baggage carriage behind began to gallop in disarray, the two carriages converged upon each other and they were well and truly ditched. There were loud, coarse noises, further shots and an anguished cry from Cordelia. It all happened so quickly that no one could make much sense of anything. Captain Argyll had vanished and Winthrop, as white as a sheet and blustering, was attempting to open the carriage door. It was jammed and his panic was incalculable. Seraphina looked about her and realised at once that they were the victims of a highwayman.

She heard the cock of a pistol and further shots. Cordelia whispered that they ought to remain still. Doubtless the outriders and Captain Argyll combined would overpower them. Seraphina nodded. Her confidence in the captain was enormous. Still, if they were armed . . . Captain Argyll had climbed down from his box. Had he taken his pistol with him when he did so? Perhaps he was lying lifeless even now . . .

"I must get to him!"

"Sit still, Seraphina!"

A long, low whistle, then the sounds of hooves flying across the paddocks. Cordelia, sitting unnoticed in a pool of seeping blood, felt faint and a little sick. She heard fumbling with the door and her eyes widened in fear. If it was a highwayman, then Captain Argyll must be injured at the very least. He would not permit common felons of the road to approach them without a fight. Her muscles tightened imperceptibly and she could see a similar nervousness cross Ancilla's pretty, butterfly-like features.

"Take off your necklaces!" she whispered to both Seraphina and Ancilla before struggling with her own.

"What?" Winthrop sounded outraged. "Hand over your gems to those rapscallions? Never! I shall scold them roundly for their impertinence and so I tell you!"

Neither Misses Camfrey bothered to reply. Ancilla already had her string of pearls dislodged from her neck and was now working at unscrewing the pretty matching earrings. Seraphina was not wearing a necklace, but she silently edged off a pretty little gold bangle that she'd insisted on keeping despite Cordelia's small efforts to economise. Blood trickled down Cordelia's arm, staining her light carriage dress of sprigged lawn as she pulled at the small cameo. A gift from her papa. She put the thought firmly out of her mind.

Lord Winthrop was still protesting loudly that they should not forfeit their gems. The door opened and the stench of sweat and alcohol assailed the occupants' senses. Cordelia felt her heart sinking, for they would surely be overpowered.

"What is the meaning of this?" Winthrop shifted in his chair uneasily.

" 'And over the pretties and none shall be 'armed. Quickly now!" The man's tone was urgent and he repeatedly looked over his shoulder as if hearing something. Cordelia wondered what had become of the outriders and why he was looking so uneasy. Perhaps they were not dead, just stunned.

The intruder seemed in a tearing hurry, but then, it was twilight and his felony might be witnessed by any passing chaise. Since highway robbery was a hanging offence, she supposed she could understand his agitation.

Perhaps they could make it work for them. If he would only take the bounty, he might be in such haste to disappear that they'd be allowed to pass on their way, or at least live.

When Winthrop moved forward, a blunderbuss was pointed rather inelegantly at his face. "Don't move! 'Urry up, I say!"

Lord Henry looked disdainful. "You shall hang for this! I am a magistrate of the peace! Allow us to continue on our way and I shall dismiss this matter from my mind."

"Oy! We 'ave a sense of 'umour! Very good, guv! Now 'and over the stash!"

The womenfolk practically begged Lord Henry to desist from argument and give the man what he wanted. Lord Henry's outrage, though, was growing every mo-

ment. Cordelia felt very close to an uneasy faint, for
her arm was aching, and though she was only losing
blood slowly, the anxiety of the situation was causing
an unsteadiness that had her swaying. Seraphina's fingers clenched over a bottle lying discarded from the
hamper. If necessary, she would hit the man over the
head, though her aim would be slightly off due to the
rocking of the carriage.

"Lord Henry, cease being a dolt and give the man
the gems!" Ancilla's tone was suddenly imperious and
Winthrop was so startled by the unexpected admonish-
ment that he meekly handed over the loot.

The man's eyes narrowed when he noted the paltry
takings, but he was fidgety in the dusky twilight and
anxious to get on. Disappointing, for the well-appointed
carriage had promised of more. Still, a quick glance at
the ladies indicated that there was indeed no more to
yield.

When the highwayman's eyes rested on Winthrop,
they rounded in satisfaction, for the man was wearing
several ornate seals and a signet ring that, if not a ruby,
was almost certainly a garnet of high calibre. When the
thief pointed to them and bade them be removed.
Henry turned a spluttering, purplish colour, and Cordelia, in her weakened state, nevertheless feared he
might have an apoplexy. She was faintly aware of noises
in the background, but she was too riveted on the scene
within to give the matter much thought. The man released the safety catch of his overlarge blunderbuss, and
at last, with the sharp click, Winthrop stopped dither-
ing. He pulled off his treasures and gingerly proffered
them to the highwayman.

"Mighty wise, guv!" The felon nodded approvingly.

Whilst his attention was momentarily diverted,
Seraphina raised the bottle above her head. Too late!
He caught sight at once of what she was about. More-

over, the noises echoing around him were suddenly brought home to him. Torn between teaching the party a very good lesson and escaping with his hide intact, the highwayman chose the latter. Just as Seraphina was preparing for the worst, his face disappeared from the window. The sound of hooves once again, then a certain eerie stillness before a yell of surprise. Against the darkening sky, the highwayman's henchmen—a threatening, foul-smelling creature—dropped in front of their very eyes.

Then Frederick was upon them, prising open the door with a stick from the meadows. He ordered the outriders—lying impotently sprawled across the ground—to resume their positions. As he did so, the thundering of Arabian hooves, ever steadier, was upon them. His grace the Duke of Doncaster slid off his horse and cast a meaningful, speaking glance at Frederick.

Frederick! The coincidence was uncanny. He would have laughed had the situation been anything but as dire as it was. How strange that of all the music masters in the world, it was Lord Argyll that the Camfreys had chosen to employ. When he'd offhandedly suggested Seraphina's tutor accompany them, he had little *dreamed* that Frederick would finally land up accepting his offer to be his guest in this ridiculous guise. Was he to be placed in the servants' quarters?

The logistics were fascinating, but the duke did not allow himself to linger on them. He'd instinctively responded to Frederick's call and the blood was still pounding through his veins as in one summary glance he took in the exact series of circumstances that had just occurred.

When the highwayman had chosen to strike, his eyes had been focused entirely on the outriders. It was unfortunate for him that he'd obviously not noticed the captain dismount, the better to slow the horses and inform the ladies that they were on Huntingdon grounds. The outriders had been quickly disabled and forced to lie prone on the floor, but Frederick had seized the opportunity to creep round from the other side and take the felon by surprise.

Not before, however, he'd emitted the high-pitched whistle that both Seraphina and Cordelia had heard in the confusion. If Rhaz was anywhere about, Frederick knew he would respond. The whistle was unique between them, used in the heat of Iberian battles and panic situations only. Frederick had whistled almost unconsciously, but the effort was not *entirely* derived from instinct, for he'd half anticipated the duke to turn up at some stage, his grace more than likely being prepared to greet his guests as they entered the estate. Consequently, in the split second Frederick had had to think, he had taken the chance that Rhaz would be within hearing distance at least. One last peacetime chance to pair up together against an unseen enemy.

With a slight twitch to his lips, the fifth Duke of Doncaster surveyed the scene of the crime. As usual, Captain Argyll had acquitted himself well, but *that* was to be expected. Rhaz almost had it in him to be sorry for the poor, unconscious second highwayman. Being coshed over the head by the likes of Frederick must be no small matter. But then, neither was a hanging. His eyes turned grim as he caught sight of Cordelia, mildly deflecting Winthrop's loquacious outpouring of rage. The way he was talking, he had single-handedly saved both chaises and the damsels within.

He was just working himself up to the climax of his piece when the duke's eyes met those of his soul mate. The anguish in them was unmistakable. So, too, was the silent plea. A moment later he was noticing the brown stain that was discolouring her gown quite fearfully. He barked an order at the second outrider and sent him scurrying for help and further coaches from the extensive Huntingdon stables. Then, *entirely* ignoring Winthrop, he nodded at Frederick and heaved the heavy gilt door open.

Lord Winthrop fussed within and was the first to step out, proclaiming loudly that no one had seen fit to attend to the horses. Casting a disdainful stare at the miscreant, who still lay in a heap at the captain's feet, he strode off to examine both teams' fetlocks. He declared the bays as "right as a trivet" but equivocated a little on the condition of the chestnuts. He might have spared his breath, for no one, least of all his grace, was listening.

Rhaz addressed Ancilla, though his eyes never left Cordelia's face, and his arms were stretching out for her long before Mrs. Camfrey understood the full import of his words.

"Miss Cordelia is hurt. I shall have to take her down from the chaise, though I fear movement may be painful. I shall try to be gentle."

Ancilla nodded, but Seraphina, her attention drawn to the stained carriage dress and the sleeve that even now was reddening, exclaimed in horror. "Delia! Are you all right, my love?"

Cordelia nodded, though by now she was feeling far weaker than a few moments before. The duke's hand was brushing soothingly against her own and in minutes—probably more likely seconds—his hand was placed firmly around her. She had little recollection of being lifted out of the excellent equipage, but for a vague sense of quickening pulses and overall well-being. If her arm ached, it seemed of little or no account, for Rhaz held her. Indeed, his grace cosseted her as if she were the most precious little package on earth. The bewildering sensations, all following one after another, finally took their toll. Though her head swam, she was aware of two salient facts beyond the sweet, deeply masculine scent of his most noble grace. The criminal was apprehended and she was safe. Upon these confused thoughts, she closed her eyes and fell into a heady, highly uncharacteristic and remarkably intoxicating swoon.

FIFTEEN

There was a moment's silence as all eyes turned to
Cordelia. Lord Winthrop returned from his inspection
of the horses, cast his eye upon the duo but refrained
from comment, other than to mention, rather sardoni-
cally, that it was a shame that the first highwayman had
made good his escape.

No one paid him any special heed, which quite
overset him. Accordingly, he announced to a strangely
silent group that, since they all had addled brains, it
must be left to him to truss up the prisoner and sternly
question him when he came round.

Relieved to give the baron some activity beyond
merely upsetting his betrothed, Frederick handed him
some rope from the corded picnic basket and allowed
him to occupy himself in this prudent, slightly priggish
manner. Rhaz was still holding Cordelia, the expression
in his eyes softer than anything Frederick had ever witnessed before. He seemed happy to just stand mutely
with his burden, gazing upon the soft, delicate lashes
that were now firmly closed against the peachy, sun-
streaked sunset.

For an instant, Frederick's heart leaped in sudden
hope. Surely it could not be *Seraphina* with whom the
duke's interest lay? And yet, everything seemed so certain. Even now, the duke was quietly lifting his eyes from

the still dazed Cordelia and asking, with considerable concern in his voice, whether Miss Seraphina and Mrs. Camfrey were not too shaken from their ordeal. His eyes rested, for a moment, on Seraphina, and Frederick felt close to throttling him. Instead, he unclenched his fists and stilled his heart.

No doubt there would be time enough to catechise Rhaz on his intentions. In the meanwhile, the debacle of this carriage trip had to be attended to before an oncoming stage or curricle was overturned. He promised to attend to this and his grace threw him a grateful glance. Ancilla noticed the gesture between these two apparent strangers and something flickered at the back of her mind. She said nothing, however, for Seraphina, was treading gingerly out of the coach and staring with bright-eyed interest at the prisoner.

It was left to the captain, then, to point out the urgent need for Cordelia to return to the house. "If she has lost blood, your grace"—he stressed these words to remind Rhaz of his lowly role as music master—"she must be instantly attended to. I suggest you take her back to your house whilst a doctor is called for."

Rhaz agreed, but he was very conscious, for the first time, of observing the proprieties. He had no wish for it to be whispered that he had compromised Cordelia. Accordingly, he begged Ancilla to join him on the trip back up to his home. Ancilla would willingly have agreed, but for two facts. Whilst Cordelia could conceivably ride up on Rhaz's mount, there was no suitable horseflesh about for Mrs. Camfrey to commandeer. Then there was the necessity for sidesaddles and the fact that Seraphina would need chaperoning if she were left with two gentlemen. All things considered, it would probably be better if his grace took Cordelia, for he could hardly be expected to seduce her whilst she was in such a dismal state. Not even the harshest critic could raise a quizzical brow at the arrangement. Of course, Mrs. Camfrey took rather too optimistic a view of gossiping, tongue-wagging society, but she remained in happy oblivion to this.

"Your grace, I am in the greatest agitation over Cordelia! I have not brought up my girls to swoon becomingly. If she is in a dead faint, I fear it must be just that. Take her immediately, if you would be so kind. His lordship, Seraphina and I—oh and Captain Argyll of course"—she nodded to him encouragingly—"shall follow you just as soon as we are able. You will send word to a wheelwright?"

Rhaz nodded, hardly trusting himself to speak. Nothing mattered beyond the fact that his darling was ill, suffering the rigorous effect of a stray bullet. Without another word, he carefully eased her into the saddle and mounted himself.

Instantly, her breathing became less ragged and she regained all of her faculties. They were all crying out, of course, but not from pain. Cordelia decided not to examine those faculties too closely, for if she did, the spectre of both Winthrop and her dear Seraphina might loom to haunt her.

The steadying trot of hooves across brambles and grass allowed her to rest. Presently, she was able to shut her mind to the delicious sensation of his grace's abdomen rubbing up close next to her. She was even able, at times, not to notice his strong arms tucked up against her and the reins, nor the way he smelled and the tantalising way he gently spoke to her through her pain. It seemed like a blissful age before the hunting box was finally reached. Rhaz drew her down very gently by the waist and snapped his fingers so that, by a ripple effect, a dozen house servants or more came rushing outside to do his bidding.

Still holding Cordelia close against him—she felt as

light as down in his arms—he begged the doctor to be called and two fresh carriages sent down from the stables. As an afterthought, he called for a smith and a wheelwright, but truly his preoccupations were elsewhere.

Cordelia protested feebly that she could be set down, for whilst her arm was undoubtedly aching, it appeared to have stopped bleeding. Rhaz raised his brows and ignored her, loath to set down his precious cargo no matter what the reasoned logic. Instead, he held her ever more fiercely against him until the flush upon Cordelia's cheeks could not be attributed to the heat or excitement, but rather to his intoxicating intensity. When she finally was settled down, it was not, as she thought, to await the arrival of the good doctor although that man had, indeed, been summoned.

She was startled and bemused when his grace the duke condescended to kneel beside her, wiping her brow and murmuring gentle nothings as his practiced eye took stock of the situation through her modest, though decidedly becoming, gown.

His hand was upon her shoulder, gently, ever so gently, testing the thin film of material that so elegantly encased her arm. It was loose in places, but near the wound it was damp and matted, so Cordelia winced a little at his cursory examination. His tone was very gentle as he rang the bellpull and checked that Cordelia rested comfortably against the brocade sofa.

When his manservant arrived, Miss Camfrey cast a startled glance at the perfection of his livery and the silvery powder with which his wig was brushed. Even in her pain and tumultuous emotions, she could see that the butler was dressed to the first stare. Still slightly dazed, she allowed her thoughts to wonder to Rhaz's indisputable rank and fortune. He was second only to a prince and here he was, ministering to her needs as humbly as one of his own servants. She shook her head at the wonder of it, then scolded herself for a widgeon. His grace was obviously a gentleman of the first stare. He would accord such civility to anyone in need. Such was the magnitude of both his good nature and his breeding.

The thought had a twofold effect on Cordelia. Her exultant, tremulous response to Rhaz abated somewhat. He was merely a man—albeit a startlingly attractive man—doing his duty. No more should be read in the light of his eyes than the civil, concerned care of a host to his guest. The second effect is harder to describe. Perversely, because Rhaz was impartial, because she knew he would treat *any* fellow human being in such a predicament in such a way, she could not help her deep admiration strengthening. What it strengthened *to*, however, only her heart knew, but the sentiment was intense, deeply painful and astonishingly clear.

Miss Cordelia Camfrey—formerly sensible, heart whole and *utterly* responsible—had fallen in love.

"How long shall we have to wait here, do you think?" Lord Winthrop was growing pettish as he eyed the groaning, semiconscious prisoner from out of the corner of his eye.

"I do not believe too long, for his grace has attended to some alternative transport for us. We shall just have to be content to wait."

"Content to wait? Can we not do something more positive? The beasts are getting restive and I could *swear* one of them is coming down with a chill!"

The words were politely murmured at, but since no one seemed about to do anything more dramatic than search among the squabs for suitable blankets upon which to seat themselves, my lord's grumblings might as well have fallen upon deaf ears. Accordingly, with a persistent eye to the prisoner, Lord Winthrop was finally prevailed upon to partake of what was left of the picnic hamper.

It was fortunate that Rhàz's staff was so thorough, for despite the fact that his lordship had made quite substantial inroads into the basket, there were still some cold wild pheasant, stuffed game, chestnuts, cranberry apples, miniature perigord pies and an abundance of delicate jam tartlets to keep the party more than satisfied with the fare.

With Lord Winthrop's surprisingly knowledgeable help, Frederick had managed to clear the paths so that any further disaster might be averted. The ditched carriages might look rather sorrowful in their present state of decline, but fortunately they could do no further damage either to each other or any oncoming equipage.

Though both Ancilla and Seraphina were obviously shaken, their natures were robust enough to put the unpleasant incident behind them. Beyond a quite natural concern for Cordelia, Frederick was gratified to see that they did not put on missish airs or appear more squeamish than they were. Seraphina, indeed, was setting her mind to enjoying the wonders of the new countryside and her music master was more than happy to oblige her with pleasant, idle talk of Hawthorn, fly-fishing and some of the many wooded ambles that might be enjoyed between here and Clarence, the next town.

"You seem to know Huntingdon quite well, Captain Argyll!"

Ancilla broke in on his thoughts, and if he were not as in excellent control of his features as he habitually was, Frederick might have coloured. A slip! He must take care not to let it happen again. The Camfreys were not to know of the many happy times he had spent with the duke on the Huntingdon estate. He smiled and replied that, though he could not know this area particularly well, he had spent many a happy hour in a neighbourhood quite similar to this. He could not be pressed into further reminiscences, but instead took the opportunity of rummaging through the baggage coach and emerging with an old black violin case. Seraphina noticed that the clasps were of dull gold, but she did not take in anything more, for Frederick had reverentially opened the heavy box and removed both the instrument and the bow. His eyes caught hers and she smiled. When Frederick looked just so, even the direst of calamities seemed insignificant. Her pretty lips instantly responded and she sensed, rather than saw, the captain's sensuous reaction. His fingers seemed to tighten for an instant over the strings. When she glanced at him again, the moment had passed.

Ancilla set down the remains of her repast and smiled encouragingly. "What an excellent thought, Captain! If you play for us this impromptu picnic shall have all the makings of a large-scale banquet!"

Lord Winthrop cleared his throat unhappily. Somehow, he felt slightly put upon. That an excellent excursion to one of the most famous stables in all England should boil down to this! A detested concert! He begged Frederick to choose a short piece, for as he said, music gave him indigestion at mealtimes.

Seraphina put her hands to her lips to avert an unladylike snort. Even Ancilla, his staunch ally, gave a suspicious-sounding snort and begged him to come of his high ropes and learn a thing or two for a change. Outvoted, his lordship could do nothing more than appropriate a large portion of the picnic blanket and maintain a dignified silence.

Frederick carefully rubbed rosin into the fine, sandy strings of pure horsehair used for the bow. When he

was done, he took a moment to tune the violin, calling
Seraphina to sit close by him so that he might teach
her the technique. Ancilla noticed how her daughter's
cheeks glowed with animation and how eager she was
to test the weight of the violin in her hands. "I do believe they smell of April and May!" The startled thought
at once gave substance to all the other little suspicions
she had been formulating for quite some time.

Impossible, of course! Captain Argyll was a mere im-
poverished employee . . . Even she, who had no notion
of economy, could see that the matter was quite ineligible. And yet, Seraphina was positively glowing, her
bright eyes brighter than usual, as if sprinkled with starlight. How very sad if this blooming fruition of woman-
hood should be dulled before its moment of perfection.
Ancilla bit her lip. Had she been bullied by the dowager
duchess? Of *course* she had. But had the dowager duchess been speaking the truth abut her son's intentions?
She took leave, for the first time, to wonder.

If only life were simpler! Of *course* she would like her
daughter to be a duchess. She would be quite dreadfully
remiss and improvident if she did not. And yet, were
there not other, more important things? Her eyes grew
faintly misty. How unlike her to grow wistful! And Cordelia? For the first time she questioned the wisdom of
pairing her off with the baron. It had seemed like so
excellent a match at the time, but now, judging him up
close, she was not so certain. Could Cordelia find happiness with such a pompous, opinionated, horse-crazed
personage? She hoped so, but honesty compelled her
to doubt. Even a morning and half an afternoon spent
in a closed chaise with him was enough. Still, whilst not
handsome he was not intolerable to look at . . . or not
entirely intolerable. . . . He was certainly rich and that
must count for something . . . or must it? Ancilla's well-
ordered world was being turned topsy-turvy by these

unconventional thoughts. *It must be the weather,* she decided. *Or perhaps the afternoon's enterprise.*

She would have been unsettled to know *quite* how distinctly her younger daughter's thoughts mirrored her own. Frederick gently removed the violin from Seraphina's arrested grasp and began to play. He started with Boyce, then moved on to a fascinating medley of the themes of Beethoven, Salieri and the more modern Haydn. Seraphina understood them all, but none seemed as poignant to her as the unknown themes that the captain tentatively began to play when Ancilla's concentration was waning and Lord Winthrop's snores could all but be detected.

The notes were at once so haunting and so sweet that tears stung the back of Seraphina's eyes. Frederick was playing for her, heart and soul, and as he improvised, the music acted as a secret bond between them, a means of communicating all the yearning, unrequited utterances and longing of the soul that was possible in the circumstance of a penniless suitor and a bride destined for another.

When he finally stopped, it seemed time had stood still, though darkness was now falling in earnest and the horses were stamping their feet restively upon the ground. Winthrop, long startled awake by the urgent neighing of a chestnut, was beginning to bluster about the time help was taking. He was not to know that, even as he complained, two pristine chaises were making their stately way towards him. Even before they arrived, however, the familiar sound of a cantering Arabian stopped him dead in his tracks.

"Good Lord! *Someone* is an excellent horseman! Cantering at breakneck speed and never a stumble over these elderberries and hawthorn bushes! Can it be the duke returned?"

His question was not long without an answer, for al-

most before the words were out the rider was upon
them. Winthrop's jaw fell quite ludicrously when the
most salient and astonishing aspect of this spectacle was
revealed to him. The Arabian, as magnificent a beast
as he had anticipated, was saddled not, as he would
have suspected, for a man of the duke's stature. Instead,
he was furnished firmly but becomingly with a sidesaddle. As he gaped his amazement, a woman slid down
from her perch and glared at him.

SIXTEEN

"Begging your pardon, sirs, have neither of you thought to rub down the teams? I warrant they need the attention after the shock they have just had! And have any of you thought to have a bottle of lint and codseed oil handy? No? I thought not." She lifted her nose rather disdainfully in the air and turned her plump, rather well-rounded form to the tethered chestnuts and bays.

Frederick was caught between amusement and indignation at her high-handed, contemptuous stance. Ancilla was merely bemused, wondering, sotto voice, *who* they had the honour of addressing. Seraphina was ready to fall about into spasms of laughter—the afternoon's passions and excitements were taking their toll on her—and Lord Winthrop merely stared. A more *magnificent* woman he had never set eyes upon.

The lady was still scolding when he sheepishly cast a glance at Miss Camfrey and her mother, shrugged his shoulders significantly and trailed off after her. She was inspecting the livestock in much the same manner as *he* had done and pronounced the bays to be remarkably well, given the circumstances, but the second chestnut to be ailing. She *tut-tutted* over his fetlocks and drew from her capacious pocket the indispensable lint and codseed oil she had inquired about previously.

Treating Lord Winthrop in much the same manner
that she would a street urchin, she demanded that he
furnish her with a handkerchief and stand back so she
might attend to the stallion in her own particular manner. Lord Winthrop drew from his pocket a very fine
cambric handkerchief, entwined majestically with his initials threading through each other in gilded thread.
Above the initials, the heraldic crest of the baronetcy
was clearly visible. The lady did not blink. She merely
stretched out her hand and applied the murky substance to the cloth. Then, speaking in the gentlest, most
sublime tones Winthrop thought he had ever heard,
she cajoled the horse to stand still. Lovingly, she applied
the ointment, then bandaged the fetlock with the
damp, greasy cloth.

"When he is safely stabled I shall apply a warm posset.
How long, do you think, has he been left standing?"

"An hour?" Lord Winthrop made to consult his fob,
then realised that he could not. The wretched highwayman had made off with all his seals. Speaking of
which . . . He looked towards the spot where the ac-
complice was now bound and well and truly trussed up.
He was beginning to moan and Winthrop wondered
whether this angelic vision would feel intimidated. If
she did, he was quite prepared to catch her in his
strong, manly arms. . . .

"Are you certain he cannot escape his bonds?"

"Have no fear, madame! I attended to the matter myself. You are safe and I shall see to it that you come to
no harm!"

"Indeed?" She was noncommittal as she ventured
near to the prisoner.

"I always favour a half hitch to a reef myself. Mind
you, you appear to have done a good job." A glimmer
of a smile crossed her features as she nodded at Winthrop in approval.

His lordship felt as if he was back at Harrow under her close scrutiny and condescending praise. It was a long time since he had found himself at a loss for words. Fortunately, however, Captain Argyll stepped into the breach and delicately inquired whether the lady would like to take a seat beside them upon the overlarge carriage blanket. She blinked and pinkened slightly, for despite her gruff ways—especially when it came to matters of horseflesh—she was as prone as any young lady to fascinating gentlemen with excellent manners.

Lord Winthrop hastily pushed himself forward, begging the lady to take up his own vacated space. The lady positively preened at the novel situation of having two young men pay attention to her. She was in a quandary over which polite offer to take up when Lord Winthrop suddenly begged her for the recipe for the lint and codseed oil, for as he said, he'd heard it worked wonders with sprains, though its efficacy with relation to a loose shoe was still, to his mind, in question.

The lady gazed at him with sudden respect. "Sir," she said, "I have long been of the opinion that a loose shoe can always be averted with a little care. In the rare instances of a horse stumbling and loosening the shoe himself, I find that a decoction of apple blossom and thyme has very efficacious effects. *Not,* of course, sufficient to *cure* the condition, but certainly enough to sooth the animal before a smith can be found."

Winthrop nodded seriously. "Very true, very true. What exact proportions do you use? My estate yields a quite nice little crop of apple blossom, but I've never thought to use it in such a way."

The animation on the stranger's face was quite palpable. There was now no question of where or with whom she would sit. She was so lost in the exchange of various equine potions and recipes that the other three members of the ditched party were quite forgotten, or at least assigned to the periphery of her attention.

Lord Winthrop appeared to be held in a similar thrall. Seeing this, Ancilla felt a stab of discomfort. If his attentions were so fickle, his interest so all absorbing and alien to Cordelia, what possible happiness could arise from a betrothal of that nature? If only she had heeded Cordelia's urging to economise! If she had, Cordelia might not have so readily accepted this . . . this . . . Oh! She had no ladylike description word for the addlepated, bottle-brained gentleman.

Lord Winthrop was happily oblivious to all these musings, his attentions wholly wrapped up in the loquacious opinions of the strange personage that had descended upon them. *He* didn't think her dull brown hair sadly lustreless—he thought the shade resembled *exactly* one of his prize mares.

The captain glanced at Seraphina and winked. Suppressing a slight giggle, she basked in the glory of their mutual amused comprehension. Both still wondered who the unknown virago was, but since they were perfectly certain the mystery would shortly unfold, they were content to enjoy each other's silent company. If truth be told, Frederick was *not* content—he rather wished the duo and even his dear Ancilla, of whom he was fast growing fond, to the devil. Seraphina's soft lips were far too inviting to require an audience. Still, as the spectre of Rhaz's proposal still loomed over them, he could only still his quickened senses and try to assign his sudden desires to the devil.

Fortunately, it was not long that this silent tension was allowed to interplay between them. Seraphina, too, had felt a breathlessness that threatened to envelop her entirely. Before the interesting situation was allowed to develop, however, the new conveyances were heard to be rattling on the horizon, and it was not long before the rattling of wheels and the whinnying of horses were upon them. The duke had wisely sent along three under grooms and his head groom himself to take care of the remaining animals, unharness them from the useless carriages and await the arrival of the local magistrate to take the felon into custody. Lord Winthrop was eager to announce that he was a magistrate and therefore particularly qualified to take these duties on board, but Frederick mildly reminded him Huntingdon was beyond his jurisdiction.

Lord Winthrop took issue with this, declaring himself perfectly capable of assuming his duties anywhere, and he was just beginning to glare balefully at the presumptuous music master, who appeared to have ideas far above his station, when Mr. Cording, the local magistrate, made his appearance. Beyond an overheard glare at Frederick, Lord Winthrop conceded defeat and handed the prisoner over with exemplary speed, only annoying Mr. Cording a smidgen by offering several voluminous and unwanted words of sage advice.

The new beasts were fresh and eager for exercise. Consequently, when the party *did* arrange themselves on the mint squabs, it was not long at all before the chimneys of Huntingdon could be spied unfurling welcoming smoke. A few minutes beyond that and Miss Camfrey, her mama, Captain Argyll, Lord Winthrop and the fussy little woman with the oversharp tongue were alighting to the welcome of several footmen, the housekeeper and sundry maids awaiting instruction.

This was given by the stranger so confidently and efficiently that none had qualms that the baggage would be forgotten or the rooms unaired or the dinner too meagre for their needs. The arrival of the chaise had been accompanied by the clanging of a yard of tin, so the lord of the manor, his grace the noble duke, was down the front steps in a twinkling to welcome the guests and set their minds at rest about Cordelia's health.

"She has lost blood, but the bullet was not lodged, so it is a flesh wound merely. A few day's rest and Miss Camfrey should, I hope, be fully recovered. I have taken the liberty of sending a missive to Dr. Siddons of Marlborough Street. He does not usually make country calls, but he owes me a favour and I fancy I shall be able to persuade him."

Ancilla looked at him anxiously. "You are certain she should not be seen by a village doctor?"

The duke smiled. "Absolutely, ma'am! I am convinced Miss Cordelia, though badly shocked, will convalesce excellently. The Huntingdon doctor, though very pleasant, is, I fear, rather prone to quackery and leeching. I believe we ought to spare Miss Cordelia from his ministrations if we possibly can."

Seraphina lifted her hands to her face in horror. "Indeed, *yes*, your grace! I cannot *bear* to think of Cordelia being blooded. It is beyond the question!"

He threw her a friendly glance that was not missed by the oversensitive Frederick. In that moment, his jealously loomed so large that he was very inclined to throttle his dearest and most noble friend. Rhaz, catching the caustic glance sent his way, was surprised and somewhat confused. In a private moment he meant to tease Frederick about his comical charade. Now, he was not so certain he *wanted* a private moment with his excellent friend.

He wondered, for a moment, whether Frederick had tumbled to the fact that he had written to Mr. Beckett, offering to stand patron for the composer. If Lord Argyll had, he might well have a *reason* to be furious, for such an act would have gone badly with his insufferable pride.

Still, Mr. Beckett's polite rejection of the offer on the

grounds that Frederick was a rapidly rising star in his own right had meant that Rhaz had not had a hand in his startling success among the ton. Every ball his grace now attended appeared to have Frederick's soulful, fashionable themes strummed out or fluted with touching eloquence.

"Your grace, I hope you are not such a gudgeon as to leave your guests standing outside in the chill night? They have had a fair dose of the outdoors, I assure you. Invite them in and have done! I hope the wax candles have been lit as I ordered?"

His duke cast Frederick a look of mock dismay. Instantly, the stiff distance that had risen up between them vanished. *This,* Frederick inferred, must be the famed Miss Moresby. He had heard his softhearted friend grumble too much about her chatelainage of Huntingdon to guess anything else. She was lucky. If he were the duke and she his cousin, he would have booted her out a long time since. But that was Rhaz. Too softhearted under his firm exterior for his own peace of mind.

His grace shrugged almost imperceptibly, as if reading Frederick's dire thoughts. Suppressing a wink, he solemnly ushered the party in and asked whether they had all been introduced. In the sparkling candlelight, Miss Moresby appeared to more advantage than usual, her brown hair acquiring some of the light's lustre and her unfortunate plumpness appearing less obvious in the dimmer lit space.

"Indeed, no! I am most anxious for an introduction. Most anxious!" Lord Winthrop had removed his beaver and was staring at Miss Moresby as if one transfixed. His words, however, held a pompous condescension that made both Ancilla and Seraphina exchange secret glances of mirth.

Rhaz saw immediately how the wind blew with Winthrop. Perversely, he was torn between delight at the cunningness of his plan and ire that Lord Henry could be so faithless to the fair Cordelia. Delight won out. After all, the baron's meeting with Miss Moresby had been the whole ridiculous purpose of this suddenly enlarged excursion.

His manner was smooth and graceful as he took his cousin's hand and presented her to the group, whose interest in her varied from mild curiosity to burning regard.

Miss Helena Moresby, belatedly remembering the manners she had sadly forgotten on first formulating her acquaintance with the group, dropped a slightly off-centre curtsy and announced that she was delighted.

If *she* wasn't, Lord Winthrop very clearly *was*, and as Rhaz slipped away with Mrs. Camfrey to check on the condition of their patient, he buzzed about Helena as if he were a man awakened from a very long slumber. It would not be long, the duke thought, before he would be wishful of crying off from his betrothal. Quite how this was to be achieved was a matter still puzzling the duke, for it would be unthinkable in Winthrop to do such an ungentlemanly thing. Still, something would have to occur. . . .

"Miss Camfrey, I have brought your mother! Show her, my dear, that she need have no qualms on your behalf." The duke's tone was light, but his *own* heart held fears.

Cordelia was looking wan, despite her cheerful aspect and obvious determination not to be a burden upon the household. "See, Mama! I am as right as a trivet!"

"I am pleased, Cordelia! Such a nonsensical thing to happen! And on his grace's estate, too."

"For that I must apologise, ma'am. The miscreants

shall be well punished. A hanging is most likely, though we are still trying to locate the first varmint."

"No!" Cordelia sat up and winced a little in pain.

"Beg pardon?"

"Not a hanging, I beg you! The poor devils have probably not had anything to eat for a sennight. Cannot you leave them be?"

"To set a lawless example to their peers? I think not, Miss Cordelia." Rhaz's voice was suddenly hard. The anguish of seeing his loved one soaked in blood was not something likely to induce compassion in his breast, though the fact that Cordelia, the aggrieved party, should feel this way further increased the intensity of his feelings for her.

"But—"

"Hush! We shall speak of this later."

Cordelia nodded and rested back on the pillows. She was still feeling a trifle light-headed though she would have scorned to admit it.

"Is Seraphina below stairs?"

"She is, with Captain Argyll, Lord Henry and the most peculiar—" Ancilla remembered herself and coloured. "Beg pardon, your grace! I had forgotten Miss Moresby was your cousin."

"Think nothing of it, Mrs. Camfrey! Miss Moresby is extremely capable and I am certainly fond of her in my own way, possibly in smaller rather than larger doses. But I have to agree, she *is* peculiar!"

"How intriguing! I shall have to come down and see for myself!"

"Certainly not!" The duke and Ancilla spoke in unison.

"You shall stay up here, Cordelia, and rest. I'll not have Lord Henry prosing over you downstairs until you are utterly knackered."

"Mama!" Cordelia was *shocked* at the unmannerly expression.

"Now don't be coy, Delia dear! Cant expressions are very useful in dire emergencies. Besides, I am perfectly certain his grace will overlook the irregularity."

"Indeed I will, Mrs. Camfrey! And may I add my own plea to yours? Stay upstairs where you are comfortable, Miss Cordelia. A flesh wound can sometimes become quite surprisingly nasty if care is not taken." He flashed her such a blazing look of sincerity and—was it passion?—that Cordelia's heart beat faster but she could not be certain. Still, something either in his tone or his stare made her desist from further objection. Besides, she felt delightfully cosseted and not having to make small talk with her betrothed came as an unexpected relief.

"Very well then. I shall allow myself to be petted to death!"

The ironic twinkle was back and Rhaz was so relieved that he grinned for some heart-stopping seconds in her direction. Neither noticed the thoughtful Mrs. Camfrey leave the room, though for once she was not too scatty to take care of proprieties. The door, when Rhaz finally noticed, was three inches ajar.

"Do you play chess?"

"Chess? I adore it!" Cordelia smiled at the duke and thought that if they played he would surely win, for his very person was the most immeasurable distraction to her.

"I have recently acquired a new set. Will you give me the felicity of playing with me? Everyone I have applied to thus far has turned me down." For an instant, Rhaz's thoughts flew to Frederick, who had declined the offer of a game the night before both their lives had became so thoroughly entangled with the Camfrey sisters.

"Certainly, though I shall be a bit clumsy with my arm in a sling!"

"You are too graceful to be clumsy, Miss Camfrey! I suspect you shall be a challenging adversary."

"Why, your grace?"

"Because you have keen intelligence and ready wit. Do you wish to toss for white or shall you claim a woman's prerogative?"

"We shall toss, your grace." Cordelia's voice was firm.

It must be reported that the next few days were probably the happiest of Cordelia's life. Dr. Siddons arrived during the late afternoon of the following day. He *tuttutted* over the wound, nodded approvingly at his grace's makeshift treatment of the injury and at the firm sling and declared himself satisfied. Cordelia won several of the games the duke harangued her to play, but her concentration was sadly impaired by the duke himself. This, however, was not an unfair disadvantage, for his grace's wits were similarly addled by the laughing, silver-eyed woman of his dreams.

Aramiss and Drixon duly arrived from Winthrop's estate in Hertfordshire and were most satisfactorily coupled with the duke's finest stallions. As a consequence, Lord Henry was in his most effusive, amiable element, the intricacies of the procedure argued about at length with the charming Miss Moresby, who had no patience for a woman's reticence about such earthy matters.

Despite his grace's insistence that she use his first name, Cordelia resisted, ever conscious that his heart belonged to Seraphina, not to her. At times she puzzled over the matter, for certainly, he did not seem unduly inclined to spend time with her delightful little sister. Had the duchess possibly mistaken the matter? But, no, Ancilla had declared she was emphatic on this point.

His mother surely must know best what was in his heart? She was probably in his confidence. Cordelia sighed and determined to enjoy every innocent moment she shared with the man.

This she did, enjoying strolls through the topiary gardens when she was a little stronger, ever conscious of the duke's magnetism. It seemed they shared the same tastes in practically everything, for when his grace showed her his extensive library, she became so animated that he had to smile rather delightedly and show her all of his especial treasures. She was so knowledgeable about editions and folios that the duke was hard-pressed to satisfy her voracious appetite for what he had to show and discuss with her. Only one thing marred the precious time.

Th duke asked her, rather abruptly, what she was doing betrothed to a fool like Winthrop. She was so shocked at the suddenness of the question that she'd found herself defending Lord Henry when all she wished to do was concur wholeheartedly with the duke. When Rhaz pressed her, oversetting her reasoned arguments that Winthrop was both amiable and kind, tears threatened to well up in her eyes. Rhaz was so gentle that she was forced to say she had no need of his sympathy, for Winthrop was both rich and titled. This gave the duke pause. Though he scrutinised her closely, she did not seem to him to be the type to marry for reasons so base as this. Cordelia looked miserable, so he turned the subject to lighter matters, but there was no doubting a small distance had developed between them for those few moments. He longed to take her in his arms and order her to tell Winthrop to go to the devil, but he restrained himself. Cordelia, he hoped, would prove her mettle and come to this point herself.

Presently, it was time for the visit to end. Cordelia's return to health was now complete, so there could be little to delay the inevitable. His grace promised that they would soon be reunited and all the guests naturally assumed he referred to the onset of Christmas. He did not, for his cunning mama had given him no hint of what she intended. When he waved the party good-bye then, it was with the simple hope that matters would come to a head as if by some miracle. He earnestly hoped that Winthrop would soon relinquish his rights to Cordelia, for if he did not, his grace knew he would go slowly insane.

He walked slowly back to the house and ordered preparations to be set in tow for his departure. It was his duty, of course, to return to his principal seat for Christmas. The dowager duchess depended on it and, though she was a devious old soul, he loved her. Home, then, but after that . . . After that, he would have a certain very definite conversation with Miss Cordelia Camfrey of the silver eyes.

SEVENTEEN

The duchess was in her element, ordering all the dust covers removed from the most unused wings of his grace's large, almost palatial residence. Since such an undertaking was beyond the powers of even his own extensive staff, she'd blithely consulted the register of superior housemaids and spent a lively morning interviewing several dozen at the very least. Those fortunate enough to have passed her beady-eyed scrutiny were now set busily to work, dusting, polishing and sweeping just as if his grace's residence were not *always* immaculate in appearance and irreproachable in aspect.

Several times the cook held up his hands in horror and vowed to send in his notice, for the dowager duchess seemed to forever confuse the menus, change them at will and scratch illegible notes all over the carefully inscribed name plates. This was only marginally better than her inspection of the pickled partridges and her wholly unsolicited advice on the best way to dress a plover. Her grace seemed to look with disfavour on the common method of employing bacon to preserve and insisted that all the poultry be laid about in charcoal. This fine state of affairs did little to appease the already stressed cook and kitchen hands. Even the scullery maids fell under the duchess's watchful scrutiny until the jangling of nerves was matched only by the clattering of pots and kettles and pans as nervous fingers dropped where ordinarily they would not.

Finally, it was up to the much tried housekeeper to respectfully implore the duchess to remain within her own domain and not to venture again into the kitchens. After extracting a promise that the footmen be decked in new liveries to complement the green wooded shades she had chosen for all the drawing rooms and reception areas, her grace was finally dislodged from below stairs.

She had a merry time redraping all of the upstairs rooms with fine muslin silks in holly green and cherry red. When that was done, she purloined several of Rhaz's best hothouse flowers in order to make scented potpourri. The head gardener was nearly stuttering in agitation as her attention moved from his blooms to his carefully tended citrus trees.

From his hothouses, she snipped off nigh on a hundred limes, oranges and lemons, the better to produce spicy pomanders laced with jasmine and whole cloves.

Actually, the household breathed a little easier with this particular activity, for there was no denying the aroma it produced was pleasant to the senses and pervaded the house with the fresh, delicate scent of Christmas to come. Not a small consideration, either, was that the tedious activity of punching the cloves through the fruit kept the duchess more than occupied for some several days.

The ducal residence resounded with the chopping of wood, the sweeping of chimneys, the polishing of door knockers and the painting of stuccoed terraces inside and out. Throughout the commotion, Rhaz, Lord Doncaster, cast a wary eye to the residence, pleased with the outcome but anticipating a revolt from within.

Every year his staff threatened to leave and every year they stayed on, mindful of the goodwill that pervaded his estates and the loyalty that they owed him. Once the duchess had been relegated to the decoration of receiving rooms and other public areas, equilibrium was restored and the imminent revolt turned to the usual anticipation of the festivities that lay ahead.

Already, church bells were beginning to peal as novice bellringers practiced the all-important commission assigned to them. The first flakes of winter were falling and, with them, the pinecones that were so integral to the season. Many a housemaid could be seen escaping the drudgery of polishing for the novelty of collecting them up in great baskets, the better to decorate fireplaces and add a woody scent to all the ready fires that were to burn in their grates.

Somewhere in the middle of all this, the Christmas party arrived. The duchess nodded in blithe satisfaction, for it appeared her schemes were working. The snows were falling in abundance, and as she had hoped—no, *planned*—it looked as though all the Christmas guests would be snowed in. Ample time for Rhaz to make Seraphina's acquaintance!

And what a *charming* sister she had, she thought, looking from one young woman to the other as they alighted from the chaise. Strange that she had not taken much account of Cordelia on her visit to Ancilla. Ah well, handsome was as handsome did. Miss Seraphina was undoubtedly a beauty, and if Rhaz's roving interests could at last be forced to settle, the younger Miss Camfrey would do very nicely indeed.

It was all his grace could do not to rush to Cordelia's side, take her in his arms and kiss away her cares. As it was, he noted her troubled brow with vexation and wished with all his heart that matters could come to a head. To this end, he had earlier delighted Miss Helena Moresby with more finery than she had ever before beheld. Consequently, her plump little figure, though never likely to cut a dash, looked a comely sight to the good Lord Winthrop.

Over the next few hours, if Rhaz had not been so nearly involved himself, he would have laughed aloud to see the stolid Lord Winthrop alight upon her like a bee to honey and murmur terms of endearment that were more than liberally laced with words like "saddles" and "bridles" and "piebalds" and "bays." Lord Henry alone was permitted to enter into a discourse on the relative merits of splints and liniment bindings on fore-legs and hocks. To him, Helena excitedly divulged the ingredients of her particular potion for curing restive-ness in flighty greys. This Lord Henry noted down with interest and in turn offered grave advice on the correct consumption of hay and other dried grasses.

Frequently, Cordelia cast a speculative glance on the pair and rather wished that they could arrive at some kind of understanding. The betrothal was becoming more and more painful to her, for whilst she could have countenanced the match when her heart was whole, she realised in perfect faith that this was no longer so. Whatever happened and whoever the debonair Lord Rhaz finally took to wife, she knew of a certainty that her heart was his. If Seraphina made a match of it, she would reconcile herself to being his sister. She could ask no more.

But she could not share her life with another or pro-duce an heir when it was Rhaz and Rhaz alone who could unlock the secrets of her soul and the desires of her body and soul.

She spent hours pondering the conundrum until fi-nally, on Christmas morning, her patience snapped.

The day dawned bright and sunny, though snow lined the paths and glistened like so many twinkling stars. There was an air of anticipation all about as ser-vants bustled here and there, excitedly preparing for

the midday feast that was to be as sumptuous a meal
as Doncaster Place had ever known. All of the steps
were draped in holly and ivy and fir, and red berries
sprouted merrily from many of the succulent, verdant
green leaves. Rhaz proclaimed himself satisfied when
he viewed the spectacle, and just as he always did on
Christmas morning, he took the opportunity of thank-
ing his staff, who had lined up in formal rank from
lowest scullery maid to the most senior gardeners,
cooks, abigails, housekeeper, butler and personal valet.
All turned towards him with light shining in their eyes,
for in truth Rhaz was a very well-loved master and the
residence of the fifth duke could not have been hap-
pier or better run.

In a mellifluous voice he thanked them for the year's
work, for the topiary gardens and the vineries, the
cleaning, the calculating, the cooking, the boot shining,
the pressing and the incalculable little things that
served to make his household so exemplary a home.
He, then, in the true Carlisle tradition of Christmas,
drew forth a ceremonial bag of green velvet and withdrew from it shiny shillings, penny pieces and golden
sovereigns that made the younger household staff gasp
in wonder. He handed the coins and the bag to his
housekeeper, who bobbed a smiling curtsy and promised to distribute the largesse. Looking on from the
faintly green-tinged crown glass windows Cordelia
could not suppress a smile. The sight had so much
charm and Christmas spirit it was bound to delight, no
matter how heavy the heart of the beholder.

She turned to be faintly admonished by Lord Henry,
who eyed her with a disapproving stare and announced
that she might "catch her death" in nothing but one
of Ancilla's castaway day dresses of scarlet merino. Cordelia had spent a careful evening gaily decking it with

shining military style buttons and delicious holly green trim.

"Indeed, no, Lord Henry. I am perfectly comfortable I assure you." But the light dimmed from her eyes nonetheless, and the round-headed windows that looked beckoning before now looked dull and lustreless.

Rather than leaving the point, Lord Winthrop manfully pressed it, pointing out that "dear Miss Moresby" advised a posset against the cold and was herself wearing sensible kid half boots and a riding habit of thick, dark wool. By this time, Cordelia, though patient by nature, had had more than enough of Lord Winthrop's homilies. To have those of Miss Moresby added to the list seemed the outside of enough. She nodded politely, however, and murmured something singularly inane but appropriate to the occasion like "Is she really?" or "How delightful!" or some such thing. Encouraged, Lord Henry expanded further until it seemed to Cordelia that the whole of this magical Christmas morning would be spent listening to the secondhand, hackneyed and rather unoriginal sentiments of her betrothed.

It cannot be commended in her, of course, but the fact that her patience suddenly faltered was understandable under the circumstances. Just as Lord Henry was muttering that "dear Miss Moresby" might be prevailed upon to give her a pointer or two about the correct alignment of a sidesaddle when alighting a frisky beast, Cordelia found her eyes flashing and her tolerance sadly astray.

In rather ringing tones for the disciplined young lady she generally proved to be, she asked Lord Henry rather testily why he did not simply ask Miss Moresby to become his betrothed, since the whole process of re-educating her to Miss Helena's ideas would be tedious indeed.

To her astonishment he seemed rather struck by the

idea. Her sarcasm eluded him, for he was simpleminded
and filled with too inflated a sense of self-importance
to suspect she might be bamming him. Accordingly, he
cocked his head to one side and gave the matter his
due consideration much to Cordelia's mingled astonishment and relief. Eventually, however, he shook his
head rather regretfully and came to the ponderous conclusion that he could not.

"Why ever not?" Cordelia was ready to push him into
it if she had to.

"Confound it, woman! You know perfectly *well* why I
cannot. A man cannot throw his cap after two young
ladies and I have already made an offer to *you!*"

"Well, *un*offer then!"

"Withdraw my word as a gentleman? Never!"

The two glared at each other, both thoroughly irri-
tated and equally miserable. They were at a complete
impasse until Cordelia suddenly realised that, if Winthrop *wanted* to be released, then it would not be churlish of her to oblige him.

Accordingly, she heaved a profound sigh that Winthrop interpreted as regret and she as relief, and she
declared that, if honour precluded *Henry* from doing
the deed, it did not so preclude her.

"Call me a jilt, Lord Winthrop, but I hereby release
you from all your former declarations. You are free to
betroth yourself where you will, for I find, quite unaccountably, that we do not suit."

Lord Winthrop *tut-tutted* and begged her not to take
matters too much to heart. Though she could never
possibly be quite as singular a female as Miss Moresby,
she nevertheless could take comfort in the fact that she
had several excellent points and needed only the guid-
ance of some superior male to steer her course when
she tended to stray. With this pronouncement he very
genially offered to be this stabilising influence on her

character, albeit in a guise different from husband. Cordelia was just formulating a scathing reply when he good-heartedly continued, saying that he accepted his release simply because he knew the Camfrey family would always be well cared for and thus pecuniary concerns would no longer be an uppermost consideration. At this, Cordelia's mouth dropped, for truly she could not conceive what the addlepated windbag was talking about.

"I refer, of course, to your sister's imminent betrothal to Doncaster. She may consider herself honoured indeed that despite her flightiness she has managed to land such a prize."

At this, Cordelia found her tolerance stretched to the limit. Rather wryly she concluded that, in releasing Winthrop from his word, she had done them *both* an immeasurable favour, for as sure as anything she would have throttled him in a sennight had she had the misfortune of actually becoming his wife.

There was a moment's uneasy silence between them whilst each stared at the other a trifle uncomfortably. Finally, Lord Winthrop made Cordelia a deep bow, pressed a clammy hand into hers and assured her that he was a very happy man.

Cordelia dimpled and the hapless Henry must have realised his faux pas, for he mopped his brow and began retracting his former comment, explaining that he was actually miserable—quite the saddest man on earth.

Miss Camfrey murmured rather inaudibly—for she was caught between exasperation and a chuckle—that he had better not let Miss Moresby overhear him say such a thing.

He blanched. "Indeed, no, madame! That would be quite dreadful indeed." At which, he made a last quick bow in Cordelia's direction and edged himself busily down the corridor.

Cordelia turned back to the window, strangely calm
for one who had just whistled away the chance of becoming a wealthy young lady of rank and title. The bub-
ble glass glistened for a moment in the sunlight and
she had to squint slightly to look through it. The first
snows were falling white on the ground and the ready
ranks of under butlers and parlour maids were slowly
dispersing to resume household chores and last-minute
errands before the season's joy was finally upon them.
Cordelia was just turning away from the window when
her eyes were arrested by the sight of Rhaz, dark hair
unmistakable against the snow, looking up at the
rounded window as if by impulse. She could not be
sure, but she was almost certain, by the imperceptible
lifting of her spirits, that he had seen her. He raised his
hand to his mouth and allowed a kiss to float slowly
upwards in the cold sunshine. Cordelia closed her eyes
and could almost feel the intangible caress settle upon
her lips in a teasing, wonderfully poignant invitation
for more. Her hands were still guiltily touching her lips,
her face flushed as though the embrace had been real,
rather than an ethereal salute of the spirits, when
Seraphina tripped into the sunshine and headlong into
Rhaz's strong, ready arms.

Cordelia noted with mingled amusement and chagrin
that the naughty creature had decided to forgo a bonnet and that her footwear was more suited to the dance
room than to the frosty, slippery Christmas morning.
Not surprising then that she should plunge headlong
into the duke's arms, for first sleet is notoriously slippery and elegant buckled pumps—no matter how fashionable the satin—are not likely to offer much
protection against a sprained ankle or an icy fall. The
fifth duke was though. Very handsomely he scooped
her up in his arms before laughingly settling her down
again and conversing with her with a sudden earnest

frown that constricted Cordelia's heart and forced her
to turn from the window.

She was unused to missish tears, but she could not
deny the sting at the back of her eyes as she realised
she would have to resign herself to her fate more
quickly than she had imagined. If Rhaz was in love with
Seraphina, there was nothing more in the world she
could hope for than to maintain the honest friendship
of both. She adored Seraphina and would never con-
template providing the smallest obstacle to her happiness. The ready understanding that had seemed to
develop between herself and his grace must be allowed
to die a natural death. The sentiments she felt for him
were not at all sisterly and best forgotten, given that she
wished to spare both him and Seraphina all pain. If she
felt pain, then so be it—it would be private. The relief
of not imminently having to wed Lord Henry coursed
through her veins once more. That, she knew, would
have been untenable.

To give one's heart to a man was one thing. To marry
another under such circumstances was untenable to her
innocent, honest thinking. She sighed as she caught
sight of herself on the glass that reflected her figure
and merry, sprigged Christmas trim. Doubtless she
would soon be putting on caps and sitting with the
dowagers at the season's festivities. She dully reflected
that, if she could not have Rhaz, she did not care.

EIGHTEEN

Unbeknown to Cordelia, the conversation that was ensuing in the forecourt was very dissimilar from the one her mind insisted on superimposing on her fantasies. Seraphina had indeed fallen headfirst into the duke's strong, capable arms, and whilst he had broken her fall and thus spared her the indignity of careering face first across the icy path, his words upon catching her were not nearly so loverlike as Cordelia supposed. He was scolding her, in fact, for being such a widgeon as to career headfirst into his impeccable morning coat of Bath superfine, superlatively cut by Weston and fitting so closely to his frame that it could almost be taken for a second skin. Seraphina had rather pertly commented that the garment was too close fitting to crease, so his grace need have no fears on this score. At which, his grace had set her down firmly on her own two feet and chuckled throatily at her impudence.

"Have you no sensibility, Miss Seraphina? I daresay it is not at all the thing for a young lady to be noticing matters relating to my intimate attire!"

"I daresay not, your grace, but etiquette is one lesson I simply cannot get the mastery of!"

The duke's eyes twinkled appreciatively. "Touché, Miss Seraphina! Perhaps your sister and I are not suitable teachers! Is it possible that it is *we* who are at fault?

I am given to understand that, if the tutor is able, *any* instruction may be satisfactorily accomplished. Do you not find this to be the case?"

His tone grew suddenly serious and he eyed the younger Miss Camfrey speculatively. He was interested in her answer, for if, as he suspected, his good friend was smitten, it was as well that he approved of her character. Frederick would never want a biddable wife—heaven forfend!—but one open to reason would be essential. He watched as Seraphina coloured quite delightfully, her recalcitrant locks flowing freely from her shoulders, blithely regardless of the fact that they should be safely tucked up beneath a bonnet of gay chip straw at the very least.

Seraphina's sky blue eyes darkened almost imperceptibly to lapis lazuli. "I am not sure I understand the direction of your thoughts, my lord! If you consider my music master to be having an undue influence on me—"

"I did not say undue."

The words hung in the air between them until Seraphina's eyes widened suddenly into comprehension. "You mean . . . ?"

The duke nodded. "Exactly. I mean that I consider him to be having some influence upon your behaviour and outlook and that—if I may say so, madame—resounds entirely to both your credits. You will make an excellent wife, Miss Seraphina!"

Seraphina looked into the handsome, searching face and felt a strange jerk of the heart. Not because the man before her played havoc with her senses—his jaw was too firm and his features too dark for her taste—but because he spoke of marriage, and in a sudden, quite overwhelming fit of sudden self-knowledge, Seraphina knew she could not have him for all the teas of the orient.

"Your grace, I am sorry. I have tried to love you—indeed I have—but I find I simply cannot!" She blurted out the words so quickly that they fell from her lips in a tumble the duke found hard to decipher. "You are excessively handsome and undeniably charming and I do so *wish* to love you, but you see . . . you see . . ." She bit her lip, too shy to continue. Impossible to confess she was in transports over a mere music master when the highest-ranking peer of the realm was doing her the singular honour of offering for her hand!

The duke's smile was wry as he took her hand in his and walked with her a little way from the prying eyes at the windows and into one of the private shrubberies that ran off from the more formal winter gardens. He was not to know that at least two sets of eyes wistfully witnessed the unorthodox, unchaperoned action.

The elder Miss Camfrey drew herself up tall, dried her eyes firmly and made for her chamber. There were some urgent, last-minute adjustments she needed to effect to her dress. If these adjustments required more than a few tears, a disgusted sniff at some particularly nasty smelling salts and a stern lecture on how not to behave like a silly, moonstruck halfling, none but herself was the wiser.

Frederick's laughing, sky blue eyes blazed sudden, icy fire as he watched the wrenching spectacle of his dearest friend compromising his only true love. If he were so reckless with her reputation as to take her unchaperoned into the briar rose garden, it could mean only one thing: He had taken her there to propose. Though he might wish, at that moment, to thrust a dagger through the heart of his dearest friend, he did him the justice of knowing that Rhaz did not play fast with respectable, well-bred young women. Before the day was out, the engagement would be announced.

Frederick's heart was heavy as he watched the last of

Seraphina's delicious train of ribboned silk disappear
behind the yew trees and roses. Christmas seemed suddenly but a dreary thing to the normally effervescent
Lord Frederick. The letter from Mr. Beckett rustled in
his pocket. Ironic to think that the tidings it bore had
the power to alter his life and they were now as useless
as the parchment the words were written on. What use
were stupendous royalties and sudden financial freedom
when the woman he loved was plighted to another?

Slowly, he crossed to the stables, eyed up most of the
horses with disfavour and settled on a long, lonely but
much needed walk. He hardly noticed that his shining
doeskin top boots were almost knee-high in snow or
that, even as he walked, soft flakes were falling about
him. Cold and the endless need to march ever onwards
had been miserable features of the Iberian campaign,
but they made him well equipped to cross several paddocks without thinking, taking the slippery, ice-en-
crusted styles as unconsciously as he took air.

Many a surprised labourer looked up from his tilling
to see the tall, muscular figure appear as if from nowhere. Though he was dressed unpretentiously, there
was no doubting he was a gentleman born and bred.
Accordingly, several caps were doffed in his direction.
The actions were wasted, for Frederick, Lord Argyll, was
far too lost to see.

The duke beckoned to Seraphina and she haltingly
stopped two inches from his immaculate garb. Her eyes
were cast down, so she could not see the glimmer of
humour that crossed the duke's aquiline features as he
bade her take the white stone seat beside him. Gingerly,
she did so, taking care not to let her train get caught
up in some of the thorns that tangled with the sweet
scent of the roses.

"I am devastated to learn that my suit does not please, Miss Seraphina!" The duke could well have asked *what* suit, but he desisted, finding it more amusing to elicit the information from Miss Camfrey herself.

Seraphina nodded earnestly. "I am very afraid your mama will be displeased, your grace!"

For an instant, the duke scowled in filial outrage. He might have known the meddlesome dowager would have a hand in this somewhere! He said nothing, however, merely nodding gently and allowing her to continue.

Seraphina, finding him less of an ogre than she feared and needing a confidant since she dared not tell Cordelia the impecunious direction her affections were taking, peeked up at the duke and decided she might as well confide in him as anyone, since he was not likely to lecture her nor was he likely to break her confidence. Accordingly, satisfying herself on the point that he did not expect her to suddenly change her mind—he gravely assured her that he did not—she settled down to pour her heart out and confess to the unsuitable attraction she felt for a mere captain—a gentleman possibly, but fallen upon hard times definitely.

Rhaz listened to her words with interest. True, she was a mischievous little sprite, *quite* unlike Frederick's usual predilections, but he reckoned that her case was not entirely without hope. Indeed, having watched his good friend carefully over the last few evenings, Rhaz could swear Argyll was well on the way to formulating a sincere attachment. His thoughts ran to the teasing conversation he'd introduced and Frederick's uncharacteristically clipped answers. If he had formed a preference for Miss Camfrey, then his annoyance at the lighthearted teasing was explained. He wondered whether Frederick, too, was suffering from the same delusion as his love and concluded that he probably

was. Somehow, the Camfrey household was suffering
under the startling misconception that he, Rhaz Carlisle, the fifth Duke of Doncaster, was about to make
some kind of declaration to Seraphina of the auburn
hair.

How wrong they were! How could their thoughts not
lead them in another direction entirely? Surely it was
obvious that he was smitten beyond belief with that
which was out of reach to him: Cordelia of the laughing
eyes and jet black hair, of quiet strength and strong,
dispassionate honesty. Cordelia of integrity . . . Cordelia of his life.

Seraphina was looking at him expectantly, awaiting a
response. He raised his brows. She repeated the question, her cheeks flushed from the effort of fabricating
a reason why both he and she would not suit.

"Could not you say, your grace, that I am too flighty
for your tastes? I am, you know!"

Since the words were uttered with a certain naughty
pride, the duke did not think it necessary to politely
disagree with her. Instead, he nodded quite seriously—
though the lights behind his deep, dark eyes belied his
tone—and announced that she was too flighty by far.

Seraphina nodded and reflected further on why they
would not suit. "Could not you say I would make an
extraordinary duchess, your grace? I would forever be
muddling people's rank and getting up to pranks quite
unfitting to my station!"

When the duke replied that undoubtedly this was so,
Seraphina looked at him suspiciously and tapped her
little, elegant foot crossly against the soft, orderly grass.
"Well, then, your grace! I cannot see why you persist!
Release me at once, I beg you, that I may go *force* the
good captain to take some notice of me!"

The duke was diverted for an instant. "Am I to understand the good music master has desisted from all attempts to attract?"

Seraphina blushed a little, remembering certain intimate moments, certain electrifying glances, the touch of his hand upon her back, his mouth. . . .

"Captain Argyll has been everything that is a gentleman, your grace! He is simply suffering from a curmudgeonly belief that, since I am intended for you, it is improper in him to entertain hopes!"

The duke looked at Seraphina in some surprise. How could Frederick—addlepated as he sometimes was— have so misunderstood the situation? Had Rhaz not practically *told* him that he was in love with Cordelia? But what exactly had he said? Thinking back, Rhaz could only deduce that it had been an episode of errors, for if he had not mentioned Cordelia by name, Frederick might well have thought his interest arrested in Seraphina. Certainly in looks she more closely conformed to his usual type. . . . In a heartrending flash of insight he realised how his good friend must be suffering. He jumped up, startling Seraphina with the suddenness of his actions.

"Miss Seraphina. I bid you pardon. I must go, but I beg you not to worry your beautiful head over this business. I shall have the lover's knot untangled for you before the day is out!"

"But what shall I tell Mama? She shall be so excessively cross with me for refusing someone as illustrious as yourself!"

The duke looked at her and a grin lit up his often stern features. "My dear Miss Seraphina! Take a moment, I beg you, to reflect a bit. Here, let me help you with your pins. You are in the most abominable shambles and I would hate anyone to think it the result of our little tête-à-tête!"

Seraphina blanched at the prospect. "Indeed, no! I am in a scrape again, am I not?"

"Not if you allow me to clip up these lovely locks of yours. Hold still. I have a sister, so I am used to such trifles."

The duke wisely refrained from mentioning the countless lovers who had also helped him to perfect the practice of acting as a ladies' maid. He looked Seraphina up and down critically, adjusting the hem of her gown just so, unsmoothing a ruffle just there. At last he was satisfied and rewarded her with a smile.

"Have no fear, Miss Seraphina! All will be well. By the by, reflect, as I said, on what has occurred between us. You need not suffer a scold from your mama, for as sure as I am standing here I cannot recall ever having asked for the pleasure of your hand!"

"True!" Seraphina dimpled mischievously. "You must think me a hopeless hoyden! I preempted you, did I not?"

Rhaz grinned. "As a matter of fact, Miss Seraphina, I shall have to say *not!* Marrying you was the farthest thought in my head!"

"Oh!" Surprise battled with startled annoyance in Seraphina's heart. It was lowering to think that the honour of attracting a duke had not been hers, after all.

"But . . . but . . ." She felt ridiculously silly and was at a loss to fathom why the duke had been so assiduous in his attentions to the family.

Rhaz winked. "I adore you, Miss Seraphina, but not as a wife. I think a sister would suit me charmingly."

Seraphina blinked until she finally understood the import of his words. "You mean . . . ? You cannot mean . . . ?"

The duke nodded. "I know it is not very gentlemanly of me, but I hope to rid you of that pompous windbag—"

"Lord Henry? Excellent notion, my lord! I shall

help!" Seraphina was eager as she announced her intention of undermining Winthrop. Her eyes were just assuming a wicked sparkle when the duke stopped her short with a rueful shake of his head. "Leave the poor man be, Miss Seraphina! I shall deal with him in my own way, I assure you! I only hope I can convince Miss Cordelia—"

"Fustian! I shall *force* her to marry you!"

"How very unflattering! But I thank you for your sentiments all the same! Allow me, however, to forge my own path with your sister."

Seraphina sighed. "Oh, very well, your grace! But if you should change your mind—"

"I shall urgently ask your assistance! Shall we abduct her?"

"Now you are being ridiculous, my lord! We shall merely tell her it is her duty to ally the family to your great fortune."

"You shall do no such thing!" The duke's tone was sharp.

Miss Camfrey sighed. "Very well, your grace! Have it your way! I must say, though, I'd prefer *you* as a brother to Lord Henry!"

"I shall endeavour to please you, Miss Camfrey! And now, I fear, you must excuse me."

So saying, Rhaz made her an elegant bow, lifted her hand but slightly in the direction of his lips and released her.

True to form, of course, Frederick was nowhere to be found. The great house was aroar with the sound of yew logs spitting in all the grates. Rhaz was momentarily diverted from his search by the delicious smell of chestnuts and mince pies that wafted up from the kitchens and took the chill out of the pleasant Christmas morning. For an instant, he wondered whether he dared invade Cook's domain and demand some of the tasty plum puddings he knew would be cooling on racks in the same tempting manner they had all the Christmases past. Poor Cook would doubtless suffer heart failure if yet another Carlisle were to poke his noble nose below stairs where he had no business. By all accounts—both voiced and merely hinted at—his mother had done more than enough of that sort of meddling to last them all through to yet another Christmas.

His attention was distracted by the *tap-tapping* cane of the dowager herself, who eyed her son speculatively and demanded that he take some china tea with her, for he was "forever gadding about" and she was sure she would catch her death before he paid her any due attention. Rhaz, used to this maternal treatment, smiled with remarkable charm and allowed himself to be momentarily diverted from his quest.

Despite his imperious mother's dominating, scheming and thoroughly machinating ways, he was fond of her and felt a small stab of guilt that he was going to so thoroughly pull the rug from her matchmaking intentions. Accordingly, he settled her in state on one of his prized Staffordshire chaise longues, ordered a footman to rustle up a rug and a comforting potation of negus "to revive her spirits against the chill" and promised to be a very good boy in the future. The duchess regarded him suspiciously from out of her beady eyes, but since the fifth duke looked as meek as a lamb, she merely harrumphed and called for the attentions of the "sweet young lady with the divine red hair."

His grace smiled to himself and nodded. No question where the Camfreys had come by their confounded impression he was courting Seraphina. The dowager was about as transparent as a glass vase. He promised to ask the under butler to locate this guest and could have laughed out loud to watch the vexation cross his dear mama's features.

"Could not *you* find Miss Seraphina? I *despise* the practice of sending minions all over the house when one can quite as easily accomplish the task oneself."

The duke nodded earnestly. "Excellent, Mama! I shall not bother Jenkins, then, for *you*, I am certain, would wish to locate the younger Miss Camfrey yourself. If it is any consolation to you, she was out in the rose garden not long since."

The duke neglected to tell her Seraphina had been with him. The news would have cast the dowager duchess into transports, but would not serve his case well with Cordelia, should she come to hear of it. The duchess glared at him, but since she had been hoist by her own petard, she could say nothing more on that score. Rhaz took the opportunity of withdrawing speedily before her devious, scheming mind could dream up any further romantic errands.

NINETEEN

Rhaz's self-congratulations on a narrow escape came to a sudden, abrupt and quite unexpected end when his tasselled Hessians padded noiselessly across the thick-piled carpet of the morning room and into the wide, rather public area leading to the grand stairs. Almost of their own accord, as if sensing, rather than seeing a presence, his eyes moved upwards across the cantilevered steps to the third floor, where his dark gaze caught those of an embarrassed Cordelia, who had been too mesmerised by the magnificent spectacle he presented in immaculate velvet to lower her lashes becomingly or withdraw before his eyes were upon her. And they were now. Without thinking, he took the stairs as lightly as a dancer, breaching the distance between them until Cordelia felt he must surely hear the whispers of breath that shuddered from her body in strange, near painful spasms. If he did, he was inflamed by them.

Never speaking a single word, he drew her into the little-used drawing room and shut the door. His eyes did not leave hers and though Cordelia's mind screamed in agitation, her heart played traitor, moving towards him when she should have moved backwards. The action was not missed by Rhaz, who was more tempted than ever before in his life to lock the damn door and have done with the proprieties. Still, she was a guest in his home, though she would soon be its mistress. But not *his* mistress! No, he would have her as his wife or not at all.

He therefore refrained from locking the tempting little lock, but cast caution to the winds and allowed the bronze handle to remain firmly shut. This, of course, was contrary to all propriety, but my lord was having a hard time thinking of etiquette when his mind yearned to devour the beautiful young woman before him and extinguish forever the blaze of anxiety that emanated hot from her cheeks and silvery eyes. He wanted to kiss away all cares and declare her his. He wished to . . . He wished to . . . But no, that was his body speaking, not his mind. With his mind he wished to cherish, to love, to desire, to hold.

This he did, holding Cordelia close until it seemed that their bodies were moulded together and the feather-light kisses with which he covered her face were harsh brands that proclaimed her his irrevocably. He could see her eyes dilate as the nape of her neck extended towards him, yielding before he touched it. It was agony to plant a kiss as light as a butterfly when he wanted more, so much more.

He was just busying himself with her elegant pearl clasps when she remembered who he was and for whom he was destined. Cordelia was suffused with a liquid shame, for Rhaz was Seraphina's and his actions not those of a brother. She had seen them traverse the rose garden and she had come to the same conclusion as Frederick, Lord Argyll. Rhaz did not trifle with ladies' reputations. There could be only one explanation for the turn among the wild pink and cherry briar roses and that explanation would forever be a barrier between them. With an effort she pushed the duke away and allowed her misery to blaze into profound anger. Before she knew what she was about, she had dealt Rhaz a stinging blow across his face that hurt her hand almost as much as his cheek. She was glad of it, for it gave her something else to think of beyond the profoundness of her misery.

"That is for my sister, your grace! Pray do not approach me again. If I behaved wantonly this time, like a veritable hoyden—well, I admit my shame! But you acted without honour either and that I find hard to forgive! Shall we, for the sake of my dear Seraphina, pretend that nothing has occurred between us? I assure you it is the only way I know to go on!" She did not wait for a reply, but in tears fled the room.

My lord was very thoughtful as his reflection looked back at him unseeingly from the glass on the other side of the room. Mistress Cordelia had not been unattracted. With his own fingers he'd felt her, pliant in his arms. More than pliant—a willing partner . . . The memory stirred him to new passion and he had to touch his cheek in order to sober himself. A stinging blow! He suspected his little vixen had taken her frustrations as well as anger out on him.

Well, she was not indifferent, and yes, the rebuke had been earned. She was, after all, still engaged . . . He sighed. How he *wished* Lord Henry would hurry up! Matters would have to come to a head soon before he ended up doing something scandalous like . . . like . . . The naughty Seraphina's words came back to haunt him. Yes, perhaps he *would* abduct Cordelia! A little dimple played round his mouth as he thought of the logistics of such an outrageous notion. There would be the sleighs, the church bells, the mad dash across the border into Scotland, the uncomfortable damp when the snows returned and their conveyance was duly snowbound. . . . Reality shook him from this pleasant nonsense. Her grace the fifth Duchess of Doncaster was not going to be beset by scandal. She would be married in pomp and in dignity and as damn early as possible! So swearing, Rhaz slipped back down the stairs to resume his search.

From the music room, he could just catch the mellifluous strains of Scarlatti dancing through the heavy oak panelling.

He at once thought the good captain must be within, but found, to his astonishment, that it was Seraphina instead who had settled herself down by the harpsichord. She coloured when the duke stared at her in surprise. It had never occurred to him that Frederick might actually be *able* to impart some of his immense gift to the tongue-tied creature who he'd once rescued from the precipice of social disaster.

"That is very good!"

"Now it is *your* turn to be unflattering, my lord! Your tone speaks volumes for your faith in me!"

"I must confess to astonishment, Miss Seraphina!"

"Excellent, for I am practicing for the Christmas pageant this afternoon! Lady Bancroft shall be attending."

"And since she is such a shimble-shamble scuttle-headed gabster—"

"Your grace!" Seraphina pretended shock but she could not prevent a giggle escaping her pretty mouth. The duke blithely ignored her.

"She will undoubtedly frank a hundred wafers at least announcing your newfound skill!"

"I only hope she writes to the Countess of Glaston, for I shall dearly love Lila Mersham to be apprised of the fact!"

"And so she shall if I have to send round a couple of footmen to announce it!"

The duke's suddenly blithe spirit was infectious. Seraphina chuckled as she closed the instrument and dutifully replaced her gloves. As she laughed up at him, she noticed the red patch above his cheek. The sight arrested her, for she could think of no one who could inflict such a dreadful thing upon a man who was quite the wealthiest, noblest and most singularly well-endowed gentleman in all of England. The offence was one for which lesser men could be sent to prison or death and she could not help wondering at it.

The duke followed her eyes with his own and made a rueful grimace. "I had hoped it would not be too noticeable!"

Seraphina shook her head in sympathy. "It shall not be, for Cordelia is almost a witch when it comes to herbal remedies and elixirs. I shall call her for you and she will conjure up some preparation that will salve it upon the instant."

The duke's lips twitched at the irony. "In this instance, Miss Seraphina, I have to report you are at fault! Mistress Cordelia is far more likely to infect the other side than to offer a cure!"

"Infect the other side? What can you mean? An assault upon the person is not infectious, my lord!"

"I do hope not, for otherwise, I might spend the rest of my life permanently featureless. The bruise raises my cheek and causes my eye to narrow to a slit, does it not?"

"Don't be so absurd, your grace! But . . . Good God! Don't say Cordelia inflicted that upon you?"

"Indeed she did!" The duke was strangely cheerful despite this admission. He might have had to pay with a faint bruise to his person, but the scent of her hair still tickled his nose and the mere thought of her lips, her neck . . . He tried to concentrate.

Seraphina was clapping her hands in whoops. "Just wait till I tax her on this, your grace! Slapping a peer of the realm must surely be worse than some of the harmless pranks *I* have been scolded for!"

"Don't tease her, my dear! Our matters are in a sad

tangle, and until we can somehow untangle them all to our satisfaction, Christmas will seem bleak indeed. I shall talk to your music master"—he watched Seraphina's eyes widen and her blush deepen—"and I shall intercede for you with your sister. If you truly love a man who is not your social equal, I can see no reason to allow society's priggish proprieties to stand in your way. As for your sister, Lord Winthrop and me—something will have to happen. I have strange hopes, for the sun *will* cast streams of light through the windows and that has always been an omen to me."

His words were firm, sensitive, romantic and strangely reassuring. Instead of rushing off to tease the poor Cordelia, Seraphina decided to let her be. The first strains of the carollers could be heard far off in the distance. If she fetched her muff and took a brisk walk outside, she could perhaps meet them on their walk up to the great house.

The fifth duke cast a weary look at the drawing room door. He did not wish to be caught in his mama's wily net once more. No doubt, by now she would have tumbled to the fact that he had been taking a turn in the rose garden with Seraphina. His life would be hell if she did, for she would immediately start preparing for his nuptials and all but trap him into a declaration. No, he must tread carefully and not trust to the soothing properties of the negus to mellow his fiery mama. Accordingly, he did *not* take the main stairs as the waiting footmen fully expected. Instead, he doubled back across the gallery and out through a little used side entrance with a handy set of servants' stairs to the rear. He was fortunate that everyone was too busy with the last-minute business of hanging holly and mistletoe to notice his descent upon the lowly steps.

In less than no time he was striding towards the stables. If Frederick was not within—and he'd had his chamber checked—then he must be somewhere in the wilds of his woods. The snow was making everything white and glimmering, but the forests would be silent and dark, laden with snow and ready, in whispering anticipation, for the coming of heavenly Christmas.

It was unlikely that Frederick took a horse, for the man always preferred his own two feet to a stallion's sturdier four, but Rhaz was just thorough enough to check. If Frederick had taken a thoroughbred he might be anywhere upon the estate. If he had not, there might yet be time to catch him before the day's festivities and the advent of the great Christmas pageant. Given that Seraphina was performing, Rhaz guessed that Frederick would not be likely to play truant, however much his wayward, solitary heart might wish him to. Still, if some of the romantic threads that had them all caught up in muddled confusion could be unwoven before the church bells pealed, the fifth duke would be well pleased. He suspected now what ailed his friend and in all honesty he wished to relieve his mind. It was hard enough for him, knowing that Cordelia was truly engaged. There was no need for Frederick to suffer from the same sorrow when Seraphina was heart whole—or at least with regard to himself—and fancy free. A hint of that to Frederick might remove some of the gloom from his face and make him a more congenial Christmas compatriot than he was currently shaping up to be.

The familiar, warm smell of hay and manure assailed his senses as he stepped into the stables. The lofts were full of straw and saddles and sidesaddles of all descriptions hung neatly from great hooks jutting out from the slate brick walls. The deep, fragrant smell of polished leather mingled with the scent of the mares and the matched bays that pawed restively at the ground. A quick glance at the stalls revealed that, whilst several of the stallions were being exercised, they were all carriage horses and therefore unlikely to have been taken out by any of the guests. Rhaz was just wondering whether he should head for the woods on foot or mount his magnificent jet black beast when he heard a faint whispering at the far end of the stalls. Intrigued—for his grace was unused to his grooms whispering in his presence—he trod carefully past his teams and made his way to the south side of the stables. The sight that met his eyes stopped him short.

Lord Winthrop, red whiskered and blustery, was busily engaged in hanging a piece of bright green mistletoe above one of the stalls. Helena—horsy, bossy Helena— was simpering madly and blushing to the roots of her dull, deadly straight brown hair. Rhaz would have quietly retreated, but his head horseman had just entered from the far end and he had no desire for the sight to be shared amongst his grooms. Accordingly, he placed his own muscular and very substantial body between the last stall and the far entrance to the stables. Anyone glancing down would have seen only his grace the duke and none, of course, would have had the presumption to approach him.

Henry—dear, pompous Henry—announced to Miss Moresby that she was truly the fairest of creatures, deliciously rounded in all the correct places, a cosy armful if ever he saw one. For an instant Rhaz was amused, for he had never before thought of the lustreless Miss Moresby in such ecstatic terms. When she tittered a little and moved towards Lord Winthrop, however, something snapped inside Rhaz.

Perhaps it was the pain of knowing that Cordelia was Winthrop's betrothed, that unless he were moved to drastic action she would be Winthrop's wife, not his . . .

Whatever it was, his grace the fifth Duke of Doncaster found himself furious. It was bad enough that Cordelia's sentiments for him did not run deeply enough to renege on her proposal to Winthrop—but to see this! Lord Henry preferring his anaemic cousin to the glory of Cordelia and playing her false! For whatever Rhaz's private hopes on the matter, there could be no gainsaying that the man was still plighted to the love of Rhaz's heart and, accordingly, should show her the proper respect.

Without thinking of the spectacle he might be creating, quite oblivious to his head grooms and their minions, he marched up to Winthrop and grabbed him by the shirt so the poor man was spluttering bewildered inconsequentialities. Miss Moresby, he could see, was equally taken aback. She did not hesitate to push herself into the fray, inquiring quite crossly whether her cousin had just run insane. Rhaz did not wait to formulate an answer. His cheek was still faintly stinging and he had a sudden urge to rid himself of the wild feelings that were tearing at his mind. Accordingly, his fist shot out and he landed poor Lord Henry such a facer that the gentleman was obliged to sit down right in the middle of the stall and nurse his face with simple bewilderment etched all over his rather vacuous features.

"Lord Winthrop, as host to the Misses Camfrey and in the absence of any male relative on their part, I feel it my duty to challenge you. If you want satisfaction for that black eye, you may call on my seconds. I believe Sir Harvey Trump or Lord Foxton of Eddington Manor will stand for me."

Lord Henry staggered to his feet with the help of a very solicitous Miss Moresby, who looked daggers at her handsome cousin and was about to pour forth with a crashing scold when Lord Henry interrupted her.

"Beg pardon, my love. I do believe his grace and I

are at outs over a mere bagatelle. Why do you not return to the house and I shall have the matter sorted out in a twinkling?"

Helena looked doubtful, but with both male eyes outstaring her, she had no choice but to gather up her sensible woollen skirts and head towards the outer door. She had the last word, however, for as Rhaz was sizing up his victim, her gloved hands on slender, entirely masculine hips, she admonished them both to come off their high ropes and Rhaz, in particular, not to be such a gudgeon.

Her voice softening almost perceptibly, she warned Lord Henry not to dally, but to come inside out of the cold, for she had a hot posset and a sherbet soaking in perfumed cakes and Damascus fruit. Rhaz wondered whether he would be offered any of his own largesse, but he was not. With a toss of her head and a scathing glance at him, Miss Moresby was gone.

TWENTY

"Well, Lord Winthrop? Is it to be pistols?"

"Indeed not, your grace, for I can think of no more churlish way of repaying your hospitality."

"You call it hospitality when I blacken your eye on Christmas?"

For an instant Rhaz thought Lord Winthrop might grin. He didn't and his grace felt a strange relief, for surely Helena would be madder still if he returned her lover to her with a face that was cracked from the uncustomary effort of smiling.

"Well, then? How does one redress the insult offered your betrothed? Not to *mention* the insult offered Miss Moresby? If I had not come upon you as I did, you might even now be kissing her!" Rhaz's indignation was audible in his voice, though he himself had been engaged in the self-same activity not long since.

"Then I have more than one reason to regret your entrance, your grace! I would far rather be embracing the lovely Miss Helena than clashing swords at cross purposes with *you!*"

Lord Winthrop fingered his bruise. He was relieved to realise Rhaz must have pulled his punch, for the duke was renowned for his boxing prowess. The fact that he was not now in dire agony showed that his grace had

had mercy. Still, he *had* interrupted what promised to be a most interesting interlude. . . .

The duke visibly restrained himself. "Puppy! Explain yourself, for I cannot feel Miss Cordelia would be happy to know that you have breached your betrothal vows!"

"A curse on Miss Cordelia! She very roundly sent me the right about this morning, so I have every reason to offer for Miss Moresby! Not even *you* could argue the logic in that!"

Rhaz felt his heart suddenly racing most inexplicably. Not even the physical effort of having knocked down the much maligned baron had rendered this intoxicating effect upon his person. He controlled his breathing and in a calm but slightly dangerous tone asked whether Lord Winthrop meant what he thought he did.

"That Miss Cordelia jilted me? Indeed, she did, for she had a fitting sensibility of the fact that she and I would not suit. There is a certain levity, you understand, that I must deplore—"

"Deplore away, old boy! Just tell me, is she or is she not free?"

Lord Winthrop looked at Rhaz as though he were being asked a trick question. Whilst he had no wish to lie sprawled in the stalls again, his natural honesty forced him to confirm Rhaz's question. "Free to wed? Indeed she is, though now she has rejected, uh"—he cleared his throat—"so eligible a suit as mine, one can only speculate."

Rhaz grinned and dashed on the hat that had fallen in his tussle with Winthrop. "Speculate away! By the by, I take it your intentions are honourable towards Miss Moresby?"

Now it was Lord Winthrop's turn to look daggers at the duke. "Am I to understand you are suggesting anything improper between her and myself? If so, your grace, I fear I shall have to call you out after all! Miss

Moresby's principles are of the highest, the most pure—"

"Yes, yes! Her virtues are limitless! I have lived with them from time immemorial and should know! You wish to wed her then?"

"*When* I have obtained the proper permissions, yes!"

"Well, consider them obtained!"

"Beg pardon, your grace?"

"As head of the family and her only male relative, I am the proper person to whom you should apply."

"Good God! I'd not thought of that! Your grace, I beg you consider. My wealth is not insubstantial. Miss Moresby shall have—"

"Write it up, Winthrop! I shall sign the papers immediately!"

"But . . . ?"

"No buts if you please! I have a lot of untangling to do before the church bells peal! My apologies, of course, for the slight misunderstanding!"

Lord Winthrop touched his cheek speculatively. Though his lips did not move, Rhaz could have sworn he'd witnessed a Christmas miracle: the glimmer of a twinkle in my lord's solemn tawny eyes.

Winthrop nodded. "You are forgiven, your grace! I find I am suddenly infused with the spirit of Christmas!"

"Excellent! If you go on into the house, try to persuade the lovely Helena to exchange her sherbet for my cherry brandy. Then, my dear man, I can *promise* you will be infused with the Christmas spirit!"

With this lighthearted riposte, Rhaz walked back to the sixth stall and beckoned to a groom, who'd just begun polishing the bridles on the far wall. "I will take Firefly out now, Hodges! She can do with a run and I'd like to take her through her paces before the snow is too settled upon the ground."

Hodges obediently led the beast out and Rhaz fondled it gently before mounting it and leading it out into the cold under the darkening sky. Frederick still needed to be found and time was running out. The sounds of the carollers, high-pitched and fervent, were drawing steadily closer. For an instant Rhaz reflected on the beauty of the age-old songs sung to age-old tunes. His heart twisted a little, for if matters managed to untangle themselves this would, he knew, be the most memorable Christmas of his life.

The woods were dense, the thickets overgrown with brambles and clad everywhere in soft, shimmering snow. Most of the pinecones had been gathered off the ground, but here and there, a couple showed themselves as Firefly trod slowly over the green needles and white mulch that formed the forest floor. When Rhaz was wondering which fork to take, the gentle sound of panpipes floated to his ears, drowning out the breeze and the carol singers, the trotting of hooves and the odd call of the doe. He instantly knew where to turn, and following the notes as if participating in a childish game of hide-and-seek, he finally found his source.

Frederick, lying on his back, was instantly alert to Rhaz's presence. He did not turn around, but continued with his piping, the notes becoming quite tumultuous with energy and unspoken thoughts. At last, he stopped, for Rhaz did not interrupt him, but rather dismounted and came to rest on a rock beside him. Firefly pawed the ground gently and took the unexpected moment to taste some of the ferny leaves that tempted her at eye level. Thus occupied, he did not notice the conversation that took place between the two friends and erstwhile rivals.

"You will miss the festivities, my friend."

"Shall I? My apologies."

"Miss Seraphina Camfrey will be disappointed."

Frederick sat up and set the pipe down. "You shall

have to comfort her then. No doubt she will comport herself excellently at the pageant. She is an apt pupil."

If his tone was bitter, it was not through intent. Rhaz, however, noted at *once* the constraint that had come over his friend. Frederick was obviously suffering from the same delusions as the rest of his household. For an instant he reflected on how he would wring his poor, meddlesome mama's neck. If only she had not circulated the misguided, hideously inaccurate rumour in the first place, they might all, by now, be enjoying Christmas peace. Well, Frederick and Seraphina at all events. He and Cordelia—well, they still had bridges to cross. Rhaz allowed a slow smile to cross his face. He would look forward to the crossing.

"I believe she will perform better if you were present, my lord!"

"Good God, Rhaz! What are you 'my lording' me for? You only ever do that when you are funning, and frankly, though I wish you all the happiness in the world, I do not feel inclined to joke at this particular moment!"

"Do you not? I rather find the spectacle of you orbiting in love strangely ironic! Forgive me the smirk but I have to say, Frederick, how the mighty have fallen! Mind you, Miss Seraphina *is* passing handsome, but you, who have sworn ever to be a bachelor—"

Lord Argyll paled and his hand clenched into a small, but visible fist. "Rhaz, if you were not my dearest friend, I would beat you to a pulp! I beg you, desist making a mockery of me! I had thought I'd kept my feelings well under check, but apparently I have failed dismally. If the truth must be spoken between us, then, yes, I do love your Seraphina. Look after her well, Rhaz, for I promise you, friendship or not, I shall be waiting in the wings to carry her off should you ever give me cause!"

"I hope I shall not, though I fear, since I am as yet

unused to the role, I shall make quite an exasperating brother at times!"

Frederick was just formulating a fierce, burning reply when the import of Rhaz's words reached the inner recesses of his mind. "Brother? Do not you mean *lover?* What a terrible slip, your grace!" His words were formal, for the intensity of his emotions necessarily placed a distance between himself and his noble friend.

"Not at all, you foolish gudgeon!" Rhaz grinned broadly. The time for teasing was well and truly over. "It is Miss *Cordelia* Camfrey whom I intend to take to wife. That places poor Miss *Seraphina* Camfrey in the sad position of having to call me brother!"

Hope flared in Frederick's eyes. "You would not joke about such a thing, Rhaz!"

"Of course not! I am a sombre old soul. *You* should know that!"

Frederick recovered himself to cuff his dearest bosom buddy wryly. "Indeed, a regular old sawbones!" His voice changed. "You speak truly?"

His grace nodded, all trace of merriment gone from his dark, handsome features. "I speak truly, Frederick! And though my preference is for the elder Miss Camfrey, I have to say that I find your choice delightful! Miss Seraphina is more than likely to lead you a regular song and dance, but I believe most emphatically that you shall suit!"

"So do I!" Frederick chuckled. "She is a little witch, Rhaz! You have no idea!"

"I suspect I can guess!"

There was a moment's silence; then Frederick, a little uncertain, asked whether Seraphina knew of his preference. "You see, Rhaz, I believe she has been coaxed into expecting an offer from you. I declare I was never more surprised in my life when I learned of the connection."

"The *fictitious* connection I collect! My mama has a lot to answer for, it would seem!"

"True! Be that as it may, she is expecting to become a duchess. I dare not hope she would lower her eyes to the level of a mere music master, but even as Lord Argyll, I cannot possibly compete! Your wretched rank is an *absurd* obstacle to my declaration!"

"Would you love her if she had no dowry?"

"I don't believe she *does* have one! Her papa left them sadly out of kilter, though what *that* has to do with the matter at hand—"

"Bear with me! You do not expect a dowry. Why should *she* marry for rank or title? You make too much of the issue."

"Thank you, Rhaz! I wish I could be certain on that score, but I fear it *shall* make a difference! I'll marry her for love but not to satisfy a fit of pique! I will not spend the rest of my life playing second fiddle to a duke, however much I happen to be *fond* of that duke!"

He nodded in Rhaz's direction but a black scowl had descended upon his brow. "Am I not perverse? Five minutes ago I was wishing merely that she was free. Now that I know she is, I find that I want more."

"Ask her then."

"But if she refuses? If she even hesitates? I shall have to live with that, Rhaz, forever!"

"You do your lady an injustice. I know she will not."

"How can you be so certain? Apart from your charm—and I know I can compete on *that* score"—Frederick grinned for a moment—"your eligibility is aeons away from mine."

"You are no coward, Frederick. Try her. I know she will not disappoint."

Frederick still looked strangely disturbed, his normal confidence ebbing most uncharacteristically and a sure-fire sign, to Rhaz, of his natural agitation.

"Frederick! You force me to lose all self-respect and offer you a weapon with which to mercilessly tease me!"

Frederick raised his brows. "Do I? How so?"

"I shall have to inform you, Lord Argyll, that I have just been jilted in my own rose garden! It appears I cannot compete with a certain nameless captain who has the knack of entrancing a particular bright-eyed seraph and capturing her heart forever and a day! Of course, I just whisper these confidences to you, for my honour does not allow me to tell you directly *exactly* what was said. . . ."

Firefly pawed the ground in the background. She was ignored. Captain Argyll stood up.

"By all that is holy, I believe you are serious!" His words were filled with wonder and a glimmer of hope that was almost tangible in its potency.

Rhaz nodded. "For all my flippancy, Frederick, I am."

"Then I must go to her!" Frederick grinned, the spirit of Christmas finally settling on his broad, enviable shoulders.

"You may take my nag!"

"Nag? Call that brute a nag? Not on your life! I shall walk."

"Very well, I shall trot sedately beside you. We'd better hurry, for the pageant is close to beginning. I think I hear the hour chiming."

Rhaz leaped up on Firefly and there was a companionable silence between them as both anticipated the afternoon to come.

"Rhaz?"

"What is it, Freddie?"

"I have just had a thought."

"Excellent! I must congratulate you!" Rhaz's teasing tone was back. "Pray share it."

"How came you to be proposing to my girl in the rose garden?"

His grace the fifth Duke of Doncaster put his head back and laughed wickedly. "Now *that* is an interesting question! I believe the little nymph was so set on rejecting me she never actually afforded me the opportunity of a declaration!"

"Impossible! You do not mean . . . No, Rhaz! That is the outside of enough! You cannot mean—"

"Indeed I do! Would you put such a preposterous action past her?"

Lord Argyll chuckled. "I do not dare put it to the test! I think, after all, I shall not propose. Declarations are obviously redundant. I shall, instead, merely insist that she wed me and have done with it!"

"*Excellent* notion! By the by, yon Winthrop is shortly to become a relation of mine."

"You seem remarkably sanguine at the knowledge! If he were to become *my* cousin I am sure I would run a mile!"

"My equanimity is due entirely to my relief, Freddie! I've wanted to throttle the old windbag several times this past month I can tell you!"

"I consider him a lucky man that you did not! I take it he is enamoured of the fair Miss Moresby?"

Rhaz raised his eyebrows. "Fair? You must have acquired some sight defect, Frederick! At all events, they are well enamoured of each other and I am of a mind to play Cupid."

"Sly creature! I'll warrant you set them in the way of each other! I never *could* understand what maggot possessed you to invite the old windbag to Huntingdon! You could have knocked me down with a feather when I heard *his* version of events. *You,* your grace, are evidently a sight keen to mix your bloodstock with those of the Winthrop stable. Something *very* fishy there, I thought, but like a meek and mild music master, I held my peace. Wished to see the spectacle for myself! *Then*

I thought it was all a flimsy excuse to bring Seraphina down to Huntingdon. You are lucky I did not knock your block off the moment I laid eyes on you!"

"You glared at me so balefully I shivered in my shoes."

"Please! Your immaculate top boots did not quiver an inch. I know, for I envied them their dash. I am sadly outmoded in this garb, Rhaz!"

"When have you cared a button for that?"

Frederick grinned. "It is not me I think of, Rhaz. It is my poor, demented, *unutterably* toplofty valet to whom I refer!"

"Ah, well, that is another matter entirely." His grace surveyed Lord Frederick candidly. "To be frank, Frederick, he has my sympathies! Still, I doubt whether the fair Seraphina cares whether your linen is fabricated from fine lawn or not. As for your neckerchief—well, sadly, there is nothing to say on the matter. If she loves you as you are, then you may take it she loves you true!"

"Thank you very much!" Frederick endeavoured to sound indignant, but his spirit was too light to pull it off. Instead, his glorious chestnut curls ran riot across his forehead, making him look more boyishly handsome than ever before. " 'Silent Night.' Can you hear?"

Rhaz nodded. The carollers were upon them. The doors of the great house were thrown wide open and the two men, emerging from the woods and into the formal gardens, could see all the servants and guests standing at balconies, singing as if imbued with Christmas magic.

Even Lord Winthrop could be detected, mouthing a few notes as he stood protectively near Miss Moresby. Rhaz caught his breath as his eyes rested on Cordelia's slim frame, exotic in the magenta red she'd chosen to effect, little splashes of crisp green trim enhancing her style, her beauty and her freshness. Rhaz knew he was in love, but the depth of the feeling he felt at that moment was a revelation to him. At last, she was free. Now it was a mere matter of convincing her. . . . He put the thought aside as he strode up the path to the cheers and applause of the carol singers. True to form, he took the wassail basket from the waiting housekeeper and distributed the warm negus, orgeat and cherry punch to all who required it. Refreshed, the carol singers kept up merry chatter as they finally led the way to the church hall, where the nativity scene was to be reenacted and the Christmas pageant played out.

TWENTY-ONE

With the arrival of their host, the ladies filtered down-stairs. Ancilla looked as ethereal as a butterfly in a light gold and buttercup gown crossed over the front and laced charmingly at the back. She had just spoken with each of her chicks, and though she found it hard to overset her ambitious plans—sown by the feisty, med-dlesome dowager—she had given both Cordelia and Seraphina the best advice her maternal heart could of-fer. She'd urged them to follow their hearts, however hard the road, however wayward the spirit. Cordelia had heard the words with a faint sadness etched upon her brow, but Seraphina had exuded a radiance that be-spoke her name—angel.

Ancilla had not inquired too closely, but she guessed the direction of her younger daughter's thoughts. She sighed for what might have been, for what self-respect-ing mama would not have wished a connection with a duke rather than a poor, struggling music master? Still, she believed that, though some might consider her a most unnatural parent, her advice was the correct one. Captain Argyll as a man—purely as a man—would make the most exemplary of husbands, the most excellent of sons. If he had not wealth and circumstance—well, nei-ther did Seraphina. Doubtless Lord Winthrop would be able to establish him. . . .

She glanced at Cordelia. No! Over her dead body would Lord Winthrop rob Cordelia of her essence, her guileless nature and her intransigent wit. If Cordelia had to be condemned to the life of a spinster, so be it. At least she would not have to constantly explain her witticisms until she arrived at the point where she no longer made them. Winthrop was a kind man but a fool. Cordelia had never suffered fools gladly, and without gladness, her life, at best, would be inferior to its full potential.

These were *very* grown-up thoughts for the flighty Ancilla. So engrossed was she that she did not notice Winthrop take Helena down the snowbound path towards the church hall. Neither did she notice her host stop at Cordelia's side, hold out his hand, encounter a moment's hesitation in which he suffered a thousand deaths before being led deep into the fray. Of the party making their way downstairs, that left the dowager duchess, herself and Seraphina.

Her eyes flitted to the stunningly handsome young man making his way to her daughter's side. She had changed into something more suitable to the cold winter day, but looked charming nonetheless. In a figured merino edged with soft white ermine and a muff to match, Seraphina was exquisite. She had permitted her hair to hang loose from her shoulders, unfashionably unbound, but magnificent for all that. The rich auburn was reflected by the glints in her handsewn morning gown and the half boots of the same shade exactly.

Captain Argyll—clad singularly becomingly in tight cream buckskins and a saffron waistcoat, silver studded with understated buttons and a loose but elegant cravat—walked up to her, made her a smart, slightly self-mocking leg and took her hand lightly between his properly gloved fingers.

"Merry Christmas, my angel, Seraphina." He whispered the words to her, for the eyes of the entire household were upon them as they took their places on the ice-lined path.

Seraphina looked at his long, unbound, wild chestnut locks, his wonderful, healthy, unbearably handsome face, his wistful smile, his entrancing, fathoms-deep sea green eyes and smiled. "If you will have me, Captain, I am your angel truly."

"Is that a proposal, Miss Seraphina?"

She stood still, a moment, the glistening snow whiter than ever around her. "Yes."

"How very improper!" Frederick was laughing at her, his eyes brimful of love and laughter.

"Who *is* that man?" The duchess's voice boomed loudly in Ancilla's ear so that she jumped.

"He is Seraphina's music master, your grace!"

"Nonsense! Got eyes in my head, haven't I? That is Drummond's boy if ever I've seen him. My son's been as thick as thieves with him for as long as I can remember. Can't think *what* he is doing here when he's got a perfectly good home of his own to go to! And what is he doing kissing Seraphina like that? Ancilla, he is making a spectacle of himself! *Do* something!" With an outraged glare the duchess pointed her lorgnette in the couple's direction.

Mrs. Camfrey, remarkably calm despite the sudden laughter in her heart, mustered up sufficient courage to stare the duchess down. "I shall do no such thing, your grace! And as for him kissing her—well, I'm sure I hope he may!"

"You are a passing unnatural parent, Ancilla! A flighty little fussbudget. A . . . a . . . widgeon of the first stare!" Her very noble grace glared haughtily at the twinkling, *fascinatingly* elegant Mrs. Camfrey. "And if you think my son—"

"Hush! The eyes of the staff are upon us!"

"Hmmph!" The duchess fingered her cane and stepped out into the snow. "Give me a hand, Ancilla. You may be the veriest imbecile, but at least you have a steady hand. Now where are my smelling salts and my tippet? I could have sworn they awaited me in the hallway."

"Here they are your grace and a very merry Christmas to you." The housekeeper bobbed a respectable curtsy but her eyes twinkled as she proffered the offending items. In the days before Christmas, the duchess might have been maddening, but the staff nonetheless harboured a secret affection for the old tartar. She was, after all, the present duke's mama and if for no other reason, this entitled her to some small affection in their hearts.

"Hmph!" came the duchess's indelicate reply as she allowed herself to be warmly wrapped against the cold. Then, unbending a little, she pressed a sovereign into the surprised woman's hand and crossly enjoined Ancilla to hurry up.

Throngs were crowding to enter the great hall, but at the advent of the noble party, the people gave way in awed silence and whispered and clapped and even, in some unrestrained instances, cheered. At the back of the hall, Lord and Lady Bancroft had already taken their seats. Rhaz, maneuvering Cordelia up to his own box, noticed and grinned. He would bet a pony the woman would be spreading the news of Seraphina's success across all London before the night was in. Even on Christmas day, the woman's tongue could be relied upon to wag.

He spared a moment's thought for poor Lord Bancroft, who had suffered the venom and indelicacies of his wife's tongue from time immemorial. He, of course, was the product of a perfectly acceptable arranged society marriage. He looked down at Cordelia and smiled secretly to himself. Well, *that* particular trap was to be evaded like the plague. To hang with his mama and her schemes. He would wed the woman of his fancy or none at all.

Cordelia, trembling from his nearness and slightly confused that he was escorting *her,* rather than Seraphina, looked up tentatively. She was met by a gaze of such scorching intensity that she was forced instantly to remove her hand from his grasp. If the duke was ever to have such an effect on her, it would be wise to withdraw from his sphere at once. Since such an action would have been monstrous rude at this juncture, she satisfied herself with the gentle withdrawal of her hand and heart.

Rhaz, sensing this distance, was saddened. Still, he satisfied himself that as soon as the pageant was over, he would be able to have a few salient words, at last, with the delicious, delightful and thoroughly adorable Miss Cordelia. He gave her a hint of what was to come when he whispered, as they walked down the aisle, "You are mistaken, you know."

"Mistaken?" Cordelia looked at him in confused surprise. The very action was bittersweet for her, for his mouth was perilously close to hers as she turned her head and her tongue wantonly wet her own lips, possibly in deference to this unassailable fact.

"There is only *one* Miss Camfrey I have ever yearned for, night after sleepless night, day after anguished day."

"Seraphina." Cordelia's heart was heavy as she uttered the name that was normally so beloved to her.

"*No,* you widgeon! You had better think again. After the pageant you may tell me your revised answer. By the by, I have this for you."

He pressed into her open hand a small package. There was no more time for talk, for the merry youngsters of the village were beginning their annual parade.

Cordelia took her seat as if in a dream. She watched as the noble lord of the estate, his grace the fifth duke, nimbly took the stage and welcomed one and all, wishing the village and its tenants a year of peace and plenty. Tumultuous applause and cheering and chaffing before the touching little nativity scene, rehearsed half a year by eager youngsters, was performed. Following that were a series of Christmas charades and beyond that again individual performances by villagers and gentry alike. At last, the final performance was announced and Seraphina, now slightly trembling, stood up to take the stage.

Her quivering was stilled when the good captain unexpectedly accompanied her up to the small platform. Out of the corner of her eye, Cordelia could see Lady Bancroft insert a monocle with eager anticipation. She caught her breath and prayed that Seraphina's diligent tuition would pay off.

Seraphina seated herself at the waiting harp whilst, to her surprise, the captain clapped his hands for silence and announced that he intended an impromptu lyric to her accompaniment. The words, he noted loudly and with *pointed* meaning, were dedicated to the player and titled "Seraphina at Christmas."

Seraphina coloured, and suddenly, with his bright, strong eyes upon her, she forgot all nervousness and struck a light arpeggio across the keys. Frederick's eyes were brimful of amusement as he nodded and she began the haunting, melodic notes of his composition in earnest.

Her fingers were now so well practiced that the piece had become effortless. When Frederick sang, she listened with her whole heart, for the music was acting as a powerful connection between them and Seraphina felt she could not be closer in spirit to the man she had so recklessly chosen for herself than she was now. Frederick looked at her with sudden, intense, unveiled passion, and if Miss Camfrey was ever in any doubt as to the state of his heart, she was no longer permitted to be. Frederick may never have proposed, but the song could not have been a more pointed declaration if he had tried.

> *There is a star on the horizon,*
> *faint but steady.*
> *In the dark of the night*
> *it flickers, ready*
> *to rise and remind,*
> *shimmer with heady flame*
> *and glimmer and sparkle to echo*
> *a name that is forever Christmas.*
>
> *You are the isthmus,*
> *my angel, of the spirit, the might*
> *On the eve of Yuletide,*
> *on a velvety night*
> *I call, "Angel my angel,"*
> *and behold Seraph, the light.*
>
> *Scatterlings of fire,*
> *fragments of faith,*
> *Yuletide's rejoicing*
> *in starlight embrace.*
> *Glisten and glimmer,*
> *sparkle my sprite.*
> *The world is in waiting*
> *this still, silent night.*
>
> *Hail to thee, Seraph!*
> *At my behest*
> *unveil celestial secrets*
> *and sweet love's caress—*

> *that your glittering beams*
> *be reflected on earth*
> *in peace and tranquillity*
> *for mankind's rebirth.*

> *You are the isthmus,*
> *my angel, of the spirit, the might.*
> *On the eve of Yuletide,*
> *on a velvety night,*
> *I call, "Angel my angel,"*
> *and behold Seraph, the light.*

A moment's silence filled the hall before the deafening cheers. Seraphina had acquitted herself superbly and whilst Lady Bancroft's eyes had dilated a little in disappointment, the text of Frederick's song was enough to satisfy her that her friends and cronies would get their regular dose of delicious gossip. Besides, she would be the *first* to pronounce Miss Seraphina gifted and to be first in anything must be considered a social coup, after all. She therefore smiled relatively benignly on her poor, henpecked spouse and joined in the applause quite as genteelly as Lady Curruthers in the next pew.

In her seat, Cordelia glanced strangely at the duke. Had he known? She had never *suspected* the state of Seraphina's heart. His smile seemed whole and genuine and wonderfully gentle as he nodded to the unanswered question.

"I am delighted, Cordelia. I may call you that, may I not?" She nodded. "My joy is twofold, but I shall leave that to the good captain to explain. He does, in fact, have a lot of explaining to do." His eyes rested softly on Cordelia's, then widened in amusement as they glanced to the back of the hall.

"*Now* the fat is in the fire," he announced, but with such an unconcerned, mischievous grin that Cordelia was intrigued rather than concerned. She noted, too, that her grace the duchess, seated next to Ancilla, was looking close to an apoplexy. When she pointed this fact out to Rhaz, he nodded slowly and announced that her hour or so of annoyance could be regarded as an excellent punishment for her meddling ways.

"For, my darling, had she *not* planted the maggot in your lovely head that Seraphina was the object of my fancies, we would all have progressed a lot more comfortably."

"You are sure she is not?"

"Widgeon! I shall speak to you further—a good deal further on this matter when we are alone. But hush! I fancy the Earl of Drummond has something to say."

Indeed, he had! He walked steadily down the aisle, his eyes fixed furiously upon the last pair of performers. Cordelia wondered for an instant who he was and what part he could possibly play in the strange, magical unfolding of their lives. In the split second before he reached Frederick, her fascinated gaze made a ludicrous connection.

Though Frederick's hair was abundant long and unruly and this man's was fair and clipped, the resemblance between the two was remarkable beyond coincidence. Of course, the captain was more muscular and youthful somehow, but the resemblance was nonetheless uncanny.

Seraphina, staring in turn, felt something momentous was about to occur. Her fingers trembled a little as they rested still upon the lovely gilt harp provided for the occasion. Frederick moved to her side and gently rested one gloved hand upon the nape of her neck. She trembled again, but this time from the electrifying sensation and not from faint premonition. In a haze, she watched the stranger draw closer and as he opened his lips to speak, she leaned forward in anticipation.

TWENTY-TWO

"Frederick, where on *earth* have you been hiding?" the Earl of Drummond bellowed before he'd quite reached the stage. "All of London, not to mention Bath, is asking after you, bidding me give Lord Frederick this commission and that. And where are you? I cannot say! As head of the family I am starting to look like a fool! What *use* is it being earl when you cannot even say where your brother may be found? Oh, and by the by, the Prince of Wales has been dogging me for your direction. He wishes a symphony to be written in his honour."

He finally reached the platform and regarded Frederick in horror mingled with disbelief. "Good God! Has your valet run *mad*? How can you possibly present yourself in public with a cravat as mangled as all that? For shame, brother!" He glared at Frederick, but sad to say, his errant brother, rather than being repentant, was grinning from ear to ear.

"On that score you are correct, my lord! I never felt so much in need of a thorough grooming as I do this day. And now that the cat is out of the bag, I do believe I shall rectify the situation. With a deft move of the hand, he pulled the cravat loose and negligently retied it in an intricate knot that had his thunderstruck brother envi-

ous among all the *other* valid emotions passing through
his person.

Frederick smiled at the bewildered Seraphina and
took her hand lightly, raising her from her seat, and in
a single, masterful stroke, he passed the hand upwards
to his mouth, whereupon he turned it over and placed
a kiss full of promise on the palm.

"Miss Seraphina, may I introduce to you my brother,
Marcus Argyll, the Earl of Drummond? Marcus, make
your bow, I beg you, to the future Lady Argyll, my dearest heart, Miss Seraphina Camfrey."

The earl was still gaping like a fish when Frederick
decided to further make a spectacle of himself by taking
the young lady in question into his arms and kiss her
so thoroughly that the small matter of his deception
was left to another time to argue, bicker, debate and
deliciously pout over.

Again, the spontaneous applause from the delighted
audience was deafening. Only Rhaz's beloved mama
looked thoroughly disgruntled, seeing all her carefully
laid matchmaking plans gone south. As she *tap-tapped*
her cane on the polished mahogany floor, Rhaz had it
in him to feel sorry for her. Still, she ought to be a *little*
punished, he thought, for the havoc she had wreaked
on all of their lives. Thank goodness the tangle was almost untied. Lord Winthrop looked perfectly snug as
the crowds streamed out of the door and he tucked his
hand possessively into that of Miss Moresby.

Now, the church bells were chiming and throngs were
moving from the hall to the age-old church, steeped in
Carlisle history, just yards down the street.

The duchess pointed frantically and Rhaz inferred
that she wished to speak with him. Accordingly, he bade
Cordelia move on and hung back for the inevitable
scold he was certain would tumble from her lips.

This occurred with remarkable rapidity, the duchess

bewailing Rhaz's deplorable tardiness in his endeavours to attract Miss Camfrey. "And *now*"—she glared at him—"as if matters were not *already* deplorable, she must needs engage herself to your shimble-shamble friend! Rhaz, you are a slow top if ever I saw one and that I tell you! The most tedious endeavours I have been troubled with on your behalf! What have you to say to that, my son? *What?* I ask you."

The duke kissed her forehead in the most outrageous way, causing her magnificently jewelled turban of bright indigo, crimson and saffron to teeter precariously on her head in the most unregal manner. Crossly, she reached up for her pins and admonished him not to try to cut a wheedle with her, for it simply would not fadge.

Her son smiled secretively and promised her that, by the end of the day, she would not be displeased with him, for he intended to do quite *precisely* what she wished.

At this, the duchess looked at him suspiciously, poked him a little with her hideous pewter fan and inquired how he intended to achieve this miracle. He merely shook his head, chuckled a little and bade her be patient. Then, with a few timeous strides—he was anxious to make good his escape—he caught up with his guests and registered delight at their astonished pleasure.

His grace, as a Christmas surprise, had ordered sleighs rather than landaus to convey them all to church. Of course, they could have walked, but the snow and ice were slippery and his grace had no desire to see Cordelia sent sprawling whilst her arm was still tender. Besides, one did not need a *reason* to order up sleighs and sleighbells on a morning as festive as this one!

All climbed in—even the *duchess* managed to puff up and order the third driver to make room for her illustrious person. Frederick's eyes twinkled at the spectacle, for his toplofty brother Drummond had refused the privilege, considering the festivities beneath his consequence. No doubt he would feel a trifle disgruntled at having missed the fun when the duchess, ranked far higher than he, had been unable to resist.

Cordelia, tucked up neatly with the duke, Frederick and Seraphina in the last sleigh, felt she had never seen a more magical Christmas. The air was like crystal—cold, sharp and impossibly clear. She was snugly tucked up in the midst of what seemed a picture-book setting, close to the man of her dreams. Her body yearned for contact with him and she wondered whether he felt the same. Evidently he did, for his hand stole, most improperly, to her lap under cover of the delightfully cosy blanket the thoughtful housekeeper had provided in each of the sleighs. Cordelia coloured to the roots of her dark, velvety hair.

She was certain Seraphina and Frederick would notice, for there was a telltale lump under the rug that must surely announce this impropriety to the world. She stole a glance at them, then bit her lip in an ironic, amused and suddenly lighthearted smile. The rug on Seraphina's side looked *identical* to her own. Lord Argyll appeared *extremely* pleased with himself as his eyes gleamed with mocking amusement.

"I shall have words with you, my lord!" Cordelia just caught Seraphina's cross pronouncement as she leaned towards Frederick.

"Shall you?" Amusement was plain as a pikestaff on Lord Frederick's expressive countenance.

"Don't seek to cozen me, sir! You tricked me most unhandsomely and you shall answer for it!"

"How shall I answer? Like this?" The lump, most improperly, moved upwards.

Cordelia blushed for her sister, but Seraphina,

strangely, made no push to return the hand to its proper position. Instead, she leaned forward and allowed a half smile to play upon her pretty lips.

"Frederick! Behave yourself, for we are in company and we speak, if I might remind you, of your untramelled deception!" Her sister's raised whisper was now quite audible. Frederick did not seem in the *least* perturbed.

"Scold away, Seraphina! I shall square my shoulders and close my eyes, and you shall tell me when you are done. I don't regret a bit of it, for had I not deceived you, I should never have come to know you. I cannot regret that which has brought me the greatest happiness of my life."

Seraphina released her breath and sat back. Her face was bathed in a joyous light, but she willed her voice to remain stern.

"I shall forgive you on this occasion, my lord, but you need not think, in the future, to manage me with simple smiles and beguiling words!"

"Good heavens, no!" Frederick sounded shocked. "You should know me by now, Seraphina . . . full of surprises . . ."

Seraphina giggled and Cordelia wondered, for an instant, what he meant. Then her thoughts focused, once more upon the delectable, unignorable warmth upon her *own* knees. The duke was regarding her keenly, slightly questioningly.

Rhaz to look unsure! She forgot her qualms and allowed the pleasant, delectably shocking situation to continue. When she looked up rather shyly, the fifth Duke of Doncaster nodded firmly and possessively. Doubts and uncertainties vanished. Rhaz whispered to her to open her gift, so she drew it out from her elegant reticule, where she had discreetly tucked it and cast an inquiring eye upon her lord.

Seraphina leaned forward with interest. "A gift *before* church? How naughty! *Do* open it quickly, Cordelia!"

This her sister obligingly did and was astonished to find her stolen cameo lying serenely in the palm of her hand.

"Papa's gift! How did you get this, your grace?"

"By dint of a lot of inquiries, certain bullying of our beloved prisoner and a little luck! The goods were all sitting with what I believe, in cant terms, is called a 'fence' or, more commonly, a 'hedge.' Anyway, I fancied you might like to have it back."

Cordelia nodded and clasped the gift to her chest. She had not liked to speak of it, but she had taken the loss of her little memento quite sadly. "Thank you."

He nodded and turned to her sister. "Seraphina—I shall call you that, for I have hopes we shall soon be very nearly related—I have also retrieved your bangle. Lord Winthrop's odds and bobs have also resurfaced, so I hope that I may wish you all a very happy Christmas."

Seraphina thanked him prettily, but was interrupted by the elder Miss Camfrey. "Rhaz, what has become of that poor miscreant? He was not, I hope, *hanged?*" She felt suddenly sick, all the joys of Christmas dimmed.

His grace grinned. "Was it not an express wish of yours, my love, that he be pardoned? The miserable varmint has been set free and even now is probably haranguing some poor innocent! Mind you, I have taken pains to set him up in some worthy employment on one of my farther estates, so I have hopes the country air shall reform him."

Cordelia was confirmed in her notion that she loved the most noble man of her acquaintance. The glory of the day resurfaced and she fingered her little necklace with simple, untainted joy. "Rhaz"—the name still felt strange upon her tongue—"this is the best Christmas gift ever!"

"Is it? I hope not, my darling, for I have another in store for you. One that has been handed down from one generation to another of Carlisles even before the first dukedom! It is a great deal more valuable than your cameo, my love, and it has an unbreakable tradition attached to it that I hope may endure forever."

"What is it? I *adore* traditions! " Seraphina could not help herself asking, but Cordelia was too breathless to do anything but stare in a manner the duke found most unfairly provocative.

"The Carlisle betrothal ring. It is a tradition that it be worn by the wife of the eldest son of the Carlisle family. The tradition has endured for close on two centuries, I believe."

"But that is famous! Cordelia, it is wonderful, is it not?"

The full import of his words was only now striking Cordelia. She smiled at him mischievously. "Is that not rather high-handed of you, your grace? After all, I am betrothed."

"Humgudgeon! Winthrop and I had an interesting talk this morning."

"Did you?" Her tongue faltered, for Rhaz was watching her in such a burning way that every vestige of her being longed to boldly kiss him and be cradled in a way that was, she was certain, most unladylike.

"There is no reason I can divine, my lady, why you should not now become my wife."

There was a silence before Cordelia's hands tentatively stole into his and the tense moment passed sufficiently for Frederick to breathe easy and resume his own caresses under the blanket.

The sleighs were coming to a slippery stop outside the church and the chimes were pealing so merrily that they were deafening. Soon, the couples stepped out gingerly onto the snow, but were arrested by the poking, impolite cane of the Dowager Duchess of Doncaster.

"I shall not take a *step* into this church, Rhaz, if you do not tell me at once what you mean!"

The duke relented. "Very well, Mama! I shall be brief. You engineered this whole Christmas plot that I may make Miss Camfrey an offer, did you not?"

The duchess glared at him and nodded.

"Very well, then, like the *excellent* son I am, I shall meekly do your bidding.

He drew Cordelia close to him and smiled deep into her clear, honest and immensely wonderful silver grey eyes. "Miss Camfrey, merely to please my mother, I beg you, most wholeheartedly, to become my wife."

The pealing of the church bells was so sweet and insistent that it seemed all the world was hushed. The duchess, enjoying a good jest as much as anyone, threw back her *ridiculous* turban and laughed.

"You had better say *yes*, Miss Camfrey. I *always*, you may as well know, get my own way!"

The duke cast a wry look at his betrothed. Though her mouth was prim, he could have sworn she was chuckling.

EPILOGUE

"Have you news?"

The eagerness in Lord Frederick's tone was unmistakable. He was pacing the room in a quite deplorable fashion, without doubt wearing the soles of his immaculate top boots to shreds. He cared not a fig for that. Hoby, he knew, could always craft him another such pair.

Even now, at St. James's Palace, the orchestra was striking up, the delicious notes of the harp rising seductively over the triple violins and the single, tinkling bell that had been wrought from silver and designed specifically for the occasion.

The Prince of Wales would be taking his seat, wrapped warmly against the snow. If he had stopped for a moment to think, Frederick might have wished him season's joy, for it was Christmas again and the notes warming the chamber, more melodious, more challenging, more spiritual than anything that had graced it before, were Lord Argyll's own.

Tonight, however, as the church bells chimed and the yule log crackled in the grate, his thoughts, tumultuous, untramelled, deliciously poignant, remained steadfastly at home.

"I do, Freddie."

Frederick did not wait for more. Cordelia's inner radiance was sufficient. He'd seen it once before, after all, when the sixth Duke of Doncaster to-be had made his lusty little way into the world. Even now, he was lying snug in his crib, unaware that his place as the youngest little nobleman was about to be usurped.

Lord Argyll took the stairs nimbly, anxiety creasing his smooth brow. As he tapped gently and pushed the rosewood door open just a crack, his breathing eased. He paced himself and permitted his habitual air of casual jauntiness to return.

Seraphina smiled. Though a trifle pale, her face was nonetheless bathed in familiar angel light. At Lord Argyll's entrance, she puckered her lips into a delicious pout.

"Frederick, have you *no* decorum?" He was unprepared for a scold, but resigned himself to the obvious fate by a mere flicker of the eyebrow.

His heart's delight continued. "For myself, I do not quibble, but really, a simple music master ought at *least* remove his beaver when making the acquaintance of two beautiful young ladies!"

The smile gave her away. Frederick gasped and took two very quick strides to the bed. Nestled next to her very honourable ladyship lay the most adorable set of angel cherubs Freddie had ever encountered.

He stared, then stared again. Tentatively, he touched one little finger. It wrapped round his upon the instant. He repeated the favour with the *other* small bundle who was patiently awaiting his attention. The same, again.

There were no words for what Freddie felt at that moment.

"Merry Christmas, my lord."

"Merry Christmas, my ladies."

More Zebra Regency Romances

Put a Little Romance in Your Life With
Janelle Taylor